Alex stopped mere inches from her, and she resisted the urge to back away.

She met his gaze evenly, waiting for him to reveal whatever it was that had him grinding his teeth.

"Did you talk to anyone on the way here this morning?" he thundered.

Kat straightened. "You know very well I wouldn't. What's this about?"

"The story about you writing a book on your father got leaked."

Kat's stomach bottomed out. He loomed over her and she sucked in a breath, immediately regretting it. His scent assaulted her senses, a spicy deodorant and the clean smell of soap. For some unfathomable reason, her body seemed to welcome his closeness. After Colin, she wanted nothing more than to lash out at every man who got within touching distance.

So why wasn't she pushing Alex away?

Dear Reader,

As a resident of the Washington, DC, area, I am constantly fascinated by the family lives of elected officials and those around them. I see Capitol Hill staffers work themselves to the bone, sacrificing friendships and love because they believe in their leader. While TV shows sensationalize political deal-making, the staffers who advise our elected officials are no different from you and me. They make tough calls, and sometimes they make mistakes. For the most part, they're trying to do the right thing.

The Senator's Daughter is the story of Katerina Driscoll, who has lived her life in the shadow of her obligations until her father's identity brings her into the political limelight. It's also the story of Alex Santiago, a first-generation American for whom politics is about power; the power to change lives and to change how the world sees people like him and his mother. The book is about confronting the inner demons that keep us from being happy, set in the midst of Washington, DC, politics.

I am tickled to share my hometown with you. To get free book extras, including some Washington, DC, insider information, visit my website at sophiasasson.com. I love hearing from readers, so please find me on Twitter (@SophiaSasson) or Facebook (SophiaSassonAuthor), or email me at Readers@SophiaSasson.com.

Enjoy!

Sophia

HEARTWARMING

The Senator's Daughter

———

Sophia Sasson

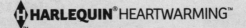

HARLEQUIN® HEARTWARMING™

ISBN-13: 978-0-373-36810-5

The Senator's Daughter

Copyright © 2016 by Sophia Sasson

Printed in U.S.A.

www.Harlequin.com

Sophia Sasson puts her childhood habit of daydreaming to good use by writing stories she hopes will give you hope and make you laugh, cry and possibly snort tea from your nose. She was born in Bombay, India, and has lived in the Canary Islands, Spain and Toronto, Canada. Currently she calls the madness of Washington, DC, home. She's the author of the Welcome to Bellhaven and the State of the Union series. She loves to read, travel to exotic locations in the name of research, bake, explore water sports and watch foreign movies. Hearing from readers makes her day. Contact her through sophiasasson.com.

Books by Sophia Sasson

Harlequin Heartwarming

First Comes Marriage

To all the men and women out there who are not afraid to pursue their goals; and to my friends and family who support my crazy dreams.

Acknowledgments

This book, and the entire State of the Union series, would not happen without my awesome editor Claire Caldwell, who really makes my manuscripts shine.

My talented critique partner, author Jayne Evans, is not afraid to tell me to hit the delete button and start all over. I love her for it.

Also, thanks to the wonderful Heartwarming authors who support each other and have created this wonderful community of sweet romance readers and authors.

CHAPTER ONE

"...SENATOR ROBERTS FACES some tough questions ahead."

The TV announcer's dramatic voice echoed as Kat opened the doors leading to the stairwell. She took the steps two at a time and burst into the hallway.

"Professor Driscoll!"

Kat turned to see her teaching assistant chasing after her. "Not now, Amanda. I'm late." Kat hurried down the hallway.

She was due to administer a final exam to juniors at Hillsdale College and didn't want to come up with an excuse for being late because of her mother. Again. She especially didn't want to look bad in front of the dean.

Almost running through the door of the classroom, Kat stepped onto the stage and set her papers on the professor's table. She opened her mouth to silence the room. Her voice stuck. Fifty students stared at her like she'd grown two heads.

"You guys are eager to start the exam," she

said nervously. Something was wrong. She glanced at the clock on the back wall. Only a minute late. Was she wearing her shirt backward? She looked down at her clothes, and then chaos broke loose.

"Is it true?"

"Why didn't you tell us?"

"What does this mean for you?"

"Are we still taking the exam today?"

Kat blinked as the questions flew at her. *What's going on here?*

"Professor Driscoll!" Her out-of-breath teaching assistant huffed up to the stage.

"The dean asked me to administer the exam so you can deal with the situation."

"What situation?"

Amanda stared at her, openmouthed. "You haven't seen the news?"

A pit formed deep in Kat's stomach. She shook her head. "What's going on?"

The cacophony of questions from the students intensified. Several were on their feet, holding out cell phones. Kat turned to see telltale flashes.

"Go to your office, don't talk to anyone and turn on the news. Go!" Amanda said.

Kat pointed the TA to the sheaf of exam papers, then turned and fled. Two more faculty members tried to stop her, but she blew past them. *It can't be Mom.* She'd just come from making sure her mother was medicated and tucked away in bed. Had she done something in the fifteen minutes it had taken Kat to make it to campus? She vividly remembered being pulled out of class and into the principal's office in high school. The principal had the TV turned to the local news and asked Kat if the woman walking around in a bathrobe on Main Street was her mother. Indeed it was, and the media had filmed Emilia Driscoll in all her half-naked glory. Not one of the reporters had thought to call for help.

How had her mother pulled off a CNN-worthy stunt in the last few minutes?

Kat ran to her closet-sized office and shut the door. As an assistant professor, not tenure track—not yet, anyway—she got an office with barely enough room for a desk and two guest chairs. There was a TV, a necessity for any political-science professor, along with the musty smell of an office without a window.

Pressing the power button on the TV, she waited for CNN to come up. It was the default channel during election season. The image filled the screen. She dropped the remote.

Her own face stared back at her. It was her faculty picture. The unflattering one where her blond hair looked lifeless, her blue eyes tired and her cheeks paler than the white background. It was her post-breakup face, the face of a woman who'd been lied to by someone she loved, cheated out of her much-deserved faculty position and forced to start over at a new college. One bad media story had done that to her. Three years had passed, and Kat was not that woman anymore.

The volume was too low, so she searched the floor with trembling hands for the remote and turned it up, stabbing at the buttons until she could hear the announcer.

"...and we'll come back to this developing story." Her picture disappeared and they went to commercial.

She let out a scream of frustration.

"Are you okay?" the professor next door called through the thin walls. She forced a breath into her lungs.

"Yes, sorry," she mustered. While her colleagues seemed nice enough, she wasn't close with any of them. That was a mistake she wasn't going to make again.

"It's understandable."

Kat went behind her desk and turned on the ancient computer. The boot-up screen was maddeningly slow. She didn't have a smartphone—an expense forgone because of the cost of the data plan on top of the pricey device. Once she got a promotion, she would treat herself to a tablet computer.

She punched in her log-in and password, keeping an eye on CNN. They were still on a commercial break. As soon as she was logged in, she opened the internet browser, which went straight to CNN's politics page. A yelp escaped her lips as she saw her picture, that same ugly faculty photo, load on the page.

Katerina Driscoll—Senator Roberts's Secret Daughter the headline screamed. Her eyes widened. She read through the article as quickly as she could, needing to blink several times when the words blurred before her. She flipped open her dated phone and called home. It rang and rang, and she swore under her breath. The mood stabilizer she gave her mother sometimes knocked her out.

This can't be true. Or could it? Her mother had mentioned that her father was a politician. Her mouth soured as she read the article. She knew Senator Roberts. Correction—she knew him the way a professor knows a subject, having lectured on the three-term US Congress senator from Virginia five times in the past month alone. He was in a tough reelection battle because he was proposing a bill to spend billions of dollars on Improvised Explosive Device, or IED, identification technology for overseas troops. The normally boring congressional election had taken the national stage since its outcome would determine the majority party in the closely held Senate. It had been an exciting few weeks for the tiny political-science department at her small-town Virginia college.

CNN came back and repeated the headline she'd just read online. It seemed the first story had appeared a little over an hour ago. Her heart pounded in her ears, muffling the words of the TV announcer. She fingered the pendant on her necklace and took short breaths to calm the sharp pain in her chest. This couldn't be happening. Not on this day.

Why do they think I'm his daughter? She flipped open her phone and called the house again. Maybe the ringing would wake her mother.

None of the articles mentioned her mother's name; all that came up was an obscure reference to a "short-lived previous marriage."

This had to be some horrible case of mistaken identity. She picked up her purse and checked her watch. Two hours until the committee would meet about her promotion. The only way to set this straight was to go home and rouse her mother.

The TV screen caught her eye and she

gasped. A new picture appeared, one from just moments ago in the lecture hall. A scrolling Twitter feed showed next to it.

VA professor said daddy isn't the smartest. #SecretDaughter

Prof Driscoll thinks @SenatorRoberts blew it. #SecretDaughter

The scrolling text was too fast to read. She went back to the computer and brought up her Twitter account. The hashtag was new, obviously being used in all the Tweets related to the story. When she typed *#SecretDaughter* into the search box, it brought up over a thousand Tweets, including a bunch from her students who were supposed to be writing an exam. There were at least ten photos of her standing in front of the class looking like a deer caught in the headlights. If possible, those images were even uglier than the faculty photo. Every crease on her tailored shirt showed, and her pencil skirt appeared to be a size too small against her newly gained five pounds. Her sensible flat shoes, good for traversing the campus, made her look short.

She struggled to take a breath but all the oxygen in the room had been sucked out. This wasn't just some small media story. It was big-time news, and she was right in the middle of it. She stood on shaky legs. The only way to put a stop to all this was to talk to her mother. She couldn't even call the CNN desk and yell at them for spreading lies. Her birth certificate, and every form she'd ever completed, had a blank next to her father's name. He was a figment of Kat's imagination, a man she'd created to fill her mother's silence.

Could the news story be true? She shook her head. Senator Roberts was a public figure, and if he was her real father, someone would have mentioned it. The only person who could refute this nightmare was her bipolar mother, who was sleeping off a manic episode. She closed her eyes, took a fortifying breath and stepped out of her office. And ran right into a solid mass. She stepped back.

"Dean... Gl-Gladstone," she stammered. The dean was an imposing man in his sixties with gray hair and a broad chest. He was well over six feet and used every inch of his height to rule the faculty. She had interacted with him only in group settings, preferring to deal with the dean through the department chief, who didn't have a notorious temper and didn't fire staff for sneezing the wrong way.

Dean Gladstone took up nearly all the space

in the tiny foyer-slash-anteroom-slash-coffee-station. They didn't have a receptionist; they barely had working phones.

"Professor Driscoll, I need a word with you."

"Of...of course." She waved him into her tiny office, wishing she had tidied up. Stacks of papers littered her desk. He strode in and took a seat. His huge frame looked comical in the tiny, threadbare visitor's chair. Kat put down her purse and sat, keeping her back as straight as she could.

"There are reporters and news vans outside this building, harassing students, asking if they know you," he said without preamble.

"What?" No one had been there when she'd walked in just twenty minutes ago.

"I have guards escorting them to the campus gates, where our jurisdiction ends. I've had to request more security."

Kat swallowed. How was she going to get out of here?

The dean continued in a dramatic, gravelly voice. "Now, I've come to tell you that this school does not welcome such publicity shenanigans. You should have disclosed you were the senator's daughter when you applied for your position here."

She put her hands on her lap so he wouldn't

see them tremble. "Dean, I have no idea why they published that story. I don't know my father—he left before I was born." Her voice was tinnier than she wanted, but at least she'd managed to keep it steady.

"Surely your mother must have said something about him."

You'd think so, wouldn't you?

She shook her head. "My mother was quite traumatized by my father's desertion. It made her so sad to talk about it that I stopped asking. I really have no idea where this story came from. Believe me, I wouldn't do anything to jeopardize this college."

"Regardless, until it dies down, for the safety of the students, you need to go home and stay there."

Kat's heart sank to her toes. She couldn't keep the tremble out of her voice as she asked, "Are you suspending me?"

"Not yet. But I'm not allowing you on campus. I'll have your colleagues cover your exams and deliver them to your house for grading."

Not again. Kat swallowed, trying to dislodge the big lump in her throat that threatened to choke her. It sounded like a reasonable course of action; they were a small school, and security consisted of old-man Pete and his sidekick. They couldn't deal with the likes of

CNN. But she knew this was the step before suspension. They'd let her grade the last papers and then fire her. If a big university took issue with a page-three newspaper article, a small-town college wouldn't put up with national headline news.

And today of all days. "Dean, I hope this won't affect the APT Committee's discussion." The Appointments, Promotions and Tenure Committee was scheduled to meet today to go over Kat's record and determine whether she qualified to become a tenure-track professor.

"That remains to be seen."

He stood, and Kat followed suit. "I recommend you not talk to the media unless you can conclusively refute what they're saying and take the attention off yourself...and this school."

She nodded dumbly. He left, and she collapsed in her chair. For two years, she'd been working toward the promotion by taking on classes that no other faculty member wanted, mentoring extra students on their dissertations and writing as many papers as she could. She had even learned how to blog, working herself to the bone to make tenure. Now this! Her luck couldn't be this bad, could it? What if the story was true? Emilia had been moodier than usual for the past several months. Kat had chalked it up to a medication adjustment, but what if…

She stood and made her way to the back entrance of the building, the one the students used to cut through the large quad area between classes. Opening the door just a crack, she peeked out. There was a man in a business suit with his back turned to her and a phone pressed to his ear. He wasn't dressed for a college campus, but he didn't have a microphone or camera, so she stepped out and walked over the grass to the faculty parking lot.

As she hurried past, she sensed him move. "Miss Driscoll?"

Ignoring him, she kept walking as fast as her legs would go. His footsteps fell heavily on the concrete path behind her, so she broke into a flat-out run. The parking lot wasn't that far; she could make it. Keys were clipped to the side of her purse, and there was a can of Mace attached to them. *Always keep keys and pepper spray within easy reach.* Her fingers closed on the metal and she automatically unlocked her car, comforted by the beep. Her pulse raced, and her finger was on the alarm button. Thankfully there was no one next to the car. *So close, only a few more steps.* The car was within touching distance when she felt someone grip her elbow. She froze for a millisecond, but then her self-defense training kicked in. She screamed and whirled, instinctively pushing out with her hand. *Go for the nose, eyes or throat.*

The man in the business suit deftly stepped back before she could connect with his Adam's apple. He held out his hands. "Miss Driscoll, I'm Alex Santiago. I work for Senator Roberts."

Her chest heaved, trying to squeeze air into her lungs. He wasn't even out of breath.

Kat put a hand on the car and willed her heart to calm down. She studied him while she struggled to gain control of her breathing. Hair dark as night, styled and tamed. Taller than her five-foot-four frame. Lean, but he looked like he had muscle underneath his well-tailored suit. Big, dark eyes, skin the color of sand. A firm jaw, high cheekbones, the hint of a five o'clock shadow. He didn't look like the typical congressional staffer, but he dressed like one. Dark gray pin-striped suit, light blue French-cuffed shirt, red tie, an American flag pinned to the lapel. He was senior staff. If he was legit.

"It's Dr. Driscoll." Kat crossed her arms. He stepped back, his lips twitching into something that looked suspiciously like the beginnings of a smirk.

"*Dr.* Driscoll, I'm sorry to scare you, but I need to talk to you. Urgently."

He pronounced each word carefully, in the precise manner of someone who had had language training.

"And why should I talk to you?"

He put his hand in his breast pocket and removed a plastic-encased identification card. It was a federal ID that listed his name as Alejandro Santiago.

"We're on the same side here."

Really? I don't even know what side I'm on. Definitely a Washingtonian. "How did you get here so fast from DC?" The capital was a three-hour drive away.

"CNN gave us a heads-up they were running the story."

"Then why didn't you give *me* a heads-up?"

"We didn't know if you needed one. But we did try to reach you. No one answered your office phone, and we couldn't find your cell number on such short notice. We even tried you at your home, but it just rang."

Kat bit her lip. She vaguely remembered the phone ringing when she was trying to calm her mother. Usually only telemarketers called that number, so she'd ignored it.

"So what's going on?"

"That's what I'm here to find out. The story

caught us by surprise." He raised his brows. "I'm hoping you can shed some light on what they're saying."

"Me? What does Senator Roberts have to say about it?" she countered.

"He's in the air, on an overseas flight. He won't be landing for another few hours."

"You don't have a way to reach him?"

"We have to wait until he lands." His gaze shifted a bit and she narrowed her eyes at him. He seemed sincere enough, but no way was she trusting him.

"I'm on my way home to talk to my mother. Give me your card and I'll call you when I have some information."

"So you didn't leak this story?"

"Excuse me?"

"Did you give this story to the media?"

She put her hands on her hips. "Do I look like some crazy woman, desperate for fifteen minutes of fame?" His eyes roamed her body and she reddened. "This story is ruining my life. I want it retracted, and as quickly as possible."

"Then you and I have the same goal. I'll come with you."

"That's not wise, Mr. Santiago."

"Alex. And I don't think you have a choice." He pointed behind her. She turned to see no fewer than ten people rushing toward her through the gates that separated faculty parking lot from the street. This time there was no doubt who they were. Cameras were already flashing and outstretched hands held ominous-looking microphones.

"Give me your keys."

She stared at him. He snatched the keys from her hand. "Get in!"

"Katerina."

"Professor Driscoll?"

"Kat!" The crowd of reporters was now close enough that she could hear them screaming her name. All doubt erased, she ran to the passenger side and slammed the door shut. Alex already had the car moving before she buckled in. She clicked the seat belt in place just as he floored the accelerator, backing out of the parking lot. Instinctively, she grabbed the handhold on the ceiling. He reversed all the way to the gate. He had a hat on his head now, its bill pulled low.

"What're you doing? This is a campus—there are kids around!" If they ran over someone, her career was over. A vision of the dean physically throwing her off campus like a rag doll filled her mind.

Alex changed gears and pushed the car onto the grassy knoll to avoid a crowd of reporters.

"Dean Gladstone will—" Her head hit the side window as the car lurched. He had hopped onto the sidewalk to avoid more media immediately outside the gates. Several people slapped the car as he pressed the horn and squeezed past them.

Kat turned to make sure no one was lying on the ground bleeding to death. She let out a breath she hadn't realized she was holding.

"Are you crazy?"

"You've never had to avoid the bloodhounds before. Trust me, this is routine—for me and for them. Tell me how to get to your house."

She wanted to tell him to get out of her car so she could drive home alone, but who knew what disaster awaited there. He seemed to have some know-how, so she gave him her address and he plugged it into his phone GPS while continuing to drive like a New York City cabbie. *On second thought, maybe I'd better get rid of him now.*

"I'm going to go a roundabout way to shake off anyone following us."

She whipped around, but all she saw were regular cars in normal traffic on the small-town streets. Her head pounded. This had to be a dream. Like the one she'd had last night in which she'd shown up to class without her lecture notes and the students had laughed at her. It had to be. This was not real.

They arrived at her house to find it quiet. No media vans, no horde of reporters. Just the neighbor's yippy dog barking behind the fence like he'd never seen her before.

"Shut up, Rex," she muttered, stepping onto her front porch. She and her mother lived in a small, brick-front town house with three feet of shared front yard between them and the neighbors. She keyed into the house with Alex right behind her.

"Wait here." She motioned to the small living room with the flowered couch her mother had owned since Kat was a little girl. The woman refused to give it up. It was perfectly preserved under a plastic cover, Kat's daily reminder of what her life would be if she didn't change something. Once she got the promotion, she could move into her own place again and get more medical assistance for her mother. She could have a life. One that consisted of more than just taking care of her mother and working to get her career back on track.

Right now, she could barely afford to pay the rent on this place, let alone get an apartment for her mother. Emilia Driscoll hadn't been able to hold down a job for over a year now. The move to Hillsdale had been hard on her, and Kat didn't understand why. Her mother was from Virginia; Kat's aunt lived a short distance away. When Kat had accepted the position at Hillsdale College, she'd expected her mother to be thrilled. Instead, she had mumbled something about the past coming back. At the time, Kat had wondered if her father was still around. It was the only thing that explained her mother's reaction.

She went to the bedroom to find her mother still fast asleep. Kat closed the door and sat on the bed. Wisps of blond hair stuck to her mother's forehead, so she pushed them back. Emilia had been a beautiful woman once, with long, flowing hair, bright blue eyes, rosy cheeks and a full body. Now her hair was thin and falling out. Her slim body was all bones. Kat could never get enough calories into her. She couldn't let the media anywhere near her; they would eat her alive.

"Mom, I need you to wake up."

Her mother moaned and turned away from Kat, but she shook her until Emilia's eyes fluttered. "Katerina, what time is it? How long have I been sleeping?" She rubbed her eyes and blinked at the sunshine streaming through the window.

"Mom, it hasn't been long. I'm here because there's a problem. I need an answer to a very important question, and I need you not to lie to me, okay?"

Her mother sat up in bed and frowned. She was lucid and calm. Good—the drugs had taken effect. "Katerina, what is it?"

Kat swallowed. There was no time to ease into this. "Remember how you told me my father was a politician?" Her mother shrank back, her lips pressed tightly together. It was her normal reaction, but Kat wasn't going to let her shut down this time. For once, she had a different way of asking the rote question. "Mom, is Senator William Roberts my father?"

Her mother paled and she clutched the bedsheet to her chest.

"Oh, no. It's happened, hasn't it? He's come to take you from me."

CHAPTER TWO

"I'M WORKING ON IT." Alex bit his tongue, literally, to keep his tone polite. The Republican National Committee had been riding him ever since they figured out Roberts was going to be the make-or-break candidate for control of the Senate. The rest of the races were a foregone conclusion. Only a third of the Senate was up for reelection every six years. Virginia had been a predictable race, as Senator Roberts was well liked, but a new challenger had changed all that. Now the race was close. Tight enough to be within the polling margins of error. If Roberts lost, the powerful Senate would go to the Democrats.

"The senator needs to focus on his trip. Convincing the Egyptians to give us the technology is critical for the bill," he told the RNC chair as calmly as he could. The senator didn't need to deal with a media crisis. The whole point of his trip to Cairo was to get a firm commitment from the Egyptian government, which was not currently a friend of the United

States, to turn over the specifications for new robot detectors that could clear IEDs. As an active senator, Roberts was both campaigning and trying to get his bill passed before the election. It was Alex's job to make sure he was successful in both endeavors. IEDs were the biggest killer of American soldiers, so for every minute that soldiers were using old equipment, someone was dying.

"I'll handle it. This isn't my first campaign." He stabbed the end button on his BlackBerry without saying goodbye. He wouldn't distract the senator. The Egyptians had initially agreed to sell the technology for an exorbitant amount of money but were now reconsidering the deal under significant pressure from other Middle Eastern countries not to sell to the US. The senator was fighting overseas, so it was Alex's job to deal with the battleground that was Washington politics.

This was a big ticket, his first national effort, nothing like the small-time campaigns he had been running. He was almost a Washington insider, not just—*pull yourself up by the bootstraps, young man*—hanging around the elite. No longer the token senior staffer, the one people turned to when immigration was the issue du jour. He wasn't even Mexican. His mother was from El Salvador, a woman who legally immigrated. Yet that fact was often overlooked. All his life, he'd been around men in power. They saw him as the stereotypical son of the cleaning lady, out to work hard and make a name for himself. *Good for you, boy.*

The party leaders were waiting for him to fail. Senator Roberts had hired him when it was going to be a simple race. Still, he'd kept him on even though the party leaders were putting pressure on him to replace Alex. *Those smug men.* Alex knew that if he didn't control this media nightmare, and fast, the RNC leaders would slap him on the back and tell him he'd fought a good fight, then give him a fatherly smile and suggest he go back to the minor leagues. *You've made your mother proud, son.* They'd blame him for the bill not passing, a bill they supported only because the Democrats were against it. Men like that always won. But he wasn't a helpless kid anymore; he was a grown man who was going to fight back and beat them at their own game.

He rubbed his temples. His first thought had been that this had to be a woman looking for her moment in the spotlight, so he'd brought the campaign checkbook and the standard nondisclosure agreement to get the situation resolved quickly. But this was clearly not the usual deal.

First of all, CNN normally gave the RNC more notice for a story like this, hoping to barter for an even bigger scoop. This time it was a call for comment as they were going to air. Second, they refused to even hint at their source. No "senior White House officials" type of disguise to indicate where the story had come from. Third, the woman hadn't given an interview. If this were the familiar get-rich-quick scheme, she would've been in front of the cameras talking about emotional damage. Her photos would be picture-perfect. Instead, they were using a mug shot from the college website, and the Twitter photos were even worse. *Could this be the real deal?* She'd seemed genuinely distressed when he found her.

He clicked on the BlackBerry again and eagerly read the email he'd been waiting for. The plastic squeaked as he sank deeper into the couch. *It can get worse.*

The bedroom door opened and Kat emerged, closing it softly behind her. She was even paler than before, and far more beautiful in person than in the pictures on TV. Her blue eyes were clear and expressive, her long blond hair haloing her delicate face. A naturally beautiful woman who would be stunning if she was done up right. Yet he could tell she wasn't the type to make sure her nails were polished, hair blown to perfection and clothes immaculately pressed. She wasn't someone you put in front of the cameras.

"So?"

He already knew what she was going to say, but he needed to hear her version of it.

"Can I get you some coffee?"

He raised an eyebrow then stood.

"I'll help you make it."

"No, you sit here. I'll be right back."

He thumbed through the remaining messages on his phone. He'd made a rookie mistake. He should've sent an unknown staffer to deal with this. Yet something about her picture had gotten his spidey senses tingling and he'd decided to deal with it himself. In hindsight, he realized that if the media found him here, in her house, the story would gain even more steam. He'd already taken a chance driving her from the college. Even with his hat, he couldn't be sure someone hadn't recognized him. Kat needed to make a statement, and soon. He didn't have time for coffee.

Thankfully, Kat returned quickly with two mismatched mugs. She handed one to him. "I have cream and sugar if you'd like."

He shook his head. He'd learned to drink his

coffee plain black. Hard to deal with creamers and sugar packets while on the go.

"So?"

She sighed and leaned back into the squeaky couch, wincing at the sound. He expected her to take her time, but she got to the point. "The senator and my mother were married thirty-six years ago. Briefly. She left him then discovered she was pregnant with me. By then the divorce was final."

His deputy, Crista, had just unearthed all this. The senator was such a public figure, having always put his life and family in front of the media, that Alex hadn't bothered to dig much deeper before Roberts entered the national stage. Like the media, he'd thought the man was already well vetted and that any skeletons would have been dug up a long time ago. Another mistake.

Her face was now ashen, her eyes large and luminous. She wrapped her hands around the coffee mug and he saw waves in the liquid.

His leg jerked. He wanted to tell her it would all be okay. Except it wouldn't. Her eyes shone and she stared into her coffee. Then a sound outside caught his attention. *Great!*

He flew to the window and pulled the drapes across it. She looked up, splashing coffee on her hands.

"What's going on?"

"They're here. You need to close all the blinds." He kicked himself for not asking her to do that first thing.

To her credit, she didn't let the panic clearly visible in her eyes overwhelm her. The cup clattered as she set it down and ran to the bedrooms. He drew the venetian blinds on the skinny window next to the front door, then walked into the tiny kitchen and did the same.

"How did they find my house?" The accusation cut through the air as she emerged from her mother's bedroom.

"Probably the same way my assistant just discovered that Senator Roberts and your mother were married for exactly eight months and it was the first marriage for both of them."

Eyes widening, she stepped backward, pressing herself against the door frame. They were both standing in the kitchen and he suddenly realized how much of the small space he was taking up. Excusing himself, he walked past her and back to the living room couch. This wasn't the standard situation, but there was an easy answer—one that would get him out of here and back to work on the things that mattered.

"Listen, obviously you don't want the publicity any more than we do."

"You've got that right," she muttered, sitting across from him and crossing her arms.

He leaned forward and gave her the smile he usually reserved for female heavyweight donors. Using his classic move, he reached out to take her hand. As soon as their fingers touched, she pulled back like she'd been burned and gave him a look that implied he had cooties. A nerve in his left eye twitched. *Okay, then. We aren't going to be friends.*

"Then it's simple. Have your mother make a statement that you're not Senator Roberts's daughter and we're done."

Her head snapped up. "You want her to lie."

"Versus…what?"

"Versus telling them it's our private matter and they need to stop harassing us."

He stared at her. Was she really that naive? Then again, she was a college professor. His deputy, Crista, had briefed him on the articles she'd written. Kat was an idealistic academic who had no idea how things worked in the real world.

"You say that, and the story continues. They start interviewing your neighbors, students, Facebook friends, Twitter followers…everyone you've ever spoken to."

"Why would they—"

"People you hardly know will come out of the

woodwork with a charming—or nasty—story about you and your mother. Think about how many people want to get on national TV. This is their chance. Have you ever cut someone off in line? Left a bad tip at a restaurant? True or not, people will have all kinds of stories about you. Just look at how many Tweets your students sent."

If possible, her face went even whiter, the color completely draining out of it.

"I'm not worth that kind of attention, surely…"

He stood and lifted the edge of the curtain. She gasped. There were no less than ten trucks blocking the street and a bunch of reporters crowding onto her front lawn.

"Any second, they're going to come banging on the door. The only reason they haven't yet is they need to get their cameras ready and the uplinks to their networks established."

This time he went and sat next to her on the love seat. She moved slightly but didn't get up. "They're not going away. You're the story of the day, and the only way to get them off your back is to tell them there is no story. Discredit it, and they'll slink away."

"I don't want to lie."

"Your birth certificate doesn't have a father listed. There is no record of when your mother separated from the senator. Our spin would be that they were separated when you were conceived, so he's not your father. There's no way, without a DNA test, for them to prove you're his daughter."

Her eyes were big and wet. He wanted to look away, but he couldn't. Something pricked his heart. Risking another rebuke, he put his hand on hers, and this time she didn't move.

"Listen, I know this is hard, and I don't agree with the tactics, but they won't stop harassing you. Your mother is sick…"

She snatched her hand away with such force that the coffee cup sitting on the table teetered, threatening to fall. "How do you know about my mother?" She inched away from him on the couch. He was handling this all wrong.

The job necessitated being able to put on a number of faces, so he furrowed his brows and leaned in, his eyes conveying sympathy and understanding. He couldn't show his impatience with this woman now. *Why is she being so stubborn?* She obviously didn't want the media attention, and he was giving her an easy way out.

He felt a familiar anger bubble deep inside, and he took a breath, modulating his voice, softening it, the way he'd been taught. "I'm sorry—I didn't mean to intrude. Unfortunately, the internet has more information on all of us than we'd like to disclose. When the story first came out, I had my staff research you."

"You thought I did this for attention. Fame."

Her sharp tone cut through him. "We didn't know you. The story came out of nowhere…"

"I want nothing to do with Senator Roberts, nor do I want any part of that circus." She jerked her head toward the window. There was raw pain in her voice and fear in her eyes. He didn't doubt for a second that this wasn't a publicity stunt for her. Kat genuinely didn't want the attention. There was a backstory there, and he made a mental note to have the campaign's private investigator do some deeper digging. They hadn't had much time to search smaller, local newspapers for archived articles.

"Then make this story go away. If your mother is up to it, have her make a statement that it's not true."

"I most certainly will not do that."

An older version of Kat walked into the room. Emilia Driscoll looked frail, far thinner than Kat but with the same blue eyes and blond hair, identical cheekbones. The PI had sent Alex Kat's birth certificate, which showed that Kat was thirty-five and her mother had been twenty-two when she had her. Emilia was fifty-eight years old, yet she looked closer to seventy.

His own mother was about Mrs. Driscoll's

age, having had him when she was only seventeen, but she was vivacious, still working as a housekeeper despite his protests. Whenever he insisted she stop working, she'd tell him there was no shame in hard work, even if her occupation embarrassed him. There was no point in having *that* argument with his mother anymore.

He stood. "Ms. Driscoll, I'm Alex Santiago. I work for Senator Roberts."

Taking her hand, he controlled his grip. She seemed so fragile; he didn't want to break her fingers.

"Call me Emilia." She took a seat next to her daughter on the love seat, forcing him to go back to sitting across from them. "How is Bill?"

Alex widened his smile, giving her his disarming "I'm your friend" look. "He's doing well, ma'am. He's currently on a plane overseas, or else he'd be here himself to talk to you."

"Oh, I very much doubt that. Bill never wanted to deal with me personally. He arranged it so he didn't even have to show up to court to sign the divorce papers. Gave his proxy to a lawyer."

Alex opened his mouth to defend the senator then stopped when he saw the ice in Kat's eyes. She put an arm around her mother.

"Mrs. Driscoll, I know this is a difficult situation…"

"Look, young man, I know where you come from in DC—people have affairs and children out of wedlock. That's not how it works in these parts. I was raised better, and I won't have people believing my little girl is illegitimate."

This is going to be tougher than I thought.

"I understand how you feel, but if you don't dispute this story, they'll hound you all the way to the elections." He put his elbows on his knees and folded his hands.

"Then let them."

Kat's hand went to her neck and he watched her turn over a pendant in her fingers. "Mom, we don't want to deal with the media."

"They will pick apart your lives, sensationalize every detail," he chimed in, his voice low.

"I want Bill to claim his daughter. Publicly. It's her birthright." Emilia sat back, lips pressed together.

Alex stared at her. *Oh, boy.* Was *she* the anonymous source to the media?

"I'm not the one who started this thing, but I'm sure as heck gonna finish it," she responded to his unasked question. Something in the way she said it set his intuition tingling. *What more is she hiding?* Her fingers played with the flowered fabric of her skirt.

"We can reimburse you for your inconvenience," he said carefully.

Both Kat and Emilia glared at him and he realized it was the wrong thing to say.

"This is not about money. It's about honor." Emilia clasped her hands in her lap.

Several thoughts raced through his mind: he could have the senator call this crazy woman and talk sense into her. Or they could discredit her with the media. His phone buzzed and he excused himself to go to the kitchen.

"Yes," he barked. Crista was on the other line.

"Alex, one of the students uploaded a video from her lectures. I just emailed it."

Hanging up, he clicked on the email. The video came to life and he activated his Blue-tooth earpiece so Kat and Emilia wouldn't be able to hear it in the living room. He had to watch only a few minutes to get the gist of it.

He strode into the living room and switched to speaker on his BlackBerry. He pointed the video at Kat.

"Did you really say that the IED robots are a waste, and the money should be spent saving lives at home?"

She gazed at him unflinchingly. "I'm a political-science professor lecturing in class. I was legitimately criticizing his policies."

He pinched the bridge of his nose. "And you're a registered Democrat."

"Excuse me, but when did that become a crime?"

"It's not, unless you're the secret daughter of a Republican senator in a hotly contested race. You just gave the other candidate a two-point boost in the polls."

Her eye roll told him that not only did she not care, but she wasn't inclined to help him.

"I did a whole class on the Democratic candidate, too, pointing out his flaws. I present a balanced view to my students."

"That's good. Do you remember what day that class was?" He began typing an email to Crista to see if she could get that video. Senator Roberts's poll numbers were falling every second, and with them, his odds of getting the bill passed. If the senate rank and file thought Roberts wasn't going to win reelection, they would stop supporting him on the IED issue. Alex had spent a lot of time on things that wasted taxpayer money: initiatives that didn't improve people's lives, investments that were downright wrong. The IED technology was the one purchase he knew would save his soul, or at least give him an image other than that of his buddy lying on the desert sand with his leg blown off. He wasn't going to let anything get in his way.

"I don't want any more videos of me out

there." Kat's frosty voice pulled him back into the moment.

"Then go outside and tell them this is a non-story."

Emilia stood. "Mr. Santiago, please leave my house. Now."

He looked at Kat, who also stood and put an arm around her mother.

The doorbell rang, followed by loud knocks. They all started at each other.

Emilia Driscoll was the first to speak. "The vultures are back."

CHAPTER THREE

"CALL THE POLICE. They're not allowed to be on your property. They need to stay on the street."

Kat began rummaging through the drawer in the hallway credenza. Everything was happening so fast, she needed a minute to catch her breath.

"What're you doing?" Alex said impatiently.

"Looking for the number to the local police department."

"It's 911."

"The nonemergency number."

He picked up the phone, dialed and held it out to her. "Hello, what's your emergency?"

"Hi, it's not really an emergency, but I need the police."

"Are you in danger, ma'am?" came the dispassionate voice.

'Well, not really, but—"

Alex snatched the phone from her. "There are twenty people on the front lawn, banging on the front door and threatening to come inside. We need the police." He rattled off the address.

Kat heard the woman put him on hold then come back and ask for his name. "I can't talk right now. They're breaking down the door." He hung up the phone.

Kat stared at him.

"You lied."

"I did not lie. I stated the facts in a dramatic way. I want the police to get here quickly."

"And what if there's a real crime being committed, like a woman being raped or someone getting murdered?"

"When was the last time something like that happened in this town? Most likely, they're out patrolling the highway and you just saved a citizen from getting a speeding ticket."

"That's Washington logic," she muttered. He was a typical man, bending the truth to suit himself. If someone got hurt in the process, so be it. Driven by his own needs, he didn't care whom he trampled along the way.

They heard the scream of sirens. The pounding on the door stopped.

Kat went to the drapes and peeked out. Four police cars came to a stop, and as officers emerged, the reporters began retreating to their vans. She had to admit it was an effective idea, but she still didn't like Alex's manipulations.

He'd been playing her since they met, and she had to remember that the sincerity in his eyes was also an act.

An officer walked up to the house and she opened the door when he knocked. She ushered him in and then noticed that Alex wasn't in the living room. Her mother's eyes flicked toward the bedroom.

Kat explained the situation to the gray-haired, heavyset policeman who patted her hand in a fatherly gesture.

"You're helping my daughter with her master's thesis." Kat blinked back her surprise as he told her his daughter's name. She was one of the students Kat had recently taken on. "Tell you what—I'm not supposed to be doin' this, but I'll ticket them for parking illegally and tell them I'll arrest them for trespassing if they set foot on your lawn again. I can't stop them from talkin' to you, though. And they'll probably accost you when you leave the house and take pictures with long-range lenses through your windows. Nothin' I can do about that."

Kat nodded numbly. This had to be a crazy dream; all she could hope for was to wake up soon.

The cop stood to leave. "And another thing— I don't think they're gonna leave you alone until you give 'em a statement. I suggest you either do that or leave town. The dean is mighty upset at you, and we're a small-town police department. We can't really protect you or keep comin' out here every time these reporters cross the line."

He gave her his card and left. Kat went to get Alex out of hiding and find out why he didn't want his presence known, though she had her suspicions already. She rapped on the bedroom door and entered without waiting for permission. This was her room. Her house. He had no right to waltz in and demand things from them.

"It won't end until you deny the claim," Alex said matter-of-factly. He seemed to take up all the air in the small space. "Nice room, by the way."

She followed his gaze, considering what he saw. Her bed was made with an old Amish quilt. The dresser held some basics. There were no pictures anywhere, no clothes loosely strewn, no underwear lying around. It was a functional room, one she hadn't made home yet because it didn't feel like hers. Yet, for the first time, she felt an energy in here that she hadn't felt before. Alex stepped toward her and she resisted the urge to back away. She was in the doorway, her hip leaning against the frame.

He reached out and touched her shoulder. She looked at his hand, but the now-familiar urge to smack it away didn't bubble up. His hand felt strong and warm. Comforting. She frowned.

"I'm not the one you need to convince. I'm ready for us to denounce this whole thing. I'm up for promotion, and the last thing I need is this media circus." She checked her watch. The APT Committee would be meeting soon.

"Then let's talk to your mother together."

She nodded. "Why didn't you want the police to see you here?"

"If anyone catches wind of me, the story becomes bigger. If you deny he's your father, but I'm seen here, they'll say I paid you off."

"Like you tried to do earlier?"

He opened his mouth then suddenly turned toward the door. "Do you feel that?" He pushed past her and she realized there was a light breeze coming through the house. She followed him into the living room. The front door was open.

"Where's your mother?"

Kat looked around, her heart sinking. Alex swore under his breath just as Kat caught sight of her mother on the front lawn, her blond hair lit up by several bright cameras.

Without thinking, she ran to the front door, but paused at the threshold. Once she stepped out, her face would be all over the cameras. Alex called to her, but she ignored him and ran to where her mother was standing. Kat wasn't going to let her face the vultures alone.

Several cameras were trained on her mother when Kat reached her.

Out in the lead was a brown-haired reporter with perfectly styled hair and enough makeup to paint an entire canvas. With her skintight suit and stiletto heels, Kat thought she looked like a doll. "Ah, Miss Driscoll, I…"

"It's Dr. Driscoll or Professor Driscoll," Kat said evenly, surprised at the strength in her voice.

"Dr. Driscoll, Mrs. Driscoll, thank you for speaking to us," said the reporter in a sugary voice.

Before Kat could say anything, her mother spoke out. "I have a statement to make, but I won't answer questions." There was silence among the reporters and Kat could almost see the cameras zooming in on her mother's drawn face. "Kat was conceived when Bill and I were still married. We decided to divorce, and then I found out I was pregnant. I chose not to tell Bill. He's never known about his daughter, and Kat has never been told who her real father is. There is no more to the story, and we want nothing from the senator. We ask you to please leave us alone."

Every reporter spoke at once, but Kat put

her arm around her mother and turned her, intending to walk back into the house. No such luck. The reporters formed a circle around them, hurtling questions at lightning speed. Her mother froze. Kat sensed panic seizing her.

"Please, let us through," she said firmly. The reporters ignored her, slowly closing in on them. Her mother was breathing faster and faster, and Kat knew she was close to losing it. She tightened her grip and spoke more firmly. "Please let us through." The note of desperation was clear, but it was drowned out by the cacophony of reporters. She barely heard them as her heart drummed in her ears. How were they going to get out of this?

Suddenly, the crowd separated, like the biblical parting of the Red Sea. Kat looked up to see Alex push through. He walked confidently up to them, flanked Emilia's other side and put his arm around her, laying his hand on top of Kat's and squeezing it reassuringly. They pushed toward the door.

The reporters stayed close, sidestepping to keep up with them, lobbing questions at Alex, which he calmly ignored. He stopped a few steps from the door and held up his hand. The crowd fell silent. "The senator is on a flight. He'll comment when he lands. I'm here to make sure these good people aren't unnecessarily harassed. Mrs. Driscoll will *not* be seeking child support. In case you hadn't noticed, Dr. Driscoll is a grown woman. No further comments right now."

He was smooth as silk, his lies sounding as authentic as the truth. Once they stepped over the threshold, Kat slammed the door and threw the dead bolt.

She let out a long breath, the tightness in her chest easing. "Thank you."

He gave her a hard stare. "That was not a good move."

Her mother looked like she was about to collapse, so Kat took her to the bedroom. The doctor had warned her against using sedatives, but she felt her mother needed one now. Or maybe *she* needed her mother to take one. The situation was getting more out of control by the minute. Kat took a pill from the locked cabinet in the bathroom and gave it to her mother, urging her under the covers to take a nap. Once Emilia was tucked in, Kat went to the living room to find Alex standing in front of the TV.

"They interrupted their regularly scheduled programming to air your statement."

"It's time for the truth to come out," Kat said simply. She didn't agree with her mother's impulsive behavior, but Emilia had been remarkably brave and articulate in front of the cameras, showing more strength in the last five minutes than Kat had seen in her for the past several years.

"Well, it's now an even bigger story than it was before. Congratulations. Until something blows up in the Middle East, the president has an affair or there's a school shooting, the media will be playing that clip of you and your mother every thirty minutes."

Where was the guy who came and saved them from the reporters? Kat stepped up to him, her feet planted wide. She put one hand on her hip and shook a finger in his face.

"My mother told the truth, something I know you're not familiar with in DC. Now that it's clear we're not on the same side, why don't you get out of my house and go back to your lair."

He carefully placed the remote he was holding on the coffee table and gazed at her with a bland expression. Every cell in Kat's body was as taut as the strings of a guitar. *Breathe, Kat.* This was no different than handling a rowdy classroom. *Hold your ground.* He took a small step in her direction, closing the distance between them so his chest was no more than a hair's width away from her. Heat emanated from him, and her own temperature rose a few degrees. Normally she'd shrink away from a man standing this close to her, but she lifted her head so she could continue to gaze steadily into his eyes. *Let me see the fire beneath your cool exterior.*

Their faces were barely an inch apart. Something shifted in his gaze and his expressionless eyes turned into a warm chocolate brown. Her own nerves tingled as she caught a whiff of his spicy aftershave, and she couldn't help but look at his mouth. His lips quirked in response and she immediately forced her eyes upward. *What am I doing?*

It wasn't like she hadn't dated since Colin. Well-meaning faculty members had a never-ending stream of friends and relatives to set her up with, and she'd been on plenty of first dates where the conversation dried up long before dessert arrived. So, okay, she hadn't really allowed any of those guys to go beyond a peck on the cheek. And none of them made her toes curl, but whatever she was feeling was a result of adrenaline. Too much was happening all at once.

Alex took a deep breath, and she could feel his controlled exhalation. She should step back. Away from the tempting smell of his aftershave. Away from his comforting warmth. Her legs refused to move.

"I'm not going anywhere. The senator knows

about you now, and he wants to talk to you and your mother."

She stepped back. "You lied to me. I thought you said you didn't have a way of reaching him, that he was on a plane."

"He is." His tone kicked up an octave, almost imperceptibly so. "Planes have Wi-Fi these days, and he has access to his email. I didn't want to bother him with this, but after your mother made that statement…"

"You had no choice because we aren't just a minor nuisance anymore."

"That's not—"

"You lied to me earlier. You told me—"

"I told you he was on a plane."

"Right, not a technical lie in DC, but in the real world, we'd call that dishonest." She balled her hands into fists so he wouldn't see her shaking. "Now leave, before I call the sheriff to escort you out."

"Kat…"

"Dr. Driscoll!"

"Fine, let me—"

The shrill ringing of a phone interrupted him. *The APT Committee!* She flew to her purse and dug it out.

"Katerina Driscoll," she answered with as much normalcy as she could muster.

"Professor Driscoll, it's Dean Gladstone."

He was the only dean at Hillsdale; he didn't really need to specify, but he always insisted on formality in a school where everyone referred to each other by their first name. Kat suspected he did it to remind people that he alone had the power to change the course of their lives.

She checked her watch. The APT Committee wasn't scheduled to meet for another ten minutes. As usual, the dean got right to the point.

"We've decided to postpone the APT meeting. Yours was the only application we were considering, and I didn't think it was in your best interest to have the meeting today."

Her heart stopped. "So what does that mean for me?" She managed to control the tremor in her voice.

"Professor Driscoll, I've personally reviewed your application and I have concerns."

She swallowed. It was happening all over again, just like it had with Colin. The media were blowing up a story, and she was paying the price. It had taken all of her savings and months of effort with a lawyer to get a small-town newspaper article retracted and deleted from the internet. No amount of money and lawyers could do that with a story this big; this would haunt her for the rest of her life.

"You've obviously worked very hard, but

I'm trying to raise the caliber of faculty in this school." Kat's heart sank. He'd canceled the meeting because they weren't going to give her the promotion.

"It's hard for our little college to compete in Virginia when we have big-name universities that attract both students and faculty. We must ensure that our professors are of the highest standing." He spoke with the kind of fake British accent that ivory-tower professors often put on. She felt like Maria in *The Sound of Music* getting a lecture from Mother Superior.

She sat on the bench next to the entryway and let her head rest on the wall behind her. The dean had obviously made up his mind.

While he droned on about his standards for faculty members, Kat's mind wandered to thoughts of the senator. After all these years of wondering which shadowy politician was her father, she finally had the truth. What was he like as a man? Would he have stood by her mother if he'd known she was pregnant? Would her mother be the same woman if he'd been in their lives? Would Kat's life have been different? Would she have picked a better man than Colin if she'd had a male role model growing up? These were all questions she'd asked herself a thousand times before, and she never came up with any answers. But maybe now...

She sat up straight. When the dean paused to take a breath, she jumped in. "Dean Gladstone, I know you don't like my newfound notoriety, but it could be a real opportunity for the school to gain a national reputation."

That was what Colin had done, hadn't he? Turned the media attention to his benefit. So why couldn't she do the same? Though he was silent, she knew the dean was still on the line because she heard his breathing. So she continued.

"What if I do a few interviews with Senator Roberts and write some articles on this race and the impact of his defense policy?"

"That's an interesting idea," the dean allowed. "One significant deficit in your tenure application is that you haven't written a book."

Kat bit her lip. She hadn't written a book because her ex-fiancé had stolen years' worth of analyses and sold them as his own.

"A book would make your application more competitive, particularly one analyzing your father's policies and tracking this campaign through the election."

That was a lot more than what Kat had in mind. Maybe she should've thought through this half-baked idea before blurting it out. She couldn't commit to being away from her mother for an extended period of time. "A book would be hard to write based on a few interviews."

The dean wasn't listening. He talked over her. "I have a very dear friend at Harvard University Press, and if you can deliver a book in the next three months, I'll twist his arm to publish it before the election."

She closed her mouth. A book? Published by Harvard University Press? In the academic world, that was like hitting the *New York Times* bestseller list. She might have a chance at living down this story. Other career opportunities would open up; maybe she could even return to a big-time university. But that meant spending two to three months researching with her father...and with Alex.

"Dean Gladstone, covering my father through the election is a longer proposition than what I was thinking."

"Professor Driscoll, perhaps I haven't made myself clear, so let me be blunt. Your current application will not get you a promotion. And your newfound notoriety gives me cause to consider whether to continue your contract for next year. I'm giving you a solution—I suggest you take it."

Kat couldn't bring herself to hit the end button despite the insistent beeps in her ear telling her the dean had hung up. She closed her eyes. *What have I done?* If he didn't renew her contract, it was too late for her to find another position. Her savings account barely held enough money to cover next month's rent. She couldn't afford to lose her position. More important, her mother needed the health insurance that came as a benefit.

"I couldn't help but overhear."

Kat opened her eyes to see Alex kneeling in front of her. She closed her phone.

"This is none of your business."

"Actually, it is." He squeezed the bridge of his nose, then looked up at her. "I'm going to put my cards on the table. No bull. I have a win-win solution for both of us."

She leaned forward, searching his eyes. He was a charmer, just like Colin. But she wasn't going to be fooled. Not again.

"The senator's going to take a hit in the polls with your mother's announcement. No matter what she said, our conservative state will see him as having abandoned you. The only way to manage the story now is to invite you into the fold. Come on the campaign trail. Take some pictures with the senator so he can show that he's getting to know his newfound daughter. Your mother said she wants him to claim you, and he's willing to do that. In return, you can spend time learning about him for your book."

She stared at him. His eyes were pleading and she could feel herself melting. Alex was a trained liar. This whole situation was his fault. If he hadn't put pressure on them to lie, maybe her mother wouldn't have made that impulsive statement. But... She had a chance to find out once and for all why her father had left, and to get some answers to questions that had haunted her life. Maybe it was time she learned to use her situation to her advantage rather than curl up and wait for others to determine her fate.

"I can't leave my mother."

"Our campaign headquarters are in Richmond, just an hour from here. The senator uses it as a base to travel through the state. I can situate you there."

"Is that where you work out of?"

"I split my time between Richmond and DC."

An unwelcome pulse of disappointment went through her. She ignored it. His not being around was a good thing.

"I have two conditions."

He lifted a brow, his lips pressing together. "I'm not sure I can meet them."

"Then *I* am sure I'll be slamming the door in your face in a few minutes."

A vein bulged in his neck and she felt her

nerves spark as she took in the curve of his neck and jawline.

"Let me hear it."

She focused her attention back on the matter at hand. "First, no media. You can take some posed pictures of me and circulate them, with my approval, but I don't want to be in front of the cameras like I was just now."

He steepled his fingers and tapped them against each other. Kat found herself getting distracted by the way his fingers moved. "It'll be faster to take the attention off you if you give a statement to the media. They hound people who avoid them."

She shook her head. "I won't do it. That's nonnegotiable. Posed photos only."

He looked down before meeting her gaze, and Kat had the distinct impression she was making a deal with the devil. "I think I can manage that. What's the other condition?"

"I want full access to the senator and to campaign decisions."

He opened his mouth to protest but she held up her hand.

"I will sign a limited confidentiality clause and allow you to review my final manuscript before it goes to the publisher. Review it for factual accuracy, not to change my analysis."

His eyes locked onto hers. She didn't blink.

"That's the only way I'll do it."

"I guess there's no way the book can be published before the November elections."

She bit her lip. Under normal circumstances, he'd be right. It took at least nine to twelve months to bring a book to publication, but she wasn't writing a commercial book. She should tell him about the inside track Dean Gladstone had.

"You've got yourself a deal." He held out his hand.

She hesitated before taking it. Was she doing the right thing? Reluctantly, she grasped his hand, surprised at the roughness in his firm grip. He smiled, and she found herself staring at the way his lips moved, the way they curved, the contrast of their pinkness against his golden skin. Her body warmed from her hair to her toes.

This is going to be disastrous.

CHAPTER FOUR

KAT KNEW WHAT to expect from campaign headquarters, but no intellectual knowledge could have prepared her for the in-your-face chaos that greeted her. Flashbulbs exploded in her face as she stepped from her car onto the sidewalk. Alex was there in a flash, shielding her and passing reporters with a firm "Wait for the press briefing."

Alex thought it best to come to headquarters right from the house to draw the media away from her mother. They walked through a set of glass doors and staffers from every corner of the warehouse-like space came rushing toward her. She instinctively stepped back... and bumped right into the solid mass that was Alex. His hands went around her shoulders, steadying her. He lifted one arm and extended it, palm out. The rush of people stopped barely a foot from her. Questions and introductions were hurled at breakneck speed. Alex shooed them away and steered her over to a glass-walled office in one corner. She sank into a guest chair as Alex waved to someone.

Kat turned to see a petite redhead with black-framed glasses walk in.

"Kat, this is Crista Jordyn. She's—"

Crista held out her hand. "I do all the real work around here while Alex runs around looking good."

Alex rolled his eyes good-naturedly. "Crista will introduce you around the office and find you a computer station. I have to go to DC."

Kat stomped on the flare of disappointment. It was a good thing he wouldn't be around, as she had enough to worry about between meeting her father and researching a book. The last thing she needed was to get distracted by Alex.

"When is the senator expected back?"

Alex tapped on his BlackBerry. "He's on the ground in Cairo. He'll video call with you at eight tonight. Crista will get you set up."

Kat glanced at her watch. "I can only stay for two hours. I need to get home to take care of something."

Alex looked up. "Kat, most everyone here works well into the evening. You want full access, you can't expect to work nine-to-five… let alone just popping in when it suits you." He began to study a sheaf of papers.

Crista took her elbow. "Let's leave Mr. Crankypants to deal with his work."

He didn't acknowledge them as they walked out, and something pinched in Kat's chest. What did she expect? He was running a major campaign and a ton of staff reported to him. Why should she feel entitled to special treatment from him? She was looking for the man she'd gotten to know back at her house, the one who rescued her mother from the talons of the reporters. Maybe what she thought had been a glimpse of the real Alex was really an aberration. After all, she had plenty of experience with men who could turn on the charm when needed.

Once out of earshot, Crista whispered to her, "He'll be leaving soon and I'll get you the senator's call information. You can take it from home."

From home? Where her mother was?

She shook her head. "I want to do my share. I'll go home, then come back for the call." Kat had to make sure her mother took her evening pills, but she didn't want to upset her when she spoke with the senator.

Crista leaned forward. "I think it's great you take care of your mom like that."

Kat gave her a thin smile. *Does everyone here know about Mom?*

Crista led Kat around tables overflowing with campaign signs and papers, introducing her to the staff. To their credit, they kept the gawking to a minimum and welcomed her warmly. The place was packed with people bustling about. There were only two offices, one for Alex and one for her father. Cubicles covered most of the floor. In the center of the large space was a long conference table littered with signs. She stole several glances at Alex. He was almost always surrounded by people. The place was buzzing with energy.

He led her into a cube. "And this is Nathan Callahan. He works on defense stuff."

Nathan swiveled in his chair, pinning her with bright blue eyes. "I hear you'll be observing."

"I hope to do more than just observe. I'd like to participate and be helpful. I've analyzed a lot of the senator's policies."

Crista squeezed into the little cube. "Nathan is working on some policy briefs for the IED bill." She gave Nathan a meaningful look but he avoided her gaze. "The people back in DC, they staff the Appropriations Committee, which is really interesting work. They use Nathan's analyses to advise the senator."

"What do you specialize in?" Nathan asked. Pressed between the cube wall and Crista,

Kat felt claustrophobic. Everyone seemed a little too comfortable with physical proximity. "I keep abreast of all issues, but I have a particular interest in military policy."

Nathan quirked an eyebrow. "Interest, huh? Well, I have six years of experience—" Before he could say more, Crista shot him a searing look.

"Why don't you send Kat the briefing materials you have on the IED bill."

He frowned. "Those are internal. Have you checked with Alex?"

"The senator wants her to have full access."

Nathan opened his mouth in obvious protest, but Crista stepped forward and put her hand on his shoulder. "Nathan, trust me—the senator wants this."

Nathan's face softened. Kat suppressed a smile at the puppy-dog look in his eyes. Crista stepped out of the cube and Kat was behind her in a flash.

"Have you spoken to my...the senator today?" Kat asked.

Crista shook her head. "Alex talked to him about the deal you made and the senator sent me an email." She stopped and Kat almost ran into her. Crista pulled her to the wall as if the extra foot would give them even a modicum of privacy. "The senator has a lot of respect for Alex," she whispered. "But when he wants something done without a lot of argument, he'll email me and ask me to take care of it."

What did that even mean? Kat wanted to ask more, but Alex was storming toward them. He had taken off his suit jacket and loosened his tie. She straightened and felt Crista melting into the background, her ever-present Black-Berry back in her hands.

Alex stopped mere inches away from her, and she resisted the urge to back away. She met his gaze evenly, waiting for whatever it was that had him grinding his teeth.

"Did you talk to anyone on the way here this morning?" he thundered.

Kat straightened. "You know very well I wouldn't. What's this about?"

"The story about you writing a book on your father got leaked."

Kat's stomach bottomed out. He loomed over her and she sucked in a breath, immediately regretting it. His scent assaulted her senses, a spicy deodorant and the clean smell of soap. For some unfathomable reason, her body seemed to welcome his closeness. After Colin, she'd wanted nothing more than to lash out at every man that got within touching distance, so why wasn't she pushing Alex away?

"I didn't even tell my mother about our deal. She thinks I'm here to take care of paperwork." Her voice was squeakier than she wanted.

His gaze flicked behind her shoulder, and then he lowered his head and whispered, "Kat, if this is about sabotaging the senator's campaign…"

She stepped back. "Why would I do that?"

He opened his mouth then closed it, obviously rethinking whatever he'd been about to say. She leaned in. "I'm not a seasoned politician—I don't play games. What you see is what you get from me."

He stared at her, his brown eyes at once expressive and shuttered, as if he was processing and then denying what he knew to be true.

"Then how did the media get hold of the story?"

"It must have been Dean Gladstone."

He frowned and muttered something under his breath.

"What is it?"

He rubbed the back of his neck. "I don't have time to deal with this today." For a moment, he looked weary. "I need you to fix this."

Without thinking, she put a hand on his arm. "How?"

His eyes softened into pools of milk chocolate. They were mesmerizing. When he spoke, his voice was warm. "Give a statement to the media that you want to get to know your father. They're loving the fact that you're at campaign headquarters."

She retracted her hand. It didn't take him long, did it? "No," she said simply, her fury threatening to erupt like a volcano. She could sense people surreptitiously watching them while pretending to be on their phones or studying their computer screens.

"What? You wouldn't be lying—that's part of the reason you're here, isn't it?"

She flinched at his harsh tone. "Alex, I told you, no media jaunts. That was our deal," she said quietly.

"But…"

"Right now, it's the book story. In another hour it'll be something else. Once I step into the limelight, I'll never get out. If you can't respect the deal we made just hours ago, then it's best I leave and we don't speak again."

"Why are you so afraid of the media?"

She crossed her arms. She didn't owe him anything. He tapped on his BlackBerry then turned it toward her. His voice was soft.

"Is it because of this?"

She looked down and recoiled. It was a picture of her from three years ago, talking to the police and paramedics. She was front and center, holding a compress to her cheek; Colin was in the background with a bandage on his head. A freelance photographer had come by after he heard her 911 call on the police scanners. He sold the photo to the newspapers. The story only appeared in the local daily, but it had been enough to get her fired. How had Alex found it? She'd paid a lawyer to get a court order for the newspaper to remove it from their online archives.

She put a hand to her mouth and stepped back, staring at the incriminating caption: *Scorned professor lashes out at boyfriend.*

"That wasn't my fault."

He reached out and touched her hand. "Kat, CNN found this and they're going to run it. You need to tell me your side of the story."

Eyes wide, she squeezed his arm. "You have to stop them. Whatever it takes, you have to stop them." She knew her voice was too loud because the staffers were no longer being discreet about their glances, but she didn't care. The story couldn't get out. It had taken her over a year to live it down enough to get her job at Hillsdale College, even after the story was scrubbed from the internet. She suspected that Colin had called around and gotten her blackballed at most of the major universities.

He nodded. "I'll handle it, but you need to tell me what happened."

She sighed. Even her mother didn't know the whole story. "I had a fight with my then fiancé. He basically stole years' worth of my work. I confronted him and told him that I planned to bring plagiarism charges against him. I had proof that the work was mine, dated emails that showed the research I did, et cetera. He didn't take the news well and got violent. I fought back hard. He bumped his head and called 911, concocting a story about how I was mentally unstable. He said I attacked him first."

Alex clenched his fists. "Why would anyone believe him?"

"Earlier that day, I also found out he was having an affair with the dean of the school. I vented to a fellow faculty member, a woman who I thought was my friend. You know how you say things like 'I'll kill him' in anger? Well, later she said I was so angry, she was worried I would actually hurt him. The dean fired me and it took months before another school would even grant me an interview." She touched the pendant on her neck, rolling it between her fingers. Did Alex believe her? No one else had; the media had portrayed her as the classic woman scorned.

"Where is he now?"

Kat reeled at the murderous look in Alex's eyes. The warmth was gone, replaced by a smoldering darkness. She shrank back.

"He's still faculty at Wellingforth University," she said carefully. "Colin wanted so badly to be promoted, to be able to show his daddy that he had amounted to something. I think he believed I wouldn't make a fuss about him using my research, but when I threatened him, he lost control. He was desperate not to make a fool of himself. The university said I had to drop all claims to the book if I wanted my severance pay, which I needed at the time. If it hadn't been for that story…" Her voice cracked and she took a breath. "Every interview I went to, that article came up. With my mother's history mentioned in there, they just thought I'd come unhinged, too. Even after I had it taken down, it took a year before people stopped asking me about it. My mother, she became so distraught, I don't think she's ever recovered. We had to start a whole new medication regimen."

She blinked back tears and acid burned in her stomach. What was wrong with her? She was over it; the incident was now three years ago. She'd put it behind her. "Those reporters never bothered to get my side. I spent all my savings fighting with the courts to get the story taken off the internet."

He shook his head. "It's almost impossible to erase something that's been posted on the internet. All you did was make it a little more difficult to find, but CNN dug it up."

"Please, Alex…"

He nodded. "Whatever it takes, I'll kill the story. I can't promise other outlets won't find it and harass you, but I won't put you in front of them."

Their eyes locked and a sense of relief washed over her. It didn't make any sense, but somehow she knew Alex would protect her. He wouldn't let the old story hurt her again.

She jumped when Crista grabbed her elbow. "Hey, your computer is ready. Let's get you settled in."

Alex took a breath, his eyes a dark brew of black and brown. He and Crista exchanged a meaningful look, and then he turned and left without a word.

Kat exhaled.

"Don't worry about him—he's that intense with everyone," Crista said smoothly. Kat followed her, marveling at how she'd handled Alex. How she'd been handling him. She wondered whether there was more to Alex and Crista's relationship than boss and assistant. Hadn't she seen sparks between Crista and Nathan earlier? Campaigns were notorious for affairs.

Long hours working together with no outside life could pull anyone together. Something flared in her chest, but she tamped it down. It was none of her business whom Alex dated. She needed to focus on writing her book.

"So, Crista, what's your secret?"

Crista turned with a puzzled expression. "What do you mean?"

Kat gave a nervous laugh. "You know, with Alex and Nathan—how do you get your way with them?"

The moment the words were out of her mouth, Kat wanted to run and hide in her car. *What's with you?* She was not a gossip, nor should she care about whatever was going on in Alex's personal life.

Crista motioned toward a desk and Kat sheepishly took a seat. Crista pulled up a nearby stool and huddled in close.

"You'll hear the rumors soon enough, so I'll just give you the lowdown. Alex and I were an item, like, two years ago when I worked on the Hill for Congresswoman Burton. I broke it off. Then this job came up and Alex was man enough to hire me because I'm the best person for it."

Kat wasn't surprised given the familiarity she'd observed between the two of them, but something kicked in her stomach. What man would hire an ex-girlfriend who'd dumped him? Probably one who still had feelings for that ex.

"Why did you break up?" Kat couldn't believe she was asking the question. Despite herself, she was curious about Alex.

"I was getting too attached." Crista studied the BlackBerry in her hand. *She* still had feelings for Alex; that much was obvious. "He's a great guy—don't get me wrong. He treated me so well… It was the hardest thing I've done in my life. But he was never going to marry someone like me."

"Someone like you?"

"Alex has political aspirations. He needs a woman with a pedigree, like someone with the last name Kennedy. I joke with him about missing the boat with Chelsea Clinton. He needs a tall, beautiful, impeccably dressed woman who can stand in front of the camera and talk about world peace and saving our children."

She pointed to a stain on her blouse, something Kat hadn't even noticed. "I'm lucky if I make it into work wearing matching clothes."

Kat smiled. "Then I'm in good company." She marveled at the ease with which Crista spoke about Alex after knowing Kat for all of fifteen minutes. Kat didn't have any close friends; it had been hard for her to work on friendships when she was constantly unavailable. The few girlfriends she'd had when she was younger didn't understand why she had to run home all the time when they wanted to hang out. Eventually, they stopped inviting her to events, realizing her RSVP would always be no.

After Crista left, Kat worked on setting up her email and reading the briefs that various staff had sent her. A frisson of excitement coursed through her. She'd only studied campaigns from afar. Never had she been in the throes of something like this.

As uncertain as the decision had felt just a couple of hours ago, she knew she'd done the right thing. She would be forced to interact with people other than her students and get out of the house during the summer months. Normally, she taught a summer class, but this year the political-science department had decided not to offer courses in order to allow students to work on campaigns for college credit. Now she didn't have to dread the long summer months with nothing to do. This would be good for her.

The first email she had was from Alex, sent minutes before their most recent encounter. She opened it.

From: ASantiago@SenatorRoberts.com
To: KDriscoll@SenatorRoberts.com
Subject: Welcome

Kat,
Despite the circumstances, I'm glad you're here. I look forward to getting to know you. Welcome.
—Alex
PS: Consider changing your name to Kat Roberts.

Kat reread the email. The nerve of him!

"He has a point, you know."

Crista's voice startled her. She whirled in her chair to find the woman standing behind her, openly reading the email on her screen.

"Excuse me—isn't it rude to snoop?" Kat winced at her snarky tone. After Crista had been so open with her, Kat should be a little nicer, but she wasn't used to such unfiltered sharing.

Crista laughed and gestured around her. "There's no privacy here on purpose. People jump ship on campaigns all the time. That's why strategies are closely guarded secrets and Alex and I have access to every email that goes out on our servers. That's actually what I was coming here to tell you—and to give you this paperwork to sign, which includes a privacy notice that says you have none."

Kat stared at her. Was she serious?

Crista nodded at her screen. "And he's right. The optics would be much better if you changed your name. Maybe not right now, but closer to the election."

Kat didn't have the words to respond to the casual tone Crista used, as if they were talking about her switching from regular to diet soda instead of changing her entire identity.

She finally found her voice. "I will not change my name. It's my mother's name, and I'm proud of it."

Crista shrugged and walked away.

Kat turned back to her screen and hit the reply button. She glanced over her shoulder to make sure no one else appeared behind her.

From: KDriscoll@SenatorRoberts.com
To: ASantiago@SenatorRoberts.com
Subject: You are unbelievable

Alex,
Asking me to change my name is not the way to welcome me. The answer is NO.
—Kat
PS—next time you want to welcome someone, try chocolates. I prefer mine dark and nutty, none of the sugary, cherry-filled kind.

Satisfied, she took one more look over her shoulder and hit Send before she could lose her nerve. She immediately went to the next email, which was from Nathan—a terse note explaining the files that were attached. The first file hadn't even downloaded when she saw an email pop up from Alex.

Frowning, she craned her neck to peer into his office. He wasn't there. She clicked the message.

From: ASantiago@SenatorRoberts.com
To: KDriscoll@SenatorRoberts.com
Subject: Thick skin

You'll find campaign staff don't have time for sugar coating or cherry fillings.

But I'm all for a woman who likes dark and nutty.

Sent from my BlackBerry

Her face heated. She minimized the message and looked behind her before she reread it. Was he flirting with her?

"Here you go." She nearly jumped out of her chair as one of the campaign staffers she'd met earlier appeared. He handed her a Black-Berry. "It's all set up for you. Use this instead of your personal phone from now on—hackers are likely monitoring your text and phone messages so they can sell something to the media."

She opened her mouth to ask the pimply-faced intern if he was serious, but he turned and left before she had a chance. She deleted Alex's emails and went back to reviewing the documents Nathan had sent. Whatever game Alex was playing, she would not indulge him.

Hours passed like minutes. Kat immersed herself in the policy briefs she'd received. The analysis was fascinating and unlike the academic ones she was accustomed to. Nathan's arguments could almost convince her the IED bill was justified. *Almost.* She made several notes for her book.

When she looked at her watch, she realized with dismay that she wouldn't have time to go home and make it back before the scheduled call with her father. She walked to Crista's desk and asked if they could move the video chat to another day. Crista handed her a tablet computer. "Here, this works on cellular. You can take the call from your car so your mother won't find out."

Kat blew out a breath. "What exactly do you know about my mother's situation?"

Crista continued tapping away at her computer. "Everything. We researched you when the news story broke and were able to get the claims made on your health insurance, so we're aware your mother is on mood stabilizers. I assume that's why you need to go home."

Fire erupted inside her. Kat gripped the tablet so hard, her fingers whitened. "That type of information is private. How did you get it?"

Crista turned in her seat, finally focusing her eyes on Kat. "Don't be upset. Privacy is an illusion. We hire a firm to do investigations for us—every high-profile campaign does. In this electronic world, information is abundant."

Kat muttered her thanks for the tablet and rushed out to her car. Someone had moved it to an underground parking spot the senator used when he needed to come in and out of headquarters without battling the media. She was shaking with anger, but there was no point in taking it out on Crista.

It took her several minutes of clicking her electronic key to find the car, but she was relieved not to encounter a horde of reporters waiting for her when she did. She sat with her hands resting on the steering wheel. Something buzzed and pinged in her purse, and she reached inside to retrieve the BlackBerry. It was an urgent text from Alex.

You ok? Crista says you seem upset.

She resisted the urge to throw the device out the window. She tapped back a message.

Privacy is important to me.

The response was almost instant.

We're a small campaign staff. It's not personal.

What did that even mean? Not personal? It was the very definition of personal. There were at least thirty people inside that campaign office and they all knew every intimate detail of her life.

She put the phone in her purse and started the car. In two hours, she would be talking to her father for the first time. She needed to prepare herself. The BlackBerry buzzed and pinged insistently. She put the car back in Park and picked it up.

The senator is looking forward to talking to you. Need anything?

Yes, she needed to go back in time, before the story broke, when she was all set to get her promotion. A gnawing ache grew in her stomach. Had she miscalculated? Alex made a good case for how her working on the campaign was a win for both of them, but she didn't trust him. What was the play? She put the phone on silent. She needed some quiet time to think.

Kat's mind whirled as she drove home, and she was grateful that the rush-hour traffic on I-95 had abated. She made it home in less than an hour. The news vans were gone; they'd left after Alex had made a statement that she was moving to Richmond to work on her father's campaign. He'd even gotten her to roll out an empty suitcase when they left the house earlier in the day, explaining that the media didn't have unlimited resources. They would take the stakeout to Richmond, and they had. Alex was a smooth operator. Just like Colin.

She entered the house and found her mother sitting in the living room with the TV on. Kissing her on the cheek, Kat noted her color was better.

"How're you doing?"

Her mother's eyes were bright. "You didn't have to come back early. I took my meds."

Kat raised a brow. Every evening was a battle to get her mother to take her medications. There had been several days when she'd actually resorted to mixing them in her food or tea. But the pillbox containing her mother's daily medications was empty. Nothing in the trash. Had her mother flushed them down the toilet?

Kat didn't want to re-dose her—too much was just as bad as not enough. She'd learned that the hard way. In the past year, the medications had gotten more complicated than ever. Her mother's doctor seemed to be getting stricter about dosages and schedules for both sedatives and mood stabilizers.

She went back to the living room and sat with her mother. Emilia was in better spirits than Kat had seen in months. They watched the news in companionable silence. Her name was mentioned in a three-minute story but it had stopped being top news. Alex had made a statement outside headquarters a few hours ago saying that the campaign had asked Kat to write an honest report on her father's defense policies. She rolled her eyes.

"He's quite the charmer, isn't he?"

Kat couldn't agree more.

"I'm glad Bill is finally going to know you," Emilia continued. "I tried contacting him, you know, after the divorce. To tell him. But he wouldn't take my calls."

Kat turned to her mother. She'd spent years trying to get her to talk about her father. "I thought you said you didn't tell him."

"Because he never gave me the chance. He was so angry with me for leaving him."

Kat's eyes widened. She'd always thought

it was her father who broke things off. "Why did you leave him?"

Her mother sighed. "We had a whirlwind romance in college during our senior year. He asked me to marry him on our third date. Graduation was coming up, and he wanted me to come with him, to his home in Northern Virginia, so we could be close to DC. I hardly knew him, but he was charming and so handsome. I was young and didn't know any better. After we were married, it all started."

Her mother stared at the TV. Kat picked up the remote and turned it off. "What started, Mom?"

"First, his mother told me I needed to change the way I dress. Be more like Jackie O. She took me shopping. I hated those clothes—they were itchy and uncomfortable. Then Bill took me to a cocktail party where they were talking about the Cold War. I spoke up and told them what I thought, that we needed to focus on jobs at home, not on stockpiling weapons and hunting down spies."

She shook her head. "Bill laughed at me, called me a silly woman. I was so embarrassed. When we got home, he told me I had no business making those comments. My job at those parties was to smile and look pretty."

Kat's heart ached for her mother. For most of

Kat's life she'd been sick, but once in a while when her medication was just right, Emilia showed Kat a glimpse of the intelligent and vibrant woman she was. She had often wondered whether her mother would have been a different person if she hadn't been heartbroken over her father.

"There was always something. I didn't know how to host a proper dinner party or smile properly when the photographers snapped our picture. I started staying home more and we drifted apart. I could tell I wasn't the wife he'd hoped for. Then one night I heard his daddy tell him that I was going to ruin his dreams of becoming president. He told his father he'd made a commitment to me, and as a good Christian, he wasn't going to break his marriage vows. He said he'd just have to give up his dreams. That's when I left."

Kat put her arm around her mother. Emilia wiped her eyes. "I loved him, Kat. I wasn't going to be the reason he didn't become the great man I knew he could be."

"Did you tell him why you left?"

Her mother nodded. "I told him we weren't right for each other, that he needed to marry a woman who could be his first lady. He was so angry with me…wouldn't talk to me after I left…said I'd abandoned him. Then you came and I had a new purpose in life. By then he'd remarried and had a perfect new wife. I saw them on TV, the perfect couple. She looked great on camera. I figured if I said anything he might sue for custody, and I'd lose you, too."

So that was when it had all started. Kat's aunt had told her that undiagnosed postpartum depression had made her mother spiral out of control. But what if it was heartbreak, too? She squeezed her eyes shut to keep from crying. "I don't have to do this, Mom. I don't need to know him. I'll quit the campaign."

Her mother grabbed her arm. "No, Katerina, I want you to know your father. I should have found a way to tell him. You need him now."

Something in her mother's tone gripped her heart. "What do you mean, Mom?"

Her mother shook her head. "It's time, Kat. It's time."

Kat wanted to press her mother, but a look at the wall clock told her it was almost time for the video call with the senator. Muttering an excuse about a grocery-store errand, she left. She drove to a nearby coffee shop and parked in a dark spot.

After powering up the tablet and following Crista's instructions to sign into the video chat app, all she had to do was wait. The senator would initiate the call. Her heart was pounding so loudly, she was sure he'd be able to hear it on the other end. She took out the BlackBerry to distract herself and noticed several messages from Alex. She must've missed them when she was talking to her mother.

Do you want to come to DC tomorrow? Briefings on the IED bill.

Would be good experience for you.

Hello?

Good material for your book.

Kat? I see your BlackBerry is online. Are you ignoring me?

This is not how I expect my staff to behave.

She'd seen the other staffers constantly glued to their phones, but she refused to use the holster that would let her clip it to her person. Crista went as far as to say that she only wore clothes that allowed her to attach the BlackBerry. Kat thought about how to play this with him. Going to Washington, DC, tomorrow? It would be a three-hour drive for her, and she'd have to leave well before dawn to avoid the horrendous rush-hour traffic in DC. It was a long trip for one day. But she would get to spend it with Alex, away from campaign headquarters. Maybe she could grill him about his endgame, find out what he was up to with her.

She thought about how easily she'd melted under his intense gaze. Was it a smart idea to spend more time with Alex? She punched out a message.

Chill. My BlackBerry was in my purse.

His response came seconds later. The man must have lightning-fast fingers.

Keep it on you at all times. That's an order.

Really?

I don't take orders from you.

She waited.

You do if you want to work on the campaign. DC tomorrow. Be here by 9.

She stuck her tongue out at the device.

I'll be there at 8. Be available to sign me in.

She was not, in fact, going to take orders from him, and tomorrow was a good opportunity to tell him face-to-face.

The tablet chimed and her father's face lit up the screen. With trembling fingers, she touched the answer button.

CHAPTER FIVE

KAT ARRIVED AT the Hart Senate Office Building well before eight in the morning. After a sleepless night following the brief conversation with her father, she gave up on sleep to get an early start on her drive.

Why was she so upset about the conversation? What had she expected from a man who didn't know she existed and didn't know anything about her? Still, the whole exchange left a bad taste in her mouth. But she couldn't think about that now; it was going to be a long day and she needed to focus her energy on the meetings ahead.

She used a home health service for her mother for times she needed to be away. It was horribly expensive, but with her class schedules she couldn't always be around to make sure Emilia took her pills. Kat had scheduled a nurse to come check in on her mother twice a day for the summer months. She didn't want the campaign staff gossiping about her needing to leave to take care of her mother. The expense would drain her savings account, but there was nothing that could be done about it. Hopefully, her work on the campaign would pay off with a promotion.

Washington, DC, was alive at this early hour, with staffers rushing into buildings holding steaming cups of coffee. It was a pleasant morning; the heat of the day hadn't hit, and the famous August humidity was still a couple of months away. The dome of the Capitol rose above all the rooftops. A law limiting the height of buildings effectively eliminated buildings taller than thirteen stories. It gave the city a light, airy feeling. She loved coming here and wished she didn't have to rush home after the briefings. The Smithsonian museums were free for visitors and contained some of the world's greatest collections.

Maybe while she was working on the campaign, she could ask Aunt Luce to come look after her mother for a night or two so she could stay a few days in a row.

She checked her phone. Alex had emailed her an agenda for the day, and it showed back-to-back meetings all morning. He'd left a visitor pass for her so she wouldn't need him to sign in. Most of the congressional members had offices in buildings around the Capitol to accommodate their vast staffs and allow the general public to visit them without the hassle of the Capitol building's security measures. A subway system connected the office buildings to the Capitol.

Kat stopped outside the building to marvel at the marble facade. Despite lecturing on what happened between its walls, she'd never actually been inside. She followed a rush of staffers into the building and stopped. The ninety-foot atrium rose before her, drawing her eyes upward to Alexander Calder's famous *Mountains and Clouds* sculpture featuring black aluminum clouds over black mountains. As people moved around her, Kat stood and stared. It was awe inspiring to experience something she'd only seen in pictures.

"It's quite something, isn't it?"

His warm breath tickled her ear, and she froze.

"I'm not sure I like it."

"Oh?" Alex didn't move. Just stood there, smelling of clean soap and fresh coffee.

"The sharp angles, the blackness of the sculpture. It seems illusory."

"Any why is that so offensive to you?" His voice was sardonic.

"This is one of the most powerful buildings in the world. The most senior senators of our Congress use these offices to make policy that affects the lives of people around the globe, whether it's international aid to disaster victims or sending troops into battle. Everything should convey the gravitas of the power and responsibility here."

She felt him step away from her and turned. He was eyeing her with open curiosity.

"For once, I agree with you. Come, let me show you to our offices."

She followed him through the atrium and to the elevators. They went up to the dual-level suite of offices for the senator. He quickly introduced her to the staff, who all greeted her with the same warmth—and barely concealed scrutiny—that the campaign headquarters staff had.

He showed her to a cramped area that the staff used for their break room. There was a laptop on a small table. "Space is a premium here, so we can't give you a desk, but you can use this space when you come visit if you need to check email or make a call. This is also where we keep the coffee."

He refreshed the cup he'd been holding then held out the pot for her. She grabbed a disposable cup and let him fill it.

"Alex Santiago pouring a cup of coffee—now, that's something I didn't think I'd ever see."

He turned and smiled broadly. Kat studied the woman who had sparked such a brilliant response from him.

"This is Mellie Rodgers. She is the senator's highly capable executive assistant." Mellie was almost as tall as Alex and was impeccably dressed in a pale pink suit that would've made Jackie O look fashion-challenged. Her auburn hair was styled in a chignon, and her pinch-toed maroon shoes probably cost as much as Kat's rent. All of a sudden she felt frumpy, despite the fact that she was wearing her best suit, a tailored navy pinstripe with a gray silk blouse underneath. Of course her shoes were sensible flats since she'd known she'd have to walk a bit from the parking lot at Union Station.

"What he means is that I'm the person who keeps tabs on the senator's whereabouts and keeps Alex in check." She reached out and straightened his tie. It hadn't been crooked, but was now. "If you need anything, Katerina, you let me know. Apparently we're to roll out the red carpet for you."

Kat stared at Mellie's retreating figure. "What did she mean by that?"

Alex took her to his office and shut the door. He glanced in the mirror on the back of the door and adjusted his tie. Kat suppressed a smile.

"You'll find a lot of interesting staff in this office and working for the campaign. We unfortunately have to indulge donors who make significant contributions by giving their children jobs."

"That should be illegal." Kat knew she sounded naive, but she couldn't help it.

"That would make my job so much easier. During campaign years we can send them to headquarters or one of the field offices, but all of the staff here have been with us for a number of years."

"Why are you telling me this?"

"Because it's understood that staff who get their jobs because of who their daddies are get limited access and responsibility until they prove their worth."

"Oh," she said simply.

"But you are the exception because the senator has said that he wants you to be fully involved."

She took a big sip of her coffee, nearly burning her mouth.

He went behind his desk. The office wasn't large, but it was certainly bigger than her closet office at the college. He had a carved wood desk with some trinkets on it but not a lot of the personal junk that normally littered desks. By the window was a more functional wood table with a computer, printer and various office paraphernalia.

The wall was decorated with photos of Alex with the senator, the president and various high-ranking congressional leaders. There was one picture on his desk that was hidden from view, turned away from where she was standing as a guest. In the corner was a pole with the US flag. His office looked like it could belong to an old, stuffy man, not at all like the other work spaces she'd seen in the rest of this modern building. It was an office with gravitas.

"So how did your conversation with the senator go last night?"

"It was fine."

"Just fine?"

"Would you like me to wait in the break room while you prepare for our first meeting?"

He blinked then shrugged off his jacket. His muscles flexed beneath the plain white shirt. When did he find the time to work out?

"Take a seat."

She sat in a plush leather guest chair.

"I understand Nathan sent you the policy briefs for the IED bill. I want to hear your thoughts."

She took another swallow of her coffee. "It was an interesting analysis, taking into account perspectives I hadn't considered when I did my lecture earlier this semester."

He sat back in his chair, trying but failing to control the smug look on his face.

"But my position hasn't changed. In fact, it's even more firm than before."

"Excuse me? Did you not read the statistics on how many lives the new technology could save?"

"My argument isn't with the merits of the bill. It's with the need for it. I don't think we should be at war anymore. We need to bring the troops home and use that money to improve our schools, provide better funding to local law enforcement, bolster social security, take care of our own people."

He laughed humorlessly. "You think we can just bring the troops home. Tell me, have you ever served?"

She shook her head and leaned forward, opening her mouth to argue about the research she had done, but he held up his hand. "I did a tour in Iraq as a reservist."

She closed her mouth. He had served? Maybe that explained his physique. "Our troops are in danger every second of every day. IEDs are on every street corner, and we use decades-old detection technology. Is it okay to let our men and women die out there? You're telling me you don't support our troops."

"I do support our troops. But we can't keep using taxpayer money for them to police an overseas nation when our own kids are suffering in poverty, when our elders can't afford health care, when..."

"Kat, you can't support our troops if you don't support their mission."

A knock on the door interrupted their staring contest. Mellie stepped in a second after she'd knocked, not bothering to wait for an invitation.

"Alex, I had to move your nine-thirty to now so we could fit in that DOD contractor you added yesterday."

Alex nodded. He turned to Kat. "Your job in these meetings is to listen and learn. You can ask questions, but only if they are not inflammatory. No comments or opinions."

She pursed her lips but nodded.

The door opened and a woman in a khaki uniform walked in. Her name tag said Atao. She was tall and slim with light brown hair pulled neatly into a bun and gray eyes.

"Hi, I'm Anna Atao."

Kat leaned forward. Was this woman here to talk about the IED bill? That seemed odd.

Her uniform was from the Public Health Service Commissioned Corps, which responded to public health disasters. What did that have to do with IEDs?

Alex gestured to the guest chair. "It's also Captain Atao and Dr. Atao, isn't it?"

"That's correct."

Alex introduced Kat then thumbed through a folder on his desk. "And I understand that you've requested this meeting be kept private because your supervisor, Rear Admiral McKenzie, doesn't know you're here?"

She nodded. "As you know, federal staff are prohibited from lobbying members of Congress, so I'm here to educate you on an issue important to me. However, I'm here as a member of the public and not representing the Commissioned Corps. I wouldn't normally come in uniform, but I have to leave for Brazil right after this meeting."

Alex sat back. "Now that we've dispensed with the disclaimers, I'd like to hear your concerns. I assure you this meeting is confidential."

Anna Atao didn't waste any time. "Sir, babies born with atrial septal defect die unless it's surgically repaired. The surgery is widely available in the United States and has a mortality rate of less than one percent."

She handed Alex a piece of paper. "On that sheet is the number of American babies who die each year on the island of Guam because they can't get that surgery. Even though their parents beg, borrow and steal the money to pay for the procedure, they die because they can't afford airfare to Hawaii or California. Sometimes there aren't even enough seats on a commercial flight to accommodate the baby incubator, nurse and a family member. The airlines don't help. The military has a huge base in Guam, but they won't get involved, either." The woman's pitch was rehearsed, but Kat heard a deeply buried pain in her voice.

Alex's face was impassive as he read the information sheet, but Kat saw the frustration in his eyes. "Captain Atao, this is an issue for the government of Guam. The governor needs to work with Congress if he wants more resources for the island. The military base is not available to serve civilians."

Kat glared at him.

Captain Atao stood. She put her hands behind her back and Kat noticed her fingers trembling. "Guam has no representation in the US Congress, so the people must rely on the goodwill of men like you."

"I see here you no longer reside there?"

She stiffened, and Kat watched her link and

unlink her fingers behind her back. This was personal.

"I don't."

"I'll talk to the senator and try to get you a meeting with him next month."

"That won't work for me. As I mentioned, I deploy to Brazil for the Zika virus outbreak today. I may be there for months."

Mellie knocked on the door to indicate their time was up.

Alex stood and came around his desk. "I'll do what I can, but I don't want to give you false hope. It's a tough issue."

Captain Atao blinked then thanked Alex and left. Mellie ushered in the next appointment. Kat excused herself and caught up with the captain. "Captain Atao."

She turned in surprise. "Call me Anna, please."

"Anna, what do you need for the island? Surgical facilities? Helicopters to do medical transport?"

Anna shook her head. "We need to upgrade our hospital and have a regular schedule of visiting surgeons so families don't go bankrupt trying to get to Hawaii or the Philippines."

She had said "our." Kat wondered if Anna was from Guam.

"What would it cost?"

Anna rattled off a figure. "Will you help?" Her eyes held so much hope that Kat immediately regretted her impulsivity.

"I don't have any power here, but I do want the facts in case there's an opportunity for me to say something."

"You know how parents whose children have cancer pray every day for a cure? In this case, there is a cure—a simple surgery. You have no idea what it's like for a mother to watch her baby die."

Kat reeled at the raw pain in Anna's voice. She reached into her pocket and pulled out her faculty business card with her email address. She hadn't gotten a campaign business card yet. Grabbing a pen off a nearby desk, she added her personal cell number. "Take this and please contact me. I will do my best for you."

Anna nodded gratefully then left.

The rest of the morning was a whirlwind. Most appointments were scheduled for fifteen minutes, though some of the bigger players got thirty. Kat's stomach grumbled loudly as one o'clock rolled by. She'd been too nervous to have breakfast, and now she regretted the four cups of coffee she'd downed.

Watching Alex work was fascinating. He was gracious, charming and made everyone feel like they'd gotten what they wanted from him while giving away nothing. It was quite an art form.

"Are you hungry?" he asked.

"Starving."

"How do you feel about food trucks?"

"What?"

"Come on—we have a whole thirty minutes. I'll buy you one of the best meals in DC."

She grabbed her purse and followed him out. They walked down the block to a street where four trucks were parked on the side of the road. Delicious aromas teased her nose.

"Looks like we have a choice of Italian, Mexican, crepes and fried chicken."

"So it's not the same trucks every day?"

He shook his head. "It's whoever can get parking. They go all over the city."

"What do you recommend?"

He pointed to the Mexican truck. "It's a little spicy, but to die for."

She smiled. "Why not?"

They made their way over and he ordered an enchilada. She hesitated then ordered the stuffed poblano peppers. His lips quirked. "You know that's really spicy."

"How bad can it be?"

"I don't recommend it. I'm used to spicy food, and even I don't order it."

She gave him a coy smile. "Can't handle the heat?"

The vendor called their order and they picked up the take-out containers. He pointed to a bench and they sat down.

Kat took a bite of her pepper, savoring the sting of spices on her tongue.

"You really do like it?" He sounded surprised.

She laughed. "I actually love Mexican. Did you grow up eating Salvadorean food?"

He looked at her, arching an eyebrow.

"What? You think you're the only one capable of using Google?"

He took a bite of his food. "Salvadorean dishes aren't as peppery hot as Mexican food."

"What's your favorite?"

He stopped chewing. "I was born here, and with the hours my mother worked, she didn't have a lot of time to cook. I grew up eating fast food like regular Americans."

Something in his tone made her pause. "Where did your mother work?" she finally asked.

He took his time, downing a swig of his drink. "Here and there. She worked as a housekeeper. Still does."

Without thinking, she put a hand on his shoulder. "My mother has a degree in biology. She used to be a high-school teacher but for the past several years she's barely held down jobs as a waitress, a check-out clerk at the grocery store, even a short-order cook at a fast-food joint. Making an honest living is admirable."

He scoffed. "Listen to yourself. The worst your mother had to be was a short-order cook. My mother couldn't get that kind of job. The only work offered to her were things that regular Americans didn't want to do. Cleaning toilets, hauling out animal manure, clearing sewers."

"Did you have to watch her at those jobs?" she asked softly.

He crumpled his napkin, threw it into his container of half-eaten food and closed the lid. "We should get back." Standing, he threw the remains of his lunch into a nearby trash can.

Kat held on to hers; she was starving and would find a quiet moment to finish her lunch later. Alex had already started walking and she had to run to catch up to him.

"You didn't answer my question. Did you have to watch your mother at her job?"

He whirled, his eyes shining. Of all the times she'd seen him look angry, this was the first time she sensed a deeper emotion in his eyes. Something dark lurked just beneath the surface. "Why must you persist?"

His tone should have made her shrink back, but she stepped closer to him. She didn't want to lose this moment, perhaps the only honest moment they'd had together. He knew everything about her life, had taken it upon himself to be her protector, yet she knew very little about him beyond what he showed on the surface. "Answer the question, Alex."

This time he stepped away from her. "Yes, I went with her. I watched my intelligent, capable mother degrade herself doing menial work just so she could feed me. I stood by while she suffered so I could have a better life. Now can we focus on work?"

The pain in his eyes was so raw that she longed to touch him, to let him know she saw it. But somehow she knew now was not the time to push him any further. He took out his BlackBerry and thumbed it all the way back to the office. When they entered, Mellie handed him a stack of messages and he asked Kat to sit out the next few meetings.

She followed him to his office anyway. When he turned to close the door, she put her hand on the frame. "I'm supposed to have full access. I didn't drive all the way over here for you to shut me out because I asked some personal questions."

He narrowed his eyes but she stepped closer. She wasn't afraid of him. There was a real Alex behind the facade he presented; one she desperately wanted to see. He was the only man since Colin who didn't physically scare her, and she needed to know why.

His hand remained on the door. If she wanted to get by him, she'd have to squeeze past him. She wasn't going to let him intimidate her. Two steps forward and she would be barely an inch from him. The second she made her move, he took a sharp breath then let go of the door and backed up.

Kat smiled and took her designated spot on the couch from where she'd observed the other meetings that morning—mostly constituent briefings in which various organizations came asking for money for their initiatives. They all sounded important, but her mind kept returning to Anna Atao. Kat could still hear the anguish in Anna's voice. There was something haunting about it, as if Anna hadn't been talking about just any baby. She opened the takeout container to finish her lunch.

"You know, you want me to open up to you about my mother but you still haven't given me a real answer about your call with your father."

She paused mid bite then finished chewing slowly.

"What exactly do you want me to say? He's a stranger to me. We exchanged pleasantries. He asked about my mother and to tell him about myself. It felt more like a job interview than a reunion."

"He's a good man. He probably didn't know how to interact with you. Video calls can be awkward."

"My mother tried to contact him when she found out she was pregnant. He wouldn't take her calls."

"Relationships are complicated."

Don't I know it.

"You don't abandon the people you love, no matter what," she said. She pointed to the picture on his desk, the one hidden from visitors. "Is that a picture of your mother?"

He nodded and turned it around. She stood to take a closer look. He was standing next to a small woman with black hair and dark eyes who was smiling into the camera, her face filled with joy. Alex was wearing an ill-fitted shirt, his bushy hair tousled and his arm around his mother. Kat picked up the frame. "How old is this?"

"That was the day I graduated from college. Made her sacrifices worthwhile."

The pain in his eyes was so fresh, her heart ached for him. She longed to ask him more, but a knock on the door signaled their next meeting had arrived.

Kat returned to the couch and opened the briefing folder for the meeting. The new arrivals were senior management at a defense contracting firm. Both were well into their sixties. One man was tall with a comb-over, while the other looked like his hair plugs were falling apart. They spent the first few minutes talking about mundane things. As with every other meeting, the men eyed Kat with obvious interest but were polite enough not to engage her further when Alex introduced her "observer" role. Kat watched Alex enthusiastically banter with them as if they were the only people he was meeting with all day. She'd watched him do this all morning, and she was exhausted just from watching.

Then they got down to business.

"Alex, m'boy, if the senator wants to continue with the IED bill, we've got to support the other guy. You know we manufacture the EAGLE. You'll put us out of business." Comb-over shifted, the chair creaking under his weight.

From the reports she'd read, Kat knew the EAGLE was a robotic IED detector that a soldier could operate from a thousand meters away. The problem was how easily its sensors jammed with sand and malfunctioned in the heat. According to the reports, the Egyptians had improved the EAGLE technology, testing it extensively in desert climates.

Alex stood and opened a cabinet that Kat now saw contained a bar.

"Gentlemen, let me pour you some bourbon."

Kat stared as he fished out three crystal glasses and a decanter. He held up a glass for her and she shook her head. Was this an episode of *Mad Men*?

He poured the dark liquid then added ice from a bucket that had also been hidden in the cabinet. How had that gotten there? Did he have elves to stock his bar?

The men, clearly accustomed to this treatment, sat back in their chairs. Unlike the morning meetings, which had been scheduled in fifteen- and thirty-minute increments, this one was penciled in for a full hour.

"You know as well as I do that the senator needs your support, now more than ever," Alex said. "But the bill is his legacy, his last big endeavor before he runs for president. Tell me how we can make this work for you."

Hair plugs leaned forward. "A contract committing to buying the EAGLE at current levels for the next ten years."

Kat took a sharp breath. Alex gave her a warning look. The visitors didn't seem to notice. The EAGLE would be redundant if they bought the Egyptian technology, and no one wanted such a long-term engagement in Iraq.

"That's a tall order," Alex said calmly, as if they were discussing a few hundred dollars' worth of product rather than a commitment of hundreds of millions.

"You know the Egyptians have already bettered whatever they're selling the senator right now. Give us ten years and we'll get you the best technology there is." Hair plugs took a noisy sip of his drink.

"We don't want to be engaged overseas in ten years."

"But you know very well we will be," Combover said arrogantly.

Alex sipped his drink, contemplating the decision. "What would your commitment to the senator be?"

The men looked at each other then slid an envelope across Alex's desk. He opened it and pulled out what appeared to be a check.

"This is generous, but not enough."

He slid it back toward the men.

Kat felt like she was on the highway watching a bad accident unfolding but unable to stop it. Barely five feet away from her, these men were playing with taxpayer money, making a deal that affected the lives of thousands of soldiers. They were doing it while drinking bourbon and talking cavalierly about millions of dollars.

The hour felt like ten. When the men stood to leave, they smiled and wished her luck, winking salaciously at Alcx, who smiled back serenely.

The second they were gone, Mellie entered, carrying a tray with an ice bucket and new glasses. Alex helped her load the used glasses and store the new ones. Kat had seen him take several sips of his drink but now noticed his glass was mostly full.

The nauseating trend continued through two more meetings, each one worse than before in terms of the "ask" and the money they were willing to pay in campaign contributions to get what they wanted. By comparison, the morning meetings were amateur hour. None of the constituent organizations had offered money, and they'd all come armed with educational materials. For the afternoon meetings, various old men and one gray-haired woman had strolled in with checks and a sense of entitlement.

When the last meeting was done, Kat turned to Alex. "Tell me you don't actually deposit those checks."

He rolled his eyes. "I didn't want you in here this afternoon. It was your father's idea. He wanted you to see how politics actually works. After reading your academic papers, he thinks it's time you opened your eyes about the real world."

"To see what? That politicians really are crooked? That the biggest check determines the fate of the American people? You'd let babies die in Guam but give those EAGLE manufacturers millions of dollars for obsolete technology?"

"Did you see me take a single check this morning? Those organizations can't afford to buy their access, but I give them time."

"I also didn't see you give them a full hour or pour them drinks."

"That's because those were the real meetings of the day, the ones where we learn about the issues. They don't need drinks because they come armed with information and want nothing more than for us to listen. The meetings you just witnessed are what we use to make sure we have the staff and resources to get the senator reelected."

"And what about the promises you made?"

"We try to keep them, but it's not always possible. The senator is a senior member of the Appropriations Committee, but he can't guarantee we'll purchase the EAGLEs. All they want to see is that we put it in the budget proposal. It won't go in the House budget, and when we go to the conference committee for a final budget to send to the president, the EAGLE funding will disappear."

Her eyes widened. "That's so dishonest."

He laughed. "This is how the real world of politics works. And before you feel too bad for them—you think they'd give me a check for a hundred thousand dollars without knowing the score? They do it for access. They'll go to the House members next and ask them to put it in the budget. We call these types of things the pork in the budget, and some of it gets through. We're not the only ones playing this game."

"But why not take the high ground?" she whispered.

"Because the senator will never get reelected without money, and the next guy may never take the morning meetings. The next guy may never pass on the briefing paper about the babies in Guam to the senator and suggest he call the governor."

"So you're the lesser of two evils."

He shrugged.

She closed her eyes. She wasn't naive enough not to know about campaign contributions and the "chit" system in Congress, where favors were traded. She often analyzed what potential chits had passed through which hands when congressional members suddenly changed their votes on an issue. But witnessing it firsthand made it seem seedier. For some reason, she expected more from Alex, more from the senator with whom she shared her DNA.

Alex was staring at her. "You're disappointed in the senator for playing these games."

She sighed. "I don't know the man. I'm not sure what to expect from him."

"Then why is this upsetting to you?"

"I'm okay," she said defensively. She didn't want to come across all Pollyanna.

"Your father wants to get to know you."

"He has a funny way of showing it."

He quirked a brow then gestured to the couch. Opening the cabinet door, he pulled out a bottle of wine. She shook her head. "I need to drive back."

"Okay. Then how about I tell you a story."

She looked at him wearily, but he pointed firmly to the couch, so she sat down. It would take three hours to get home and she could barely keep her eyes open now.

"I've known the senator for five years—he hired me right after his last campaign manager quit. You ask anyone in Washington and they'll call me a winner. A small-time one, but a winner nonetheless. I was working for Senator Graham at the time."

"Senator Graham," she repeated. "The Republican nominee for president?"

He nodded. "It was my ticket to the big time, but I made a bad call."

He turned toward the window and stared at a partial view of the Capitol building outside. It was currently encased in wired scaffolding—repair work to restore the outer part of the rotunda.

"I told the senator that his wife was having an affair."

Kat sat back. That was certainly not public knowledge and would be a blow to the now presidential candidate. Why was Alex trusting her with this information?

"I suspected something and decided independently to have the senator's wife followed so I could give him concrete proof. Turns out, he knew about it already and took offense at my initiative."

"That's a hard call to make."

He nodded. "I've replayed it a thousand times and realized that you don't mess with your boss's family. No matter how close I was to him, family lines should not have been crossed."

She found herself drawn to his eyes, to the smoky darkness burning inside them.

"Senator Graham could have blacklisted me in Washington. My career would've been over if he had. But I heard this position was open and I took a chance. I came here and told Senator Roberts the truth about everything and begged him to take me in."

"And he did," she said softly.

Alex nodded. "Not only that—he put pressure on Senator Graham to keep quiet about me. People assumed I got a promotion. Aside from the two senators, you're the only person I've told."

"Why did you tell me?"

"Because your father is a good man at heart. My job is to do his dirty work. Don't let what I do affect your opinion of him."

Warmth bloomed in her heart. She wondered what it would be like if he pulled her into his arms. All day she'd looked at him as a reminder of what she didn't want in a man. But here he was, showing her how wrong she was. He was protecting her father, just like the little boy inside who longed to protect his mother.

"Senator Roberts offered me money."

She hadn't planned on telling him or anyone else. It was all too embarrassing. In fact, she'd been up all night wondering whether she should quit the campaign. Finally, she'd settled on staying until the senator returned so she would have enough material to write some papers to appease Dean Gladstone. In what she'd witnessed today alone, she could write several fascinating commentaries on the trade-offs that occurred all the time in politics.

This morning she'd been convinced the IED bill was the wrong approach, but after listening to some of the constituent meetings, it became clear things were bad in Iraq and bound to get worse if they withdrew the troops. Now that they were in, could they really leave? What if the country was worse off than it had been?

Besides, she needed to meet her father in person. She'd waited too long to give up that opportunity.

Alex was staring at her.

"He wanted to buy me," she clarified.

"Excuse me?"

She shifted on the couch. "Yesterday on the call, after he grilled me like I was on trial for fraud, he offered me money. I didn't fully understand what it was for, but I politely declined."

"Are you sure you didn't misinterpret? It's not like he's denying that you're his daughter. What does he have to gain by paying you off?"

"There's not a lot of analysis required when a man says, 'You know, if you're hard up, I can give you some money. I don't want people thinking my child is living in poverty.' It was like he was just waiting for his chance to say that, like he hadn't been paying any attention for the twenty minutes I'd been telling him about my life."

Alex flinched. "I'm sure he didn't mean anything by it. He was probably as nervous as you were and just meant to ask if he could do anything to help."

She sighed. "I appreciate you sharing that story, but I really should get going."

"Why don't you stay the night? We rent a town house on Capitol Hill for staffers who have to go back and forth. It's cheaper than paying for hotel rooms. I have some meetings tomorrow that'll be more uplifting. Less... mafia-ish."

She smiled at the last part. He did get it. She shook her head. "I need to go home."

"I can ask one of the interns to go check on your mother."

She looked up, touched by his consideration but also perturbed by the intrusion of privacy. Again.

She stood. "This has been an educational day, but I'd better get on the road if I want to avoid rush-hour traffic."

He got up slowly. "Kat, we're a family around here. We take care of each other. It's not an imposition. You can call to tell her who it will be so it doesn't feel like a random stranger."

Tears stung her eyes. It would be nice to take the night off. She was already exhausted, and the prospect of a three-hour drive didn't sound as appealing as spending a night in DC. She wondered whether Alex used the town house, too, or if he had his own place. They might have just shared a moment, but she'd seen so many sides of him. Which one could she trust?

"Yesterday you were lecturing me on pulling my own weight and today we're a kumbaya family?"

She sounded testier than she intended. Maybe it was the stress of the past two days. Or maybe it was the mixed signals Alex kept throwing her way that had her confused about where she stood with him.

"What's gotten into you?"

She stepped up to him. "You're what's gotten into me. Yesterday you went from being a white knight to a bear, then sent me flirty emails. Today you start out caring, then morph into a sleazy deal maker then switch to Mr. Understanding and Compassion. Can you pick a man so I can know who I'm dealing with?"

A slow smile spread across his lips. "What's your favorite kind?"

She took a step back, her stomach fluttering. "Excuse me?"

"Which Alex do you like best?" He was standing so close she could feel his chest rise and fall with every breath. "The Alex who saved a damsel in distress…"

She opened her mouth to protest that characterization of her, but all that came out was a squeak as he closed the meager distance between them. *Run, Kat, run.* He wasn't touching her, yet she could smell the whiskey on his breath, its spicy scent making her head light. She felt the steady rise and fall of his chest, could almost hear the heavy drum of his heart. Perhaps that was the pounding in her own chest.

"Do you like the Alex who bosses you around? Or do you like the one who couldn't stop staring at you yesterday? The one who had to physically leave his office so he'd stop finding excuses to come talk to you."

She gasped. He stepped closer but didn't make a move to touch her. She stood as still as she could, afraid to move a muscle.

Bending his head, he touched his lips to her hair. "Tell me, Kat, which Alex is it that you like?"

The vibrations from his voice sent pulses through her entire body. Which Alex, indeed? There was the Alex who warmed her heart, the one who frustrated her and the one who made her want to run away from him as fast as she could.

"Are there more Alexes that I haven't seen?" Her voice sounded foreign to her. She heard him take a breath, the air tickling the sensitive skin on her neck.

He moved his lips and touched her ear. Every nerve in her body was on alert, telling her to get out of here, yet she stood rooted to the spot, waiting for whatever was coming.

He softly kissed the top of her ear. His gentleness was surprising. Every inch of him screamed of a man used to taking what he wanted. Except the Alex before her seemed to be tentative, asking permission at every step.

This was a mistake on so many levels. She couldn't get involved with a man who represented everything she hated. Lying, deceit, manipulation—he was a master at it. Not to mention the drama that would ensue at campaign headquarters. Her father already believed she was out to get something from him; what would he think of her if she started seeing his campaign manager two days after she came on board? And if this became another media *thing*, her job at the university was as good as gone. There were so many reasons not to be with him. She lifted her arms to push him away, but once her hands were on his chest, she savored the feel of hard muscle beneath his shirt. Instead of pushing, she closed the remaining gap between them.

He made a sound deep in his throat and she lifted her head.

"Kat."

He whispered her name with so much softness that the chains around her heart broke. She touched her lips to his, eager to feel the strength of the powerful man before her.

Her lips slid across his. She expected him— *no, wanted him*—to claim her mouth, needed him to pull her closer. He cupped her face in his hands. He kissed her so tenderly, it left her trembling. She was sure her legs would give way any second. As if sensing that, he placed a firm hand on her waist, holding her without forcing her close. It was unlike any kiss she'd ever experienced. It left her breathless, and it ended too soon. He rested his head on top of hers, holding her loosely, as if it was the most natural thing to do.

"This Alex I can love."

The words were out of her mouth before she could stop them.

He tensed. "Kat, I can't."

The words cut through her.

She turned away, but he placed a hand on her shoulder. "I owe a lot to the senator, and he's asked that I look after you. I can't lie—I am attracted to you, but I don't do relationships. And you don't seem like the type of girl who dates someone just for fun."

She whirled. "If you've figured that out, then what's all this, Alex? Why bring me close then push me away?" She'd meant to sound outraged but the hurt rang clear in her voice. *This isn't fair.* Since Colin, she hadn't been able to feel close to a man; fear kept her away. Alex was the first man since who'd made her feel safe—however briefly.

He ran his fingers through his hair. "You're

right. I'm just not thinking. I'm being impulsive, something that's very unlike me. Since the second I saw that silly picture of you on TV, I haven't been myself."

"Great. So what you're telling me is that none of the Alexes I've seen are real."

He opened his mouth, but she held up her hand. "Your message has been received loud and clear, Alex. I'm not shiny enough to be worthy of standing at your side."

She turned to grab her purse but he caught her arm.

"Kat!"

She glared at him, then looked pointedly at her arm. He let go of it like he was touching something hot and rubbed the back of his neck. "It's not you."

She waited for the rest of the inevitable "it's me" speech.

"I'm not myself around you. I don't know what it is. I...I feel out of control when I'm with you."

He walked over to the desk and poured himself a thumb of whiskey. He lifted the glass to his mouth but stopped short of drinking.

"It's okay, Alex. Just tell me."

He set the glass down on the table with care.

"I hit a girl once." His voice was thick, shoulders slumped. Her veins filled with ice.

There must be more to the story. He wasn't the kind of man to hit a girl; he couldn't be. Seconds ticked by. Frozen, her feet wouldn't move, and even if they could, she didn't know whether to go to him or run as fast as she could out the door.

When he spoke again his voice was so soft, she had to step closer to hear him. "I was angry, and I did the one thing I swore I would never do. I was so out of control…"

The self-loathing in his voice clawed at her. She touched his arm. "It must have been an extraordinary circumstance."

He shook his head. "She made me so angry, I couldn't think straight. I hurt her."

Kat dropped her arm. It wasn't as if she was a good judge of men. If she were, she would've seen Colin for who he really was: a weak, desperate man who was so driven to prove himself to his father that he did terrible things. Who was she to say Alex wasn't the same?

"I grew up with men like that," he continued. "Men who took out their frustrations on a woman, men I loathe. Ever since that day, I've worked hard to be a man in control. I can't… I won't be with a woman if I can't trust myself with her."

You're not like that, Alex. The desperation in his voice was heart-wrenching.

"Please go, Kat."

She stared at him for a beat, then picked up her purse and left.

CHAPTER SIX

ALEX EYED THE bar after Kat left. He hated this part of his job and had become masterful at pretending to sip without actually drinking anything. Every once in a while, a donor would notice the full glass before Alex could pretend to refill it and insist he drink. When that happened, he'd shut the office door and wouldn't let anyone in for the rest of the day. He'd seen what alcohol did to men, and what men did to women when they didn't realize how much they'd had to drink. His mother's bruises might have healed, but he could still see the scars on her arms.

Scars that reminded him of the helpless child waiting outside a room hearing noises he knew were wrong; huddling in a corner like he'd been told to do when all he wanted was to charge through the doors. Scars that made him step away from any woman he cared about. And those were just the scars he could see. There were many more that his mother kept deep in her soul.

When he'd asked his mother about the wounds, she'd told him the governor didn't mean it. The governor was his mother's employer, a man people seemed to revere and admire when all Alex wanted to do was get his mother as far away from him as he could.

Alex prided himself on becoming a man who was a master of his actions. One who would never give a woman scars—of any kind. He would never allow anything to undo the hard-won restraint he kept on himself. Until now.

He was behaving differently around Kat, making questionable choices, like the one he'd just made by kissing her. What had gotten into him? He'd invited her to DC to prove to himself that he could be professional around her. He had no problems doing that with all the other women in the office. What was it about her?

Kat scared him. He had given himself a stern talking-to after he left the campaign offices, vowing to stay as far away from her as he could. She ignited something in him that no other woman had. The reins of self-control slid from his fingers whenever she was around.

He didn't feel the kind of blind rage he had as a teenager; this was something different.

But he wasn't going to risk going down a slippery slope.

He wouldn't go back to being that guy who had hit a girl. The raging bundle of hormones who'd had to look into his mother's eyes and see that he was no better than the men they both detested. Years of martial-arts training had given him the skills of self-discipline. *Yes, I can*—the mantra that reminded him he had the resolve and the inner strength to be the master of his behavior and emotions. Kat was putting those skills to the test, and he needed to stay away. The senator was due to return tomorrow, after which he would be canvassing the state, giving speeches and rallies to drum up support. Alex was going to go with him and keep Kat parked firmly at campaign headquarters. It was the only way to make sure he didn't do something else he'd regret, like jeopardize his career by getting involved with the boss's daughter. He had a plan he'd been working toward all his life, and Kat was not going to be the reason he failed.

THE CAMPAIGN HEADQUARTERS were quiet when Alex arrived. It was early in the morning. He needed that quiet to go over the information the senator had sent from Egypt last night. Alex had a whole team working on the bill, but he liked to be up to date on the latest information. While he trusted his staff, he was the one who had to make quick decisions.

Crista waved to him from her cubicle and he wondered whether she'd slept there. Hiring her had been one of his best moves since taking this position. Technically he was doing two jobs as both the campaign manager and chief of staff. He'd hired Crista as his deputy because she knew campaigns. Given their past relationship, he'd had his doubts, but she handled her job like a true professional. In the backstabbing world of campaigns, he knew she was loyal to him.

He'd barely turned on his laptop when Crista walked in with a steaming mug of coffee. She set it down and remained standing. "How did the meetings go yesterday?"

He gave her a quick rundown then handed her the checks he'd collected. As the campaign's deputy, Crista was responsible for working with the fund-raisers to keep the cash flowing. She eyed the checks. "Where's the one from the EAGLE manufacturers?"

"I'm working on a bigger donation from them."

"But they did give you a check?" The standard protocol was to deposit any checks as fast as they could and talk the donors into more later.

"They have some conditions I want to run by the senator."

Crista frowned. He understood her concern. Usually, it didn't matter what the conditions were and whether the senator disagreed with them. The idea was to get a donation and deposit it. Most mid-level contributors understood that they were buying access to the politician; any promises from staffers were tenuous at best. But with the EAGLE guys, he'd felt compelled to hold back.

"Did Kat do something?"

Alex looked up. Crista's highly intuitive nature was a great asset most of the time, but today it was annoying. "No," he said wearily. "I'll get back to you on that check—just get these ones in the bank."

She left without a word. Alex checked his watch. He had timed his visit so he could be in and out before Kat showed up. Figuring she'd take care of her mother in the morning, he'd be long gone by the time she got here.

The senator would arrive in a few hours at Dulles Airport then take a regional jet to Richmond. Alex planned to accompany him to a rally in the southern part of the state. It was yet another part of the job he hated, but it had to be done. You couldn't make change until you got elected, and winning an election required a pedigree and a healthy bank balance; both of which Alex didn't have.

While he detested meetings like the ones he'd had yesterday, they were necessary. He'd seen too many good candidates lose elections because they didn't know how to play the game. And that was why he was here: he would use his experience and connections to one day be the senator or governor who did things for the right reasons, who would make his mother proud. To give her center stage, so everyone would see her as the mother of someone important. So she could see herself as important. Not just the cleaning lady.

He went through the daily paperwork with record speed. The campaign required him to sign checks and approve reams of documents. Crista was highly organized and had things vetted for him so he could get through it quickly. He often wondered whether something could have come of their relationship. While Crista had broken it off, he knew she would've stayed if he'd given her even the tiniest indication that he was open to a future together. At the time, Senator Roberts had swayed his decision. "Alex, take it from someone who's learned the hard way—you want a woman who you can picture as the FLOTUS. A woman who sees your vision and can help you make it come to fruition."

Crista could have filled the role of first lady. She was intelligent and capable, and she understood politics. He had thought about it, but he'd held back with Crista. He wanted someone who would offer him a different perspective, who would make him think outside the box. Kat certainly did that. He sighed. But Kat was not FLOTUS material. Even as the senator's daughter, her aversion to the media and lack of willingness to rethink her ideals was a deal breaker. Not to mention the fact that he couldn't control himself around her. He had always wanted a woman who could challenge him, but not at the expense of his self-control.

A commotion near the front door caught his attention. He stepped out of his office to see an overeager reporter stick a microphone in Kat's face as she pounded on the glass. Alex and Crista were the only ones with the code to the front door. Crista typically opened it at eight in the morning, when the other staffers were expected. The media and even rival campaign workers were notorious for trying to sneak into headquarters to gather information.

Blood pounded in his ears as he threw open the door. He wanted nothing more than to shove the reporter who had the gall to grab her arm. He took a breath and gave a firm "No comment" to the obnoxious reporter.

A wide-eyed Kat, her hair escaping from the clip at the nape of her neck, stumbled in. She was wearing an ill-fitted pantsuit with a wrinkled blue shirt. And yet she was the most beautiful sight he'd ever seen. Her eyes were radiant, full of innocent hope. Just looking at her made him want to see the future in a different way.

"Why aren't you using the parking spot?"

"The garage wasn't open."

He plucked his BlackBerry from its holster and tapped out a message to the office manager to get Kat a key card that would let her in before and after hours.

"What're you doing here?" Her tone was accusatory.

"I work here."

She rolled her eyes. "You know what I mean. I thought you were in DC and wouldn't be coming here until after the senator arrived."

That was the plan he'd given her yesterday.

"Things change," he said dismissively. He tapped out another message to the campaign publicist. "I'm emailing Elle Howard—she'll take you shopping today."

"Excuse me?"

He knew without glancing up at her that she was mad. "Your clothing is unacceptable. We need to take photos with the senator today—something you agreed to. I can't have you looking like this. Elle will also take you to get your hair and makeup done." With anyone else, he would have explained it in a more diplomatic way. He sensed the steam coming out of her ears but he didn't stop. "And before you protest, just look at the pictures the media managed to snap yesterday. Is that really how you want to be seen?" He hated himself for talking to her like that, but the more distance he put between them, the better it would be.

DID HE HAVE to be so rude first thing in the morning? Kat fumed as she settled at her desk. She didn't know what to expect from him after yesterday, but his behavior was an insult. As soon as the computer booted up, she did an image search for her name. The photos loaded slowly, and she noted that her jacket appeared wrinkled even though she'd just gotten it from the dry cleaner's. She winced. Her face was pale and tendrils of blond hair had escaped her carefully constructed bun. One picture had been taken when she and Alex were walking back from lunch. Next to the suave and polished man, she looked downright dumpy.

She stabbed the mouse to close the screen. In third grade, she'd learned she would never be as popular as the other girls in school. Now she would never be as well liked by her students as the other professors. She didn't have an easy rapport with her students. Her role in life was to be the unremarkable woman. A publicist couldn't make a better version of her.

She opened her email to find a message from Elle Howard informing her that she would be coming by in an hour. Kat stood and marched to Alex's office to set him straight. Except Crista was sitting behind his desk when she arrived.

"He left already. I use his office when he isn't here," she said by way of explanation, but her fingers were moving a little too quickly as she stuffed a piece of paper into a yellow folder.

Kat sighed. "I wanted to talk to him about the publicist."

Crista nodded distractedly and glanced at the computer screen. "Elle's great. You'll like her."

"I don't need a publicist."

Crista met her gaze. "Kat, this is the first of many things you won't want to do. You're not just a campaign observer—you're the senator's daughter. Your image is important to this campaign."

"And that means you have to suck it up." Both women jumped at Alex's voice. Crista turned pale. Alex strode to his desk. "I forgot a file." He reached over and picked up the yellow folder Crista had been handling earlier.

The look he gave Kat made her pulse kick up a notch. He was always so intense; a fierce energy emanated from his every pore. "The senator is coming back to Richmond tonight. He wants to have dinner with you."

Kat began to protest, but he interrupted her. "It'll be early so you can get home to your mother."

She bit her lip. He bent down so he wasn't quite towering over her and fixed her with his dark eyes. "We're really trying to make things comfortable for you, Kat. Meet us halfway."

Without waiting for an answer, he left. Kat released a breath. "Is he always so forceful?"

Crista laughed. "No, he's usually even crazier when the senator is around."

Kat returned to her desk and had barely gotten back into the documents she'd been reading when someone tapped her on the shoulder. She turned to see a petite woman, stylishly dressed in a silk shirt, jeans and a sparkly rhinestone belt. Her dark brown hair bobbed around her heart-shaped face.

"Hi, I'm Elle," she said brightly.

Kat shook her hand, dread pooling in her stomach. Something told her she was going to hate what was about to happen.

"I know you want to get back to your work, so let's get going. We'll have you done in a jiffy—I'll drive."

Kat hadn't known what to expect, but she was bowled over by the whirlwind that was Elle. They started at a salon where Kat was ushered into a back room and put into a chair. Someone cut her hair, layering, styling and coloring it while another two women cut, polished and manicured her nails. Yet another team worked on her feet. "It's sandal season," Elle reiterated. They all worked with remarkable efficiency, and an hour after they'd walked into the salon, Kat already looked like a different woman. She couldn't have cared less about her nails, but she had to admit the hairstyle changed her entire look. Plumped from a limp, expressionless style to something out of an ad for hair products. She usually wore it pulled back, but having it framed around her face made her cheekbones appear high and refined rather than gaunt. The coppery brown lowlights they'd added made her normal blond shine.

"That's quite a makeover."

Elle laughed. "Oh, this is just the start."

A makeup artist appeared with a palette of

colors. Kat stared in horror. Her normal routine was a swipe of mascara, a dab of blush and some lip gloss. The makeup artist showed her how to use eye shadow, line her eyes, bronze her cheeks with a special brush, then use a combination of a pencil, lipstick and gloss to complete her lips. The whole thing took more than forty minutes. She felt like a clown with all that paint on her. "You expect me to do this every day?"

Elle shook her head. "This is camera makeup. Anytime you go in front of reporters or do a media interview, this is how much you need to put on. The flash and lights wash out most of the colors."

Kat reached for a tissue. "I won't be going in front of the camera."

Elle raised her brows. "I suggest you leave it on for now. I understand you'll be taking posed pictures with the senator later today."

Kat rolled her eyes. She had forgotten about the pictures she'd promised Alex she would take.

When they were done, the makeup artist began putting various products in a bag for Kat. She quickly calculated the savings in her bank account and realized that all this was far more than she could afford or what she wanted to spend money on.

Elle handed over a credit card to the manager, and Kat put out a hand to stop her. "I can pay for my stuff."

Elle waved her away. "Don't be silly. The campaign pays for all this."

What? Why was the campaign paying for her makeup? She began to argue but Elle gave her a stern look, raising her brow toward the store manager.

The next stop was a high-end department store where Kat normally didn't even dare to window-shop. They were ushered into a large room where a personal shopper had gathered various outfits in Kat's size for her to try on. As she stepped into the luxurious fabrics, she searched for price tags and didn't find any. So it was *that* kind of store.

With practiced efficiency, Elle commented on the clothes Kat tried. "You're heavy in the chest and the hips, dear, so you want your clothes to show off those features, not hide them. Boxy suits, stiff materials are your enemy. Let's find you clothes that flow with your curves."

As much as Kat wanted to defend her wardrobe, the mirror didn't lie. The extra pounds she was carrying actually flattered her in the clothes Elle suggested. She looked refined rather than frumpy, and the fabrics caressed her skin.

Before leaving, Elle insisted she wear one of the outfits she'd tried on, a pair of jeans and a dusty-rose silk blouse. "You don't have to dress up at campaign headquarters. Fit in with the rest of the crew, and the media might not even notice you come and go."

Kat had seen the clothes the rest of them wore; none of the staffers or volunteers were wearing designer jeans and silk blouses. She was about to argue then remembered she had photos and dinner scheduled with her father. It was probably a good idea to be wearing decent clothes, but she would insist on buying this outfit. Fresh anger bubbled through her as she remembered the senator's offer to give her money.

They left with more than two dozen outfits, all charged to the campaign credit card. Kat's mouth soured as she caught a glimpse of the bill Elle signed. She refused to let Kat pay for anything; not that Kat had a high enough credit limit to even buy what she was wearing. The clothes cost several months' worth of her salary. What was worse, it was all being paid with blood money. She thought about the meetings yesterday and the outrageous demands that campaign contributors made. "I don't need all of these," she told Elle, who shooed her away.

Staff at the store were watching her discreetly. They all knew who she was. They were too professional to gawk, but their curiosity was obvious. She didn't want to make a scene and have them make a story out of it for the evening news.

A mere four hours after they'd started, they returned to campaign headquarters. It was barely early afternoon. Grudgingly, Kat marveled at Elle's efficiency.

Elle drove Kat to the parking garage so they could transfer the purchases to her car. "Now remember, it's not just about the clothes, the hair and the makeup—it's also the way you carry yourself."

Kat nodded as if that made complete sense. She wanted nothing more than to get back to her desk and finish reading Nathan's reports so she could be up to speed when she had dinner with the senator. It was time to focus on her book.

She fished her BlackBerry out of her purse while she rode the elevator, to make sure she hadn't missed any messages from Alex. She stepped off absently, but the sound of people whistling and clapping made her stop. The entire staff was staring at her. People were standing up from their desks to get a look. Everyone seemed to be talking at once.

Nathan and Crista came toward her, and Crista nodded appreciatively. "You look great."

"I'm still the same person," Kat muttered.

Crista had the good sense to let it go. Kat returned to her computer and spent the next several hours poring over the analysis on the IED bill.

She knew her father had arrived when the loud hum and whir of the campaign office changed to a palpable excitement. Kat took a sip of her coffee and a deep breath. What was the protocol here? Should she stand and go up to him or wait for him to come to her desk? Was she supposed to shake his hand or give him a hug? Her stomach twisted into a thousand knots.

"Wow!"

She turned to see Alex standing behind her. She watched him study her and felt herself flush. "I guess this is what you wanted?"

He shook his head slowly. "Don't get me wrong—you look fantastic. Exactly what we need for your publicity shots. But…"

She stepped closer to him. "But?"

His mouth quirked. "It's not…you." He took a step back.

She smiled. "It's *really* not me, and I'm pretty sure it'll barely last the day unless you plan to send me to the salon every morning."

"The campaign can't afford that."

"I'm happy to return the clothes—they cost a small fortune."

"Those I like." His voice was thick and his eyes so intense, Kat's cheeks burned.

"Well, you might want to take the pictures quickly before this paint wears off." She gestured to her face to distract from the high pitch of her voice.

He cleared his throat. "Yes, well, the photographer is all set up." He took her elbow. "Let me introduce you to your father. Fair warning—the senator is a hugger."

She wanted to be mad at him, to give him the same attitude he'd shown her earlier, but she just let him lead her, taking comfort from the warmth of his hand on her elbow. She didn't trust her legs to carry her the few feet to the senator's office and meet the man who had consumed her childhood imagination.

She'd pictured her father as everything from the president of the United States to a third-world dictator. She had always wondered what it was about politics that had made her father willing to give up on his family, and the question had only grown stronger in her mind after her mother's revelations. TV glamorized public life, but after going through the makeover, she could see things from her mother's point of view; she felt like a total fraud. How could anyone live this way all the time? Was the power that alluring? She sneaked a sideways look at Alex. How important was it to him?

Senator Roberts was standing in his glass office. He was bent over a piece of paper with Crista. Alex's grip on her tightened. Her stomach flipped, threatening to send back the coffee she'd drunk an hour ago. This was the man who had fathered her, the man who had changed the course of her and her mother's life.

She already knew what he looked like, could picture his shock of white hair and bright blue eyes. Having spent hours watching media clips of him discussing serious defense policy, joking with reporters and charming the media, she was as prepared as a thirty-five-year-old woman could be to meet her father for the first time.

They were going to meet in his office so they could have some privacy; Alex had thought of that and arranged it. As it was, every campaign staffer, including the entourage that had accompanied the senator, was staring at her as she walked in with Alex.

The stir in the office made Senator Roberts look up and make his way to the door just as she arrived. Alex let go of her.

"Katerina, welcome." Her father wrapped his arms around her and hugged her tight. Being a tall man, he enveloped her. Kat heard the telltale sound of a camera and noticed a photographer out of the corner of her eye.

She tried to speak, but her throat was closed. This was the man she'd thought about during every school performance her mother couldn't attend, every father-daughter event she politely declined. The man who brought despair into her mother's eyes every time Kat asked about her father.

He released her and she looked up into his shining eyes. "It's nice to meet you, sir," she said in a thick voice.

"You are just as beautiful as your mother." His voice caught. Had he thought about Emilia in all these years? Her research on him had told her that he'd remarried less than a year after he divorced her mother. His second wife had died three years ago from cancer. He had two children from the marriage who were two and four years younger than Kat. There were a ton of photos of her half brother and sister on the internet: happy childhood shots of them at their father's rallies, at pumpkin patches and ballet recitals. Kat wondered how many of those pictures her mother had seen.

"Mom was keen on me meeting you," Kat said quietly.

The senator nodded and stepped back. "I was wrong in the way I handled things with her. I should've taken her calls. I was hurt and angry when she left, but you have to know that if I thought for even a second that she was calling to tell me about you, I would've rushed to her side."

"You remade your life pretty quickly. It doesn't seem like there would've been room for us." Kat hadn't meant to say the words out loud. The dinner conversation she'd planned revolved around safe topics like the IED bill, the practicality of his campaign promises, his plans to run for president in four years. She'd promised herself she would stick to the things she needed to write her book. A relationship with the senator was not something she needed, so there was no point in bringing up touchy personal subjects.

He sighed. "We have a lot to talk about. Why don't we do it over some good food and maybe a nice bottle of wine?"

Kat nodded, and after they posed for the photos she'd promised Alex, the senator led her out the front doors. He had parked on the street. The moment they stepped out, they were surrounded by reporters. She blinked against the camera flashes.

"Senator, what's it like meeting your daughter for the first time?"

"She's a wonderful woman and it's my honor to have her by my side," he replied smoothly.

"Ms. Driscoll, what do you think of the senator now?"

Kat's vision swam. This wasn't supposed to happen. Crista had said the campaign photographer's pictures would be circulated with an official statement from the senator so the media would stop hounding her.

Then it hit her.

The senator had purposefully parked on the street so they would have to walk out the front door together. The media would follow them to dinner and he could make a show of getting to know his daughter. Spinning away from her father, she flung open the door and stormed back into campaign headquarters. Alex was waiting on the other side.

"I had no idea he was going to do that," he said before Kat had a chance to scream at him. "The plan was for him to ask you to drive and leave his car out front so the reporters wouldn't be the wiser."

She narrowed her eyes. Was he telling the truth?

He stepped toward her. "I remember my promise, Kat. I know how important it is to you. I wouldn't betray you like that."

The door opened behind them. "Kat, are you okay?" Kat glared at the senator. She was being played. Just like she had been with Colin. And she was letting it happen to her all over again, sitting back and letting her father and Alex manipulate her to get what they wanted.

No more. It was time for her to do what she should have been doing all along. What she should have done with Colin when she first discovered his betrayal.

She smiled sweetly. "I guess we'd better take my car if we want to avoid the media."

The senator nodded and she caught Alex staring at her from the corner of her eye. She offered her arm to her father, who took it, and they walked to the elevator. She could feel Alex's eyes on her. Maybe this was a good thing; she was now absolutely certain where she stood with him. She wasn't going to let another man take advantage of her.

CHAPTER SEVEN

ALEX DIDN'T NEED a report on how the senator's dinner with his daughter had gone. There were plenty of pictures. They showed Kat leaning in, laughing and toasting with the senator. It was all fake. She was putting on a show—one he'd wished for but now felt uneasy watching. Smiles that didn't reach her eyes, exaggerated gestures… She was trying too hard to look happy. The photos were beautiful and the campaign staff were busy spreading them on various social-media sites rather than trying to get them deleted. He should be happy that she'd finally gotten the message about how to act, but he had a sour taste in his mouth. What was Kat up to?

He'd had a long meeting with the senator last night after his dinner with Kat. All of a sudden, the man wanted to explore alternate options to the IED bill. Alex tapped on his desk. Had Kat said something to him or was someone else undermining Alex's efforts? Had the EAGLE managers noticed the check hadn't been cashed yet? Had they called the senator directly? He made a mental note to talk to Crista. She was the only person on staff he could trust.

He checked his watch. *She should be here by now.* The senator was scheduled to do a stump speech then meet with a heavyweight donor afterward. Alex had come to headquarters first so he could talk to Kat. There wasn't much time; he was supposed to follow the senator all day then return to Washington to clear up a few things before leaving for Iraq in two days. The senator had come back from Egypt with a promise from the government to sell the IED technology, but the general in charge of the US presence in Iraq hadn't given his support. The general's endorsement was essential to ensuring that members of the Armed Services Committees of both the House and Senate would support the bill. The senate committee chairman was already making waves, upset that Senator Roberts was getting credit for the bill even though he was listed as a co-sponsor. It was these petty things that often derailed a bill, so the general's endorsement was essential.

Alex was better positioned to talk to the general than the senator given that he'd actually served in Iraq. The trip had been booked weeks ago, and Alex had been dreading it. He hadn't been back to Iraq since he and Nick got shipped home. The plan had been to firm up the deal with the Egyptians then seal it with the general's endorsement. Now the senator wanted him to go talk to the general about options other than the new IED technology.

The only good part of the trip was that he would be thousands of miles away from Kat. He'd spent two hours last night watching her dinner through the various news channels and social-media sites rather than clearing his inbox. What was it about her that was making him feel so out of control? A break would help him get his head back in the game. She wasn't in any immediate danger.

He hadn't gotten the full story on Colin from their research. He'd leaned hard on his CNN contact, promising her an exclusive on the IED bill to squash the old story on Kat. He had been so angry that Kat had been subjected to a man like Colin that he'd called up the guy they used for opponent research. It was a nice way of describing their dirt-gathering guru. The man had sent him a report within hours confirming that Colin was doing well and married to the dean of the college where Kat used to work. He was apparently the son of a famous academic and the brother of an accomplished lawyer. Until the book came out, Colin had been considered a failure in the otherwise illustrious family. His publication had gotten him a promotion to full professor, one of the youngest in the school's history.

It didn't take a genius to figure out the book was probably based on what he'd stolen from Kat. It was taking everything Alex had not to drive out to the address he'd gotten for Colin and give him a piece of his mind. Something had snapped inside him when he saw Kat's face as she described the incident. Further proof he couldn't trust himself around her. His BlackBerry buzzed and rang.

"Mellie."

Her voice was honey sweet. "Just checking to see if we're still on for dinner tonight?"

"I'm looking forward to it."

Mellie had just quit the senator's office yesterday to return to her "charity work," which was a socialite's way of saying she was tired of a nine-to-five job. Or in this case an eight-to-eight job. Mellie had worked hard for Senator Roberts and Alex, never complaining about the punishing hours, especially considering she was the daughter of a prominent New York family for whom the term "heavyweight donor" was invented. Her brother was the former mayor of New York City, her uncle the governor of New Hampshire. She'd been pursuing Alex since she started working in the senator's office a year ago. He had finally accepted her weekly dinner invitation. It was time for him to start thinking more seriously about his own political future. Mellie was definitely FLOTUS material. And a good distraction from Kat.

"Good morning, Alex."

Kat was standing in the doorway. Based on how lovely she looked, he assumed she was wearing clothes from the new wardrobe. Soft linen pants and a delicate blue blouse the color of her eyes. Her hair was beautifully styled, but he noted that she hadn't applied much makeup. He knew it was essential for the cameras, but it just wasn't her, and he respected that. She was gorgeous without it, anyway.

Kat smiled and he couldn't take his eyes off her.

"I hear you had a good dinner last night."

She nodded. "It was great. Thanks for setting it up." She seemed like she was about to say more, but she shut her mouth as if she'd changed her mind.

As she turned to go, he stood. "Wait—aren't you going to tell me more? Did you change the senator's mind about the IED bill?"

She gave him a stunning smile and he

frowned. Her mouth was stretched a little too wide, her eyes too cold. "We discussed it, and I think he has some valid points. I look forward to working on it with him."

This is new.

"Glad you're finally toeing the party line. I see Elle's makeover changed more than just your look."

She narrowed her eyes. *Good. I'm getting to her.* She spun on her heels to walk out. He knew he should let it be, but he couldn't help himself.

"Ex*cuse* me, Kat."

She turned from the doorway. "There's no excuse for you, Alex."

He suppressed a smirk. *That's more like her.* He walked up to her and she planted her feet more firmly, as if stopping herself from running away. He noticed for the first time that she was wearing heels, not the flats she usually preferred. He knew Elle was good, but something wasn't sitting right with him. "Can you tell me who you are and what you've done with the Kat I know?"

She lifted her gaze and he felt his heart kick in his chest. Her clear blue eyes had a new determination in them. "I thought you'd be happy that I'm finally following instructions."

I should be.

"I don't like people who are unpredictable."

"Take it up with your therapist." She turned.

"I need to know what you said to the senator about the IED bill."

"You tell me. The senator mentioned he had a meeting with you right after," she threw over her shoulder.

"We had a lot of other things to talk about—we didn't get to it."

"Then I must not have said anything important."

"Kat!"

She faced him again. "I don't understand what you want from me, Alex." *There!* A genuine reaction. The icc in her eyes had been replaced with the passion he liked to see.

"The senator came back from dinner questioning his commitment to the IED bill. Please tell me what you said to him."

A line deepened between her brows. "I told him that I thought he was playing fast and loose with the public trust, that those meetings you had with the donors were disgusting and that I was disappointed he wasn't the man I pictured him to be."

Alex stared at her. Had she really said those things? He wouldn't put it past her. She was a loose cannon. Whatever his reservations about Mellie might be, at least she was predictable.

"The conversation between me and my father was a show for the cameras. Those vultures stood right outside the glass windows taking pictures. I was mad and in no mood to be kind."

"I had nothing to do with the reporters." A nerve twitched in his forehead. Alex knew the senator disagreed with him on using the dinner as a media opportunity. Had the senator arranged this? No way. It had to be a coincidence. The man didn't call up reporters on his own; he would've needed people to do this and the campaign staff didn't do anything without Alex finding out about it.

"Senator Roberts is well-known. Someone must have called the media from the restaurant," he said dismissively, returning to his desk.

"And of the hundreds of restaurants you could've picked, why choose one where our table was right beside big glass windows?"

The restaurant had been the senator's choice.

"Have you stopped to consider what it would mean to withdraw troops from Iraq?"

"It would mean bringing our men and women home. How do we really know we are making things better for the Iraqi people? Maybe we'd be better off focusing on things that matter to people here who want jobs, good schools for their children…"

"They also want to feel safe. They don't want to go to work wondering whether their building will get blown up."

"That's fearmongering."

"You have no idea what you're talking about."

She stepped up to his desk and planted her hands on it, leaning forward.

"Then educate me. We have American children dying in Guam because we apparently can't afford to give them money to upgrade their medical facilities. Why is this technology so important that we're going to give millions of dollars to an unstable regime to get an inferior version of it?"

"Do you know what it's like to get blown up by an IED?"

"I…"

He leaned forward so they were nearly nose to nose. "You don't, because you sit in your ivory tower analyzing numbers and facts. Take a second to *feel* what it might be like. I walked down a street we knew to be littered with IEDs. Imagine what it's like taking each step as if it might be your last. To wonder whether your mother will know how to request your death benefits from the army."

She stepped back, her face white.

"I was on patrol with my buddy. The EAGLE robot jammed and he wouldn't let me go retrieve it. Said it was his turn. He pushed me out of the way and got blown up. I watched his body twist unnaturally. I had to scour the streets for his leg in case they could reattach it. Guess what? They couldn't. So now he's in a wheelchair for the rest of his life."

Her hands flew to her face. "Alex, I had no idea. I'm so sorry. How is he?"

Alex turned away from her, unable to deal with her shining eyes. Nick's story wasn't a secret, but he didn't need sympathy from her. There was only one way to repay Nick's debt.

"He hasn't been able to find a job, and he lives in a trailer but won't let me help him because he's too damn proud. The only thing he's asked is that I do what I can to make sure this doesn't happen to other soldiers."

"The only way to keep them safe is to bring them back."

He gritted his teeth. When would she get off her high horse and understand that it wasn't as simple as that?

"Come with me to Iraq. See for yourself what we're fighting for."

She took a sharp breath. He balled his hands into fists. What was wrong with him? The words had come out of his mouth without any thought.

"I can't. My mother…"

He let out his own breath. "I know. It's not practical."

She left, and with a sense of relief he turned to his computer, tapping the keys to wake it up. Staring at his screen, he couldn't remember what he'd been working on before she walked in. He gave up and shut down. It was better to leave before he did something else stupid. Why was he letting Kat into his head? What did it matter if she understood why this bill was so important to him? She wasn't any more powerful than the rest of the people who questioned him—the donors, party members and other stakeholders he dealt with every day. *Then why is she getting under your skin?* He packed up his files and made his way to Crista's desk.

"Here's the check from EAGLE," he said.

"What did you have to run by the senator?"

He shrugged. "It wasn't important."

"You asked her to come to Iraq?"

"Crista…"

She stood and grabbed his arm, pulling him back into his office and closing the door. "I've seen what you're like around her."

"Crista!"

"I'm not the only one who sees it. Nathan

said something to me this morning about how you were looking at the front door like you were waiting for someone."

He rolled his eyes. "I don't have time for this."

"I saw the emails you sent her."

"You're reading my emails?"

"I have access to the campaign server, remember?"

They had separate servers for campaign and congressional staff. The congressional emails were on a server in DC. Alex even had an entirely separate account to communicate with donors that wasn't hosted on either server. He knew how to hide emails he didn't want seen. What was he thinking sending those flirtatious emails to Kat on the campaign server? The messages were meant to be perfunctory but he hadn't been able to help himself. Just like he hadn't been able to shut his mouth before asking her to come to Iraq.

"Crista, you're reading too much into this. I need to get to the Eastern Shore."

"She's the right type for you."

"Excuse me?"

"She looked good on the cameras yesterday. I think you can get her over the media aversion. She's smart and she has a pedigree. If the senator runs for president, you'll be all set with her by your side. She meets your requirements."

His chest burned. "Let's not have this conversation again. That's not what our breakup was about." Why was Crista opening old wounds? When he hired her, they'd both agreed not to rehash their relationship.

"Yes, it was, Alex, and don't insult me by pretending it wasn't. But there is one thing I haven't figured out. Why were you with me to begin with?"

Because you're intelligent and didn't bore me to tears.

"Crista, we agreed to keep it professional. Let's not get into this again."

She pressed her lips together. "I'll talk her into Iraq." She turned and walked away.

Alex didn't know whether to stop her or thank her. Crista was wrong about Kat meeting his requirements; she was too headstrong and volatile. Arguments would be typical in their daily lives, and he couldn't afford to keep being impulsive. He needed someone with whom he was in complete control of himself. The last thing Kat needed was another violent man in her life.

CHAPTER EIGHT

WHY WAS SHE even considering it? Alex's half-hearted offer hadn't been real. She chewed her lip. She was tired of having things happen to her and merely reacting to them, changing her life to accommodate whatever disaster someone else caused. She'd realized that yesterday, when she'd stepped out of headquarters with her father into the sea of reporters. So she'd gone along with him, smiled and made conversation, all the while gathering information for her book, including a quote her father wouldn't expect her to publish. Maybe she should take the same approach with this trip to Iraq.

Alex's words came back to her. She'd never been to Iraq, and she didn't know what it was like. So who was she to pontificate on what should happen there? Getting an opinion from soldiers on the ground and speaking to locals would add dimension to her analyses, let her see firsthand what Alex was talking about. And being with Alex had nothing to do with this.

She picked up the phone, and her aunt Luce

readily agreed to come stay with her mom. Kat suspected Emilia had called her aunt two nights ago and put her on standby when Kat returned from Washington, DC, tired and barely able to walk through the front door.

Kat had never traveled internationally. She had lectured for hours on the war in Iraq without ever having stepped foot in the country. When would she get such an opportunity again? Aunt Luce could take care of her mom for a few days, couldn't she?

If she was lucky, the trip might even shorten the time she needed to spend with the campaign. The faster she wrote the book, the sooner she would get her promotion. Then she could go back to her normal life, where her world made sense and she didn't live in a fishbowl or have to deal with her father.

She tried not to think about how disappointing dinner with the senator had been. He had been charming and full of amusing tales, but beyond discussing the IED bill, there was nothing real in their conversation. They'd never gotten back to talking about her mother or shared any feelings about their newfound relationship. The only substantive moment they'd had was when he talked about his son and daughter, his voice filling with genuine pride.

"Hi!"

Kat jumped. She'd never get used to people sneaking up behind her. She made a mental note to check out the other cubicles to see if there was one that faced outward so she could see who was coming at her.

"Hi, Crista. How are you?"

Without waiting to be invited, Crista pulled a chair from another cubicle, blocking Kat's entry as she parked herself. "So, I called the home-health company you use and they agreed to increase the coverage on your mom if you want to go to Iraq."

Kat sat up straighter, irritation burning deep in her belly. "Crista, I wish you hadn't done that. It's my personal business and I don't like—"

"You're not authorized to offer the owner's daughter an internship on the campaign in exchange for them not charging you any more than what you're paying for the summer. I am."

Kat took a breath. "I…"

Crista put her hand on Kat's shoulder. "It's okay to let people help you. Nathan gets me a cup of coffee every morning because he knows I hate the stuff we brew here. Alex paid the ER bill for the IT kid when he broke his arm. We work together for fourteen hours a day— we're each other's family."

An elephant was sitting on her chest. Kat had never had a real friend, someone who would take care of her. She always had too much to ask and not enough to give. Colin had been her friend first. He hadn't seemed to mind that she didn't have a lot to offer in return for his kindness with her mother, but then he'd taken the only thing she did have that was all her own. Her professional integrity. What did Crista hope to get from her?

"Sometimes you need a friend to do something you wouldn't do for yourself, Kat. Go to Iraq, take a break from your daily obligations. Enjoy the time with Alex."

Her head snapped up. "There's nothing going on between me and Alex."

Crista smiled slyly. "I never said there was. I just said enjoy the time with him. It's hard to get his attention for more than five minutes around here—you can learn a lot about the campaign from him."

Her face heated. "Oh."

"It's okay, Kat. We're not dumb. We spend most of the day analyzing what someone meant or trying to predict what the opponent might do. We're pretty good at reading human behavior. It's obvious you're attracted to Alex and that he's got a thing for you."

"I'm not pursuing him."

Crista laughed. "Not because of me, I hope. We dated two years ago—that's like ten campaign years. If it makes you feel better, I've had two boyfriends since Alex. I'm most definitely over him, and honestly, I think he might be less cranky if he had someone. He handles everything alone."

Kat searched Crista's eyes, but she gave away nothing. "Since you're so good at reading people, you do know that Nathan has a thing for you, right?"

Crista chuckled. "See? It's not that hard to figure these things out." She lowered her voice. "I don't think it's a good idea for me to get involved with him until I'm ready for a long-term relationship. He's a forever kind of guy."

Kat knitted her brows. Hadn't Crista said she'd broken things off with Alex because he *wasn't* going to marry her? "Are you really sure you're over Alex?"

"I know what you're thinking. It's not that I wanted to marry Alex—I just needed to know there was a future if I was going to invest more time in him. I didn't want to fall hard, spend years in a relationship and then realize we weren't in the same place. I'm thirty-three years old—I can't afford to waste several years on a guy and still have a family at the end."

If that was the case, why wasn't Crista open to the idea of dating Nathan? Kat wanted to say something, but she kept her mouth shut.

Crista had extended her friendship and Kat didn't want to push it. "Well, it's hard not to be attracted to Alex, but we disagree on everything. It's never going to work between us and I'm not interested in casual relationships."

Crista smirked. "You just wait—Alex has a way of getting under your skin. So, will you go to Iraq?"

There was no reason not to. With her aunt's help and extra nursing care, her mother would be well taken care of. "I'm the only person in the world who wants to go to Iraq to take a break."

Crista clapped her hands. "Don't worry. We usually arrange security with a private company in addition to what the army will provide. There are a number of green-zone camps and the general will decide which one to send you to on the day you arrive, to minimize the risk of an ambush."

Crista continued for several more minutes. Kat should've been concerned about the fact that she'd need to wear a bulletproof vest from the second she stepped off the plane, but all she felt was an uplifting energy. The most adventurous thing she'd done in her life was to try skiing with Colin on a rare weekend when her aunt had come to visit.

Crista excused herself and returned a few

minutes later with a credit card and piece of paper. "This is your travel credit card and a list of items you need to buy. Use the credit card—the campaign will cover any of the supplies on the list."

Kat scanned the list. "Thermal underwear?"

"We have an Iraq travel guide on the network drive. Read it. The temperatures there can vary considerably. You need to be prepared. It's not exactly a honeymoon location."

Before Kat could protest, Crista held up her hands. "Sorry, I can't help it. Just take my advice and don't let Alex push you away. He's a terror in the office but he's a wonderful boyfriend."

She left Kat wondering exactly what made Alex such a wonderful boyfriend and how she was going to get through seven days in close proximity to him.

KAT LOOKED UP at the departure monitor to make sure she was heading to the right gate. Dulles Airport was a blur of world-savvy travelers walking with purpose. Two days had gone by in a whirlwind. She was grateful that her aunt had come early so that Kat could finish shopping for the "trip to hell," as most of the staffers called it.

She'd downloaded a pile of reading onto

the campaign tablet, which she hoped would get her through the twenty-hour trip. There weren't any direct flights to Baghdad from the US; it wasn't a great tourist destination. They'd be flying a commercial airline into Doha, Qatar, then taking another flight to Baghdad.

Kat idly wondered who else was flying to Iraq, given the new security concerns. Alex wanted her to have a passport that identified her as a US government employee, but they hadn't had time to get it for her, so she was traveling on her tourist one. For once, Kat was grateful to Colin for insisting that she get a passport so they could go overseas for their honeymoon. Now that she thought about it, she'd been more excited about the possible trip than the actual honeymoon with Colin.

The only glitch had been obtaining a visa. Alex had a diplomatic passport that didn't require a visa but she did. Somehow the senator managed to make the calls to get her the required visa from the Iraqi embassy in Washington. She hadn't talked to her father since their dinner, but he'd sent her a box of candy the next day with a nice note thanking her and reiterating the invitation to meet his family. The box was filled with dark, nut-crusted chocolates.

She was meeting Alex at the airport, but

they hadn't arranged a specific meeting spot, so she wheeled her carry-on onto the train that took her to their gate. Crista had advised not to check a bag if she could avoid it. Apparently, American bags had a way of disappearing during transit to the Middle East. Lucky for her, she didn't have a lot of equipment or clothes that she wanted to take with her. She kept it to basic mix-and-match clothes and a few travel essentials.

She had nearly an hour until the flight to Doha, so she purchased a latte and sandwich from a nearby coffee shop. She wasn't sure if there would be food on the plane. This was only her second time at Dulles Airport. The last time was when she'd flown out for a political-science conference. A knot formed in her stomach as she remembered the stress of that trip. Her aunt hadn't been able to come to stay, and at the time Kat could afford only a couple of hours of nursing care a day. She had to cut the trip short when her calls home went unanswered. She found her mother in bed, with the room reeking of bodily fluids. Her mother had tricked the nurse into believing she'd taken her medication when in fact she'd been stuffing the pills between her back tooth and cheek then spitting them out when the nurse left. Kat had promptly changed nursing companies.

Would her aunt be able to handle her mother for a whole week? Thanks to Crista, the nursing company was sending someone four times a day, including late evening hours, which usually came at a premium. Her mother had thrown a fit when she found out, but relented when Kat threatened not to go. This wasn't a trip where she could be back home in a few hours if there was an emergency. Crista had warned her that even with optimal connections and flight times, it took more than a day to return from Baghdad.

She settled into a seat and sipped her coffee, wondering when Alex would show up. She hadn't seen him since the day in the office when he'd asked her to come to Iraq. He'd emailed her briefing materials, but other than that, she hadn't talked to him.

Glancing out the window, she saw the plane was at the gate. It was one of the largest planes she'd ever seen. Boarding began, starting with first class. Kat checked her watch, wondering when Alex would show up. They were forty minutes from departure. What would she do if he didn't appear? There was no way she was going to Baghdad alone.

"Worried I wouldn't show?"

She breathed a sigh of relief and turned to find a smiling Alex standing behind her looking...

more handsome than he had a right to be. His jeans and untucked white polo shirt made him look loose and not at all like the buttoned-up Alex she was used to.

"You like cutting it close, don't you?"

He smiled. "I'm a seasoned traveler not checking luggage. If I hadn't known you'd be sitting here nervously staring at your watch, I'd have come twenty minutes later."

He motioned toward the line. "Let's go."

"They haven't started general boarding yet."

"Have you looked at your ticket?"

She frowned. "I'm in row ten."

"What does it say above the row number?"

"B.U.S.I."

He rolled his eyes. "We're in business class."

She gasped. "Really?"

"It's a long flight."

He took the handle of her bag and wheeled both carry-ons toward the gate, where the attendant gave Alex a brilliant smile. When they reached the plane, they stepped onto lush carpeting. A flight attendant in a beautiful burgundy suit greeted them and motioned to a staircase. Kat tried to keep her mouth closed. She didn't even know there were airplanes big enough to have two stories. Alex was seated next to her, and she avoided his gaze when the attendant showed them how to convert their seats into full beds. Relaxing into the window seat, she watched Alex remove a book and sink into his seat. The attendant reappeared and gave them drink and dinner menus.

"Are they seriously serving filet mignon and wine for dinner?"

"First class gets lobster."

"I wouldn't know. They don't even give you a drink in economy." She turned to him. "Why are we traveling business? I know these tickets are twice as expensive as economy class."

"Four times."

"Excuse me?"

"Business-class tickets are four times more expensive than economy seats on international flights."

She swallowed. He placed a hand on top of hers. "If I were traveling alone, I'd have bought the economy ticket, but Senator Roberts insisted we fly you first class. That ticket was ten times more expensive, so I made a call figuring you wouldn't mind."

"Why the unnecessary expense? I was expecting economy."

"He only travels first class, and he wants you to live like his daughter would."

"But I'm not his daughter."

"I think he wants you to be."

She pretended to study the menu. The senator already had the daughter he wanted: her half sister, Victoria. Vickie had just finished law school at Yale. Kat's PhD was from a small-time state college that most people didn't even know existed. Her father didn't want another daughter; he wanted to absolve himself of guilt.

The flight attendant returned and Alex ordered a soft drink. "I'll have lemonade," Kat said.

"She'll also have a glass of the Riesling," Alex added smoothly. Before she could protest, he turned to her. "Trust me, you'll want a glass of wine—there's something I need to tell you."

CHAPTER NINE

ALEX WAS MADDENING. Kat was on her second glass of wine; they'd already been served appetizers of crab-stuffed mushrooms and falafel. He'd filled the air with inane facts about polling data, information she already knew and couldn't care less about.

"Alex, when are you going to get to the point?"

He took a sip of his soft drink. "Senator Roberts would like you and your mother to meet his other children."

She blew out a breath. It wasn't a big surprise; she'd figured with all the media coverage, it would only be natural to meet his family.

"I don't think my mother would like that."

"For what it's worth, I think he genuinely cares about your mother."

"He has a funny way of showing it." She played with the rim of her cup.

"Why couldn't he have asked me himself?"

"He plans to. He just knew I'd be spending

a lot of time with you this trip." Alex's voice was smooth, persuasive, the way he had been with the EAGLE manufacturers.

"So he wanted you to soften me up."

He sighed. "Why can't you be happy that the father you haven't known your whole life wants you to be a part of his family? He could've just as easily decided not to have anything to do with you. What's he done that makes him such a villain? Did he beat your mother? Didn't he offer you support the second he found out about you? That's more than most men would do."

She studied him as he stared at the bubbles in his drink. "Alex, what happened to your father?"

"That's not the point of this conversation."

"No, but I want to know."

"I don't like to talk about it."

"You can tell me now or I can annoy you for the remaining eighteen hours of this trip."

His mouth twitched, even as he tried to give his signature look of annoyance.

"Come on—we can only discuss the polls for so long. If we're going to have an honest conversation about my father, I want to know about yours."

"My mother left my father when I was eight, and we haven't seen him since."

"Why did she leave?"

"Because he was a drunk who spent her hard-earned money on booze, then beat us both." The words were said so matter-of-factly that it took Kat a full minute to absorb their meaning. She placed her hand on his, sensing the pain he was so carefully controlling.

"Because of him we were forced to..." He swallowed. "That's all I'm willing to discuss." He unbuckled his seat belt and excused himself. He followed the aisle to the bathroom, but she was sure it was an excuse to get away from her. When he returned, he opened his book. Kat noticed it was the latest presidential biography.

"What do you think I should do?"

He raised a brow.

"About my father's invitation," she clarified.

"I think you should give him a chance and get to know your half siblings. Vickie is a really bright woman—you'll enjoy talking to her. Walter is younger and a little immature still, but he has a good head on his shoulders."

"I don't want him hurting my mother."

"I don't think he intends to, but ultimately it's her decision."

"Would you let your mother see your father again?"

His response was instantaneous. "Not if I could help it." He clenched his jaw. "In fact, if I saw my father again, I'd probably kill him before he could get to her." He hadn't meant to say the last part. That was obvious from the way he set his lips and turned away from her. She couldn't see his eyes and resisted the urge to reach out and pull his face back toward her so she could see them. Adjusting his seat, he picked up his book, and she knew it wasn't wise to pursue the conversation.

KAT DIDN'T FEEL as tired as she should have when they arrived in Doha. She'd taken a nap in her reclining seat, marveling at the relative luxury that four times the airfare bought. Yet when she thought of the promises and compromises that had to be made to fill the campaign money coffers, her stomach sickened. It was unreasonable of her, but she expected better from her father. From Alex.

But she couldn't control their behavior...just like she couldn't control her mother's. Even this trip. It had been her decision to come, yet Alex had arranged everything, and he was still calling all the shots.

The Doha airport was a surprisingly modern facility filled with a wide range of passengers. Kat had no trouble spending the four-hour layover watching people scurrying about.

"It's amazing, isn't it, how this airport looks just like ours, yet the people aren't the same."

Alex smiled at her. "The world looks very different outside of Washington, DC." He tilted his head to indicate a family sitting a few feet away. "What do you notice about them?"

She observed them for a few moments, trying to see past the obvious fact that the woman was veiled and the man was wearing a traditional thobe—a white, ankle-length robe—and a headdress.

"My guess is that they're from Saudi Arabia. Obviously they can afford to travel outside the country, but there's only one wife, or at least just one traveling with him. Hard to know, but let's say they're middle class." She'd read that Saudi Arabian men were allowed to marry up to four women. The rule was that all four wives had to be treated equally, so plural marriage was only common among members of the royal family, who were wealthy enough to afford four palaces, and the very poor, who could afford four tents in the desert. Although the trend was changing toward monogamy.

He nodded. "That's a lot of assumptions. But what else do you notice?"

"The woman has her face uncovered."

"You wouldn't see that at the Riyadh airport. Qatar isn't exactly a liberal country, but for a family like that, even little freedoms we take for granted, like how we dress, are regulated."

Kat hadn't covered her head. Alex had said she could wait. The Doha airport included numerous European, Asian, Middle Eastern and African travelers. Kat noticed people in traditional clothes she'd only seen in pictures, and Alex served as a tour guide, amusing her with cultural facts that she had learned through study and that he knew through experience.

"What about them?"

She nodded to a couple sitting on the far side of the waiting area, obviously distressed. The woman was crying and the man was trying to comfort her.

"Their love is forbidden."

She looked at him. "How could you possibly know that?"

He pointed to the passports they were holding. "See his passport, it's a dark green—my guess is Pakistan. And hers is dark blue, almost the color of ours, but it has a different alphabet on it. It's Indian. I can't say for sure, but I'd bet that he's Muslim and she's Hindu and their families don't approve."

"So what?"

"What do you mean?"

"Let's say you're right—so what if the families don't approve? It shouldn't stop them from being together."

"Could you be with a man who didn't understand your need to take care of your mother?"

Her eyes snapped to him. "That's not the same thing. My mother would never forbid me from marrying someone I loved."

"Yes, but in your case your future husband won't just have you to take care of—he has to be willing to accept the fact that your mother is an integral part of your life. Your husband is marrying into your family."

She raised her eyebrows, as he had just put into words one of the chief reasons she'd been attracted to Colin. Most of the men she'd dated scoffed at the fact that she still lived with her mother, but Colin had embraced her responsibilities.

"In South Asia, you don't marry the man— you marry the family. A daughter is given away and her husband's family becomes her own. Parents don't want to send their daughter into a family who won't accept her. The guy's parents probably don't want him marrying a girl who's not from their country or their religion, and who they perceive doesn't understand their values."

She turned to watch the couple. The young woman was wiping tears from her face as she embraced the man a final time before getting in line to board the plane. The man stared at her, unabashedly wiping tears from his own face. "If all that mattered, then how did they fall in love?"

"Because they don't care about the politics of their countries. They don't worry about religion. They were probably educated abroad, and that's how they met. But as they go home, reality is hitting them. They realize their parents will never accept their union and there is no way for them to be together. This might be the last time they see each other."

Kat watched the woman break from the line and fly into the man's arms. They held each other, sobbing.

"Why can't they make their parents understand?" She knew they were making up a narrative for a random couple at the airport, but she was getting wrapped up in the story.

"Because their parents are practical. They know how difficult life will be for these young lovers. They'll be ostracized from their communities. He won't be able to find a job anywhere because his wife isn't Muslim. She won't be welcomed back into her family because she'll be considered tainted. She'll lose her community and eventually resent him."

"They can live somewhere else, where these things don't matter."

"Like the US, where we're free?"

Kat nodded. For some inexplicable reason, she couldn't take her eyes away from the couple, wanting desperately to find a way for them to be together. She watched for several minutes as they held on to each other. The line dwindled and a flight attendant came and tapped the young woman on the shoulder. She shook her head but the young man gently pushed her toward the gate. The woman wouldn't go, so he gave her a kiss on the forehead and left. Kat watched him as he raced away, tears shining on his face. He didn't bother to wipe them.

"There are billions of people like them in the world, who don't have the freedoms we do. There are people in Iraq being executed. Children are kidnapped every day. We can't bring them all to the US. That's why we're in Iraq—that's why we're fighting for the people there. It's to make the world a better place, to fight for those who can't fight for themselves."

A deep ache formed in her chest. It wasn't as clear-cut as she thought. Even if the story they'd made up about the couple wasn't true, she knew there were couples out there for whom it was a reality. She knew Americans were in Iraq to fight the extremists who killed innocent people.

"What about what we need at home? Like Dr. Atao, who needs medical facilities in Guam for those babies? Or programs for victims of domestic violence."

His face twisted. *Open up to me, Alex.*

"We can't do everything," he said quietly.

"We can't save the world, either." But even as she spoke the words, she couldn't stop thinking about the couple. Despite all the obstacles, they'd found the courage to fall in love. She knew it was just a story she and Alex had made up. They could just as well have been individuals cheating on their spouses, but somehow she didn't think so. She could feel the pain in their souls.

THE FLIGHT FROM Doha was more of what Kat was used to, people packed like sardines into too small seats. Her arm was pressed against Alex's, and she enjoyed his warmth.

"There's not a lot of demand for business class to Baghdad," Alex explained.

She watched the passengers file past. The people who boarded looked like any other passenger manifest once you took away their ethnic dress. There were families with crying babies and chattering children, men with briefcases, couples and elderly individuals, some accompanied by younger caregivers.

"Who are all these people?"

"They're going home or visiting family. The normal reasons people get on a plane. The only travelers you aren't seeing are tourists."

Hers was the only white face on the entire plane. Kat brought out the scarf she'd been advised to wear and put it on, conscious of her blond hair in the sea of black and brown. "That's probably a good idea," Alex whispered.

There were no drinks or food offered on the flight. For the most part, the passengers sat in silence, though several people prayed. Tension crackled in the air and Kat couldn't understand why.

As if reading her mind, Alex said in her ear, "They're nervous. Baghdad is still unpredictable. They don't know what to expect at the airport. It's likely they'll be harassed about who they are and whether they are legitimately entering or reentering. Their belongings will be searched and items that the customs officials find interesting will be confiscated without reason."

"Why?"

"Because they can. A perfume bought in Qatar can fetch a nice price on the black market in Iraq. People are used to it—they consider it the price of travel."

When they landed, it was early afternoon. Alex placed a hand on her arm and directed her to stay in her seat until the rest of the passengers had deplaned. When they exited, it was the dust that hit Kat first. She sneezed and put her scarf over her mouth as they walked to the main customs area. The smell of perspiration clung to the air that was being ineffectively circulated by floor fans.

A woman they'd seen earlier began sobbing loudly. A customs officer hit her viciously with a stick. Kat put a hand on her mouth to suppress a scream.

Alex placed an arm around her. "Don't say anything, don't do anything. Someone will come get us."

Sure enough, a man in western clothes waved a badge and was let through the glass doors that separated them from the rest of the airport. He introduced himself as Roger Koralis then escorted them to the gate, where he handed a padded envelope to the customs official standing guard. No one bothered to check Kat's passport or the visa they had painstakingly obtained.

Roger led them to a dusty black car. He sat in the front seat while Kat and Alex got in the back. As they swung into traffic, Kat noticed there was another car in front and one keeping close behind them. Extra security, she guessed. They made their way through traffic-snarled streets, sharing the road with cyclists, wagons, even stray animals. Half-dressed children, dirt streaked across their faces, came to the windows as soon as the car stopped even for a second. Kat's first instinct was to roll down the window, but Alex firmly shook his head. They passed by streets that were littered with trash, and others that were immaculately clean and desolate.

"I thought we restored order here," she said.

"This is order," Alex said grimly. No one mentioned where they were going. Alex's gaze darted from side to side as they sat in silence and she wondered whether any of the sights were familiar to him. Was he thinking about his last time here? Her mouth soured as she remembered the story he'd told her of his friend getting blown up.

"Are you okay?" she whispered.

"Why wouldn't I be?"

She didn't push it. The firm set of his jaw and his clenched fists told her all she needed to know about how he was feeling. What could she say to comfort him? It occurred to her that she'd never had to soothe Colin. He always seemed happy and without a care in the world. Had they ever shared anything real?

Everyone in the car was silent while the driver negotiated traffic, never breaking out of formation with the other two vehicles. Every time a beggar came up to the window, Alex tensed, and both the driver and their escort discreetly placed hands on the guns holstered at their hips. Kat's eyes were glued to the sight before her. The city was a juxtaposition of normal life and an obvious war zone. Men in battle dress uniform carrying rifles were on patrol. Women wearing long, dark veils walked purposefully and children hurried along in school uniforms. Other men stood on street corners smoking or talking. Some wore the long, tunic-shaped thobes but most wore western clothing, untucked shirts and pants. Boys pushed carts laden with all kinds of goods, yelling out prices. People were going about their daily lives, ignoring the chaos around them.

The scenery changed as they left the city, and so did the tension in the car. Fewer people and buildings dotted the streets. The potholed road could charitably be called a one-lane thoroughfare. If possible, Alex, Roger and the driver were even more on edge.

"The city's secure, but out here in the country, we can't control insurgents with a rocket-propelled grenade or an IED hidden in the road," Roger remarked.

Kat's eyes widened.

"Don't worry—the car's bulletproof," Alex said. She was sure he meant to relay confidence, but she didn't hear it in his voicc.

She tried to sit back and memorize the countryside. She might never have another opportunity like this. Suddenly, a loud pop reverberated through the car and Kat was pushed against the door. Hot pain screamed through her shoulder and arm. Barely a second passed before she felt Alex's weight on top of her. His arms went around her and she could feel him shift so he wouldn't crush her.

"I got her. Get us out of here!" he yelled. She tried to move but was encased in his arms.

"Alex, what's going on?"

"We don't know. Keep your head down."

Every inch of her body was covered with his. His heart thumped wildly. Or was that pounding coming from her own chest? He smelled of dust and sweat and his hard muscles twitched, like he was ready to spring into action. "It's okay—we just blew a tire. We'll form a perimeter and move you to another car," Roger reassured her.

Alex exhaled then moved off her. Her skin cooled, but his scent lingered and she took a deep breath. She tried to catch his eye but he didn't meet her gaze; he was looking outside.

"You were willing to take a bullet for me?"

He shrugged. "The senator will kill me if something happens to you."

The driver and their escort left the car. Alex leaned forward, peering out of each window. "Whatever you do, don't move from this seat. You're safest inside the car."

He put his hand on the door handle, and she grabbed his arm. "You're leaving?"

"I need to see what's going on. Insurgents often lay shrapnel to puncture tires then kidnap the occupants. I don't believe in sheer bad luck. If something happens, hop in the driver's seat and go."

She held on to his arm, her blood thundering through her body. "Alex, *no*."

He reached into the front seat and handed her a walkie-talkie. "Press this button and you'll be connected to our security company. They'll come get you."

"You just said the car had a flat."

"It'll run for a few miles." He pressed the walkie-talkie into her hand. "Can't believe these guys didn't bring run-flat tires," he muttered.

She gripped his arm even harder. "No, don't leave. I don't want you in danger."

"Kat, I can't keep either of us safe if I'm

sitting here. I need to know what's going on out there."

Her mouth was so dry, she could barely open it to get the words out. "What if you get shot? You told me yourself—the car is the safest place to be."

He turned toward her and put a hand on her face. The gesture was absurdly comforting. She leaned into his hand, her eyes stinging with tears. "Please, let's just wait until the security guys come back." Her voice was small and whiny.

A loud knock on Alex's window had them both jumping in their seats. Kat looked out to see a car pull up beside her door. Alex unrolled his window an inch so he could hear what Roger was saying.

"Open the back door on the driver's side. We'll open the other car's door so you can get across. We'll form a barricade. Keep your heads down."

They both nodded. Kat waited until the other car door was open then released her own. She crawled into the other car, sliding across the seat quickly to make room for Alex. He was beside her in a flash. The car was moving before the door had fully closed behind him, and Roger dived into the passenger seat at the last second. Alex had brought her purse with him and handed it to her. "They'll bring our luggage if they can, but you'll need your passport."

They both let out a breath then turned to each other. She wasn't sure if it was her pulse or the bumps on the road that pounded in her ears. They'd increased their speed and were racing across the rough terrain. There were a million things she wanted to say to him. Thank him for wanting to save her life, berate him for thinking her life was more important than his, ask him to pull her into his arms so she could stop shaking. She'd never known anyone who was willing to die for her.

On her ski trip, she'd gotten stuck on a slope and couldn't navigate her way out. Colin had called the ski patrol rather than spoil his own run by walking back up the hill to help her.

"I should never have asked you to come. It's too dangerous here." He broke eye contact. She touched his arm, but he kept his face turned away from hers, so she tried punching him lightly instead.

"Ouch!" No way was he hurt. If anything, her fist would probably bruise from connecting with his hard biceps.

"I'm not an idiot," she said. "Iraq is a war zone. I read the security briefing, so I know going between the airport and military installations is the most dangerous part of the trip. And I know what happens to American women who get kidnapped. This isn't Tahiti."

Roger turned around. "Ma'am, we've never lost any of our visitors. We know how to be careful. Bad luck back there—the roads are full of debris. We may have picked up a nail in the city."

"Why don't you have run-flat tires?" Kat could almost see the steam coming from Alex's ears as he asked the question. "I'm not of any value, but she's the daughter of the ranking senate member on the Appropriations Committee."

Kat flinched at the rudeness in his voice. He sat stick straight, his fists clenched.

"I'm sorry, sir, but we only have so many cars. The tires are in short supply here. We lose at least a couple a week." He turned to Kat, probably looking for a more friendly face. "If a run-flat tire gets punctured, we can drive for several miles more at speed, but we still have to replace it. We haven't gotten a new shipment in over a month. The last cargo was confiscated by the Iraqi government."

Kat raised her eyebrows. "So now they're overtly taking things instead of asking for kickbacks?"

She could feel Alex's eyes on her as the man nodded. Alex thought she was a naive professor, and she had to admit she was. Experiencing "security concerns" was nowhere near the same as reading about them in a paper.

The man nodded. "You got it. Despite all our time here, the ongoing civil war makes it dangerous in many areas."

The dust became thicker as they drove along, covering the windows of the car in a sheet.

"Kat, there's something else I need to ask you."

She turned to Alex. She knew he'd been holding back.

"The senator would like you to give a pep talk to the troops on base. They've been here months past when their tour of duty was supposed to end, and they've had no visitors."

She bit her lip. "I'm not the right person to do something like that."

"You're the senator's representative."

"No, *you're* his representative. You know his policies."

"So do you—I saw the lecture you gave in class."

"But you believe in his philosophy."

"Kat, as his daughter, it'll mean more coming from you than from me."

"That's hardly fair. You're better qualified."

He muttered something that sounded like "fair doesn't matter in politics." "There won't be any media. It'll be just like lecturing to a class. We've even written talking points for you."

He pointed to her purse, and she noticed that he'd tucked his tablet inside. She handed it to him and he clicked on it. "I just sent it to you."

"You have Wi-Fi here?"

He nodded. "The car has Wi-Fi. It works on a satellite system."

"Guess the Iraqis can't confiscate the satellites in space." Her voice was light and the guys in the front laughed.

"Yes, but they have been known to take the receiver dish off the top of the car."

She shook her head in disbelief. How did these guys get anything done? Turning her attention back to Alex, she said, "I'll do it. Not for you, or for the senator, but for the troops." She clicked on her tablet and read through the points. "But there is no way I'm saying these things."

He sighed, as if he'd been expecting a fight. "Kat, we're two miles out. With luck, we'll be there in ten minutes. I'm not sure when they put you on the schedule, but I doubt we have time to come up with another speech. Can you just this once get with the program and stop fighting me on every little thing?"

She shook her head. "I'm not a puppet whose strings you can pull whenever you want."

He muttered something that sounded a lot like "don't I know it."

"Out with it, Alex."

"Why can't you be a team player?"

"My integrity is not for sale."

His eyes bored into hers. "The troops are here risking their lives because they believe in the mission. They're sitting here missing milestone events with their families. Many of them go back to broken homes and a country that can't appreciate the sacrifices they've made. This is about thanking them for their service. It's not the time to push your own agenda."

"I'll be respectful, but I'm not using those talking points."

THEY ARRIVED AT the forward operating base without further incident. Alex thanked the security team. He had overreacted to the situation on the road. So overcome with an insane need to protect Kat, he had lost his mind. If it had been a real threat, he would've put her life in even more danger if he got himself shot. But he'd been driven by an insane urge to stand between her and any flying bullets. In truth, if the security team had gotten shot down, his best move to protect her would have been to drive them away. Why hadn't he let his training kick in? Because he'd lost control, something that seemed to be happening a lot around Kat.

An army sergeant met them at the drop-off point and gave them a tour of the base. The sergeant explained that from the height of the war, the encampment had been reduced from having a full battalion to just one company of about a hundred US soldiers and support personnel, and an equal number of Iraqi forces that were there for training.

The general was scheduled to arrive early the next day. Kat was asked by the base commander to address the troops during the evening meal, which was coming up in an hour. Alex rubbed his temples.

Why did Kat have to be so difficult? The talking points his staff had prepared were relatively benign. He'd even taken out the part about the IED bill, figuring it'd be a nonstarter. Crista's comment that Kat was exactly the type of woman he'd been looking for came back to him. She couldn't have been more wrong. He needed to run as far away from Kat as he could. The woman frustrated him to the point that he lost all rational thought. Life with Kat would be a constant battle, everything from speeches to policy to what to make for dinner. Who needed that kind of stress? He had enough of it trying to break into the good-ol'-boy network that was Washington, DC.

As it was, the RNC was now breathing down his neck asking for more data on the IED bill. If the general didn't get on board during this trip, they would lose the support he'd spent months building. The bill had to come to vote in the next month, before the budget was finalized. Being a ranking member on Senate Appropriations gave Senator Roberts, and by extension Alex, a lot of chits to trade. The senator from Hawaii wanted a hundred thousand dollars to fund a study on improving the safety of hydrofoil ferries between islands. Alex could put that in the budget in exchange for a vote for the IED bill.

The budget was supposed to go to conference by July. If Alex didn't get the IED bill passed in the next month, he'd lose most of the votes he'd gotten by making budget promises. This was no time to get distracted by Kat.

The quartermaster handed them olive drab T-shirts and camo pants. Alex knew they'd never see their luggage. In the time it had taken the security personnel to change the tire, anyone from local villagers to hidden insurgents could've shown up. The security company would trade the bags for their own safety.

They headed to their quarters to shower and change out of their clothes, which were now dusty and a little ripe from nearly twenty-four hours of travel. On the way, Alex greeted the soldiers who were already back from patrol, surprised at how familiar everything felt. He'd signed up for the reserves in order to pay off his college loans. He was called up in the early years of the Iraq and Afghanistan wars and had gone in thinking the experience might look good one day when he ran for office.

He'd shown up with a superior attitude and a law degree under his belt. It took less than a day to be humbled by the men in his unit. They'd taught him what it meant to fight for freedom, how to put his own needs aside. Nick was serving his second tour and had shown him the ropes. Alex started out by counting the days until he was out, but when his time was up, he tried to fight it. It was his mother who'd talked him out of returning to active duty after his relatively minor injuries healed.

The shower was cold, and Alex was grateful for the sting against his skin. What was wrong with him? He'd dealt with difficult staffers before; it was inevitable when spoiled rich kids realized they'd be expected to do real work. He'd stared down powerful members of the US Congress, negotiated with tough lobbyists and industry officials. Why couldn't he get one woman to toe the party line? *Because she's not just any woman.* She was the one woman who threatened to undo everything he'd worked for in his life, including what was most precious to him—his self-control.

He made his way to the mess, desperate for a cup of coffee. He hadn't slept well on the flight, unable to stop the sweet scent of Kat's perfume from hitting his nose or admiring the way her lashes fanned over her cream-colored skin.

Kat was already in the hall, looking fresh and scrubbed. She'd pulled her hair into a ponytail. He stopped. Not even the olive drab T-shirt ballooning around her could hide how beautiful she was. The campaign manager in him wanted to ask if she could borrow makeup from a female soldier. Although there wouldn't be any media, he knew people would take photos and put them up on Facebook, Instagram and Twitter. But he didn't have the heart to tell her to change. Her beauty was in her simplicity, and he liked it.

"Are you ready for your big speech?"

The mess was set up like a cafeteria with metal tables and long benches. A small stage made of wooden crates had been erected at one end. She nodded. "I'm going to speak from the heart."

He needed something stronger than coffee, maybe a Xanax—or a blow on the head—so he could pass out and not have to witness the disaster that was coming. "Kat, this is not the time."

"I can be respectful of the soldiers without compromising my ideals."

"How long before you have enough material for your book?"

"Let's see how this trip goes." She grinned. A genuine smile that lit up her face. "Are you tired of me?"

He nodded. "You are a pain! I have several new gray hairs, thanks to you."

She pretended to study the top of his head. "I count at least ten."

"Why do you do this to me?"

"I'm not torturing you on purpose, although that is a side benefit. I'm open to changing my opinions, but you haven't given me anything that compels me to do that. Your pretty face alone is not enough."

He pinched the bridge of his nose. He was too tired to argue with Kat, and it wasn't worth it. She would say what she wanted and he'd have to deal with the consequences.

The mess hall was filling up. "Have you eaten?"

She shook her head. "I'll wait to get a tray until after I speak."

"You're a professor—you talk all the time."

"About subjects I'm comfortable with. Motivational speeches aren't my thing."

The base commander stopped by their table and chatted with them for several minutes about the training exercises earlier in the day. When the mess was full, he stood on the wooden crates and whistled. The entire hall went silent. He introduced Kat simply as the senator's daughter. She stepped on the crates, looking tiny in the big hall with her baggy clothes. Perfunctory applause greeted her. Alex started the video recording on his BlackBerry.

She stood frozen for several moments and he stood, ready to go to her side if needed. Her eyes locked on his and he nodded. Beginning tentatively, she introduced herself as a college professor and the recently-discovered secret daughter of the senator, which elicited chuckles from the crowd. "You may have seen the news coverage that I'm not the most well-behaved daughter of a prominent politician."

Alex sighed. He'd left his tablet in his room and now regretted not having another device to start damage control. He could already see several soldiers pointing phones at Kat.

"The senator's chief of staff and campaign

manager, Alex Santiago, is back there and is probably having a coronary right now." She pointed to him and all eyes turned to stare in amusement. He gave a wave, grateful that his skin color hid most of the raging red in his face.

"But here's the thing—each and every one of you is here so that our media can take a bad picture of me and blast it on TV, so I can stand up and openly oppose a powerful US senator. You're here so my students feel safe coming to college every day and are available for learning. They don't worry about their families at home, and they don't know what a missile careening toward your building sounds like. You make it possible for me to enjoy the freedoms that many in the world don't..."

He watched as she held the attention of the soldiers, doing better than the talking points. She gave a heartfelt speech and sincere thanks. When she was done, she got a standing ovation.

He looked up as the base commander slapped him on the back. "Hey, thanks for that. I gotta admit, there was some moaning among the rank and file when I told them we'd be having this during dinner. The guys aren't into stump speeches from blowhards, but this—" he nodded toward Kat "—was genuine."

She stepped off the crates, nearly toppling the makeshift stage. Several soldiers rushed to her rescue and she rewarded them with a stunning smile. On her way back, she stopped at several tables to shake hands. They were enamored with her, especially the young men. He could see the attraction and admiration in their eyes. It took every bit of self-control he had left to stay glued to his seat, resisting the urge to stand up and drag her back to his table. He didn't have any claims on her.

She returned with a big smile on her face. "I think it went well."

"If you do say so yourself."

"What's the verdict from the office?"

He thumbed his BlackBerry. Her speech was getting mixed reviews; some of the campaign staff worried that by joking about opposing her father, she was creating negativity. There were some nasty comments about her appearance. He scrolled to find something positive and came up empty. She hadn't been that bad, had she?

"Job well done, Kat."

She beamed. "I know you and I disagree on a lot of things, but at least we can agree on the fact that the troops deserve our appreciation."

One of the soldiers stopped by with a tray of

food for her, flirting shamelessly. She turned him down kindly.

"There's no shortage of handsome young men here willing to fall at your feet."

"I'm thirty-five," she said. "They all seem a little young for me."

"My guess is many of them are close to that age. You should accept one of their offers to take you out."

"I'm not really interested," she said.

"Why don't you date?"

Her brows furrowed in annoyance. "I date," she said defensively. "I'm just focusing on my career right now." She forked some mashed potatoes into her mouth then scrunched her nose.

"They make the powdered kind since fresh fruits and vegetables are in short supply," he told her.

She tentatively speared the steak, and Alex shook his head. "I wouldn't. Try the peas and bread—they're the most palatable."

"They eat this every day?"

Alex nodded. "When they can get a warm meal. A lot of times they're in the field eating MREs—meals ready to eat. Those are nasty. After a few days here, you'll give anything for something fresh."

She pushed her plate away. He wondered

whether she'd dated anyone since Colin. Was she still hung up on that jerk?

"When was the last time you went out with someone?"

She snapped her eyes to him. "A few months ago."

"What happened?"

"We could barely keep the conversation going through appetizers."

He suppressed a smile. "I can't imagine you not being able to talk through dinner. All you have to do is disagree with everything the other person is saying."

She rolled her eyes at him. "When was the last time you were in a relationship?"

"Relationship, not dating?"

"If we're going to talk about personal things, I don't want to know about meaningless dates."

Relationships were hard for him. Dates were much easier, like the one he'd just gone on with Mellie. They'd had a good time; she was a good conversationalist and they'd gotten through dinner effortlessly. The only problem was that by the end of the night, the thought of a lifetime of such dinners, filled with inane chatter, had him sick with dread.

"Crista was the last person I dated for more than a few weeks." Saying it out loud was so much worse.

"Why did you break it off with her?"

"She broke it off with me."

"So she says," said Kat.

"We weren't right for each other."

"How so?"

"When were you last in a relationship?" It was time to turn the questions back to her.

She paused. "I get it—tit for tat. I was engaged to Colin, the guy from that story three years ago. We broke up after…all that."

Alex leaned forward. "He took advantage of you."

She nodded.

"What attracted you to him in the first place?"

"He understood why I needed to take care of my mother. For all his faults, Colin was really sweet to my mom. Until things got bad, he was good to me, too."

Alex couldn't see any scenario where Colin had been good to her. "How so?"

"Until he stole my research and analysis, he didn't want anything from me. He accepted me as I am."

And I expect too much of you.

"In an odd way, I understand why he stole my analysis. He always felt so inferior to his siblings and wanted nothing more than to impress his father, to show that he was worthy of being part of his family. I guess I can empathize with that. What I can't forgive is that night when he hit me. I never saw it coming. The fear that caused… It's made it hard for me to trust. To let anyone—any man—get close to me."

Alex reminded himself to breathe deeply. The slight tremble in Kat's voice made him want to launch from his seat and hunt Colin down, make him fall at her feet and apologize until she saw him as nothing more than the coward that he was. Except, if he did that, how was he any different?

Colin had lost control. He'd let his anger at the situation override him, something Alex was all too familiar with. He wouldn't be another Colin in Kat's life.

She leaned forward. "Your turn. Tell me more about your relationship with Crista."

"I don't have much more to tell. Crista wanted marriage and I knew I'd never get there."

"Why not?"

"Because I'm not that different from Colin. I want to make my mother proud. I want to be a man who wins."

Kat opened her mouth then snapped it closed. She sighed. "I'm tired. Do you mind if I head to bed?"

He nodded, feeling a gnawing pain in his stomach. Could he be a better man? Not with Kat, he couldn't. She pressed all his buttons, and while he wasn't an angry teenager anymore, he needed to work hard to keep his temper in check. Kat didn't need a man like him. He walked Kat to her room.

"Thank you for trying to save my life today." His soul stirred as she looked up at him with luminous eyes, her fire and idealism shining through. He wanted nothing more than to cup her face and kiss her hard, to lose control for just a minute. Was she worth giving up everything he'd worked for?

He stepped back. "Things didn't work with Crista because I want a woman who can stand by my side, be my first lady. She's too smart and independent for that."

"Are you kidding me? In this day and age you think women need to take a backseat to their politician husbands? Look at Hillary Clinton and Michelle Obama. I think it should be a requirement that spouses of elected officials contribute to the public good."

Was Kat ever going to let up on him?

"Listen, I didn't mean a politician's wife can't be smart and pursue her own goals. But she does have to follow party politics. You don't see Hillary Clinton or Michelle Obama siding with the Republicans, do you?"

"You want a woman who can stick to the party line," Kat whispered.

He nodded. That was the whole point of accepting a date with Mellie. She was supposed to be getting his mind off Kat. Mellie was the kind of woman who could help him achieve his goals. So why hadn't he called her? And why was he standing here wondering whether he wanted something different? He turned and left before he did something he'd regret.

CHAPTER TEN

THE GENERAL HAD been delayed by a day, so Kat was left to find something to do. First Lieutenant Luke Williams was leading his platoon on a routine patrol and offered to take Kat with him. She was waiting for Alex in the mess hall.

"Ma'am, we're getting ready to leave. If you want to come with us, we need to find you a vest and helmet."

Nodding, she followed him out. She wasn't going to miss out on this opportunity by waiting for Alex's permission. "Please call me Kat—'ma'am' seems so formal."

The man grinned, and for the first time Kat noticed how attractive he was. He must've been the "hottie" she'd heard some of the female soldiers discussing last night.

A few minutes later, she was outfitted with a bulletproof vest and helmet. Their luggage hadn't been recovered, so she was still in the same clothes she'd been given the night before.

Luke explained that they were going to a

nearby village. There hadn't been any insurgent activity there, so their patrols were mostly to reassure the villagers and to remind informants to contact the base if they saw suspicious activity. "You'll be safe," Luke assured her. "Else I'd never have gotten permission from the base commander to take you."

She was put in the front seat of a Jeep, pressed between Luke and another man. She knew they were blanketing her in case the vehicle was hit with bullets.

There was no road to the village, so they followed a dirt path, Kat holding on to a bar overhead to keep from falling all over the men on either side of her.

They chatted about the war and she resisted the urge to pull out her phone and tape their conversation for her research. They openly discussed what it was like on the ground, how the insurgents came back the second troops withdrew, causing them to lose hard-fought territory yet again.

The weariness was obvious in the men's voices, as was their patriotism. While they were on an "easy" patrol today, yesterday they'd been canvassing for IEDs, aware that any second could mean death. The army corporal next to her had two kids back home and talked about how his wife planned to leave him because their marriage hadn't withstood his multiple deployments.

They arrived at the village and several children ran up to the Jeep. Luke went to the back and pulled out chocolate bars and MREs, handing them to the kids. "We're not technically supposed to do this, but it garners a lot of goodwill. They welcome us here and warn us if anything's about to go down because they want the chocolates."

Kat made a mental note to send Luke some boxes when she got home and to tell Crista to put candy on the packing list.

Luke introduced her to the villagers. She talked at length to a young paraplegic man, Reza, who spoke English fluently. He had gone to live with relatives in Pakistan so he could study English and get a good job to support his family. His goal had been to get his family out of the small village, which had no electricity or running water, and into better housing. Mere months after successfully moving his family to Baghdad, he was in the wrong place at the wrong time when a bomb went off. He lost the use of his legs and was fired from his job. With no income to support their life in the city, the family had to move back to the village so they could take care of him. The villagers often went days without food. His younger sister had died from hunger. The man cried openly and Kat matched his tears.

"How do you deal with this every day?" she asked Luke when they were done.

"By being here, Kat. If we left, there'd be a lot more men like him. That's why we're here."

"Do you have a girlfriend at home?"

He shook his head. "I get to go home for a few weeks at a time. I meet someone and we barely go out on a couple of dates before it's time to deploy again. Last tour, I fell in love with an Iraqi woman."

Kat closed her eyes, letting out a fresh stream of tears. She knew what was coming before he said it.

"She died in an attack."

At the end of the day, as they drove back to the base in silence, she felt an overwhelming sense of guilt. Her life back home was meaningless. She had the opportunity to influence young minds and she spewed academic nonsense at them that had no significance in the real world. In all the lectures she'd done on defense policy, not once had she talked about the impact to soldiers' personal lives, never had she discussed people like Reza and how their lives had been shattered by decisions made in Washington. She had already started writing her book, critical of the IED bill and of the military's presence in Iraq generally. She'd even used the example of Captain Atao's children in Guam, whose lives could be saved several times over by the money being spent on the IED bill alone. But as heart-wrenching as it was not to save the lives of those babies in Guam, how could they leave people like Reza in Iraq with no hope? If only there were a magic wand she could wave to make the world a better place, one where there was enough money to feed people *and* save babies.

Her heart was gripped in a vise. What had Alex accused her of? *Not feeling.* Maybe that was what she'd been doing all these years. Keeping herself behind a lecturer's podium so she could analyze things from afar. Maybe that was what Colin had offered her, a chance to experience the life she wanted without becoming emotionally involved. But that wasn't what it would be with Alex. Even being near him pushed her to emotional extremes. It was what scared her most about him. There would be no protecting her heart if things didn't work out.

When they returned to base, Luke invited her to have dinner, the intent clear in his eyes.

"How can you ever open your heart after what you've been through?" she asked.

He gave her a wide smile. "Precisely because

of where I am, Kat. Every day I'm breathing, my life is a gift and I don't waste a second. So what do you say?"

She smiled and shook her head. "I'd just break your heart. I'm unavailable."

"Does it have something to do with that bad-tempered guy who's walking over here like he's going to kill me then take you away, cave-man style?"

Kat turned to see Alex thundering toward them and couldn't help laughing. She nodded. "Don't tell him—it'll just make his big head grow even bigger."

ALEX HAD BEEN sitting in the operations center all day, monitoring the field communications to make sure that Kat was safe. *What a waste of a day.* He had a million emails to go through, reports to read, not to mention meetings he could've scheduled with field commanders in Iraq. Instead, he'd spent the day obsessing about whether Kat was going to get blown up. And now she was standing there flirting with GI Joe, laughing it up like they were on a date.

"What did you think you were doing?" he bellowed as soon as he was within hearing range.

"Educating myself," Kat said in that maddeningly sweet tone she used when she was being condescending.

"Have you not learned anything from yesterday? Do you not understand how dangerous this country is?"

"I was perfectly safe with—"

"And you, Lieutenant. Did you consider what a lucrative target this woman could be? She's a prominent senator's daughter. She—"

"With all due respect, sir, the threat was extremely low, she was well protected and I had permission from the base commander."

Alex and Luke were the same height, and he fumed at the obvious amusement in Luke's eyes.

"Luke, I'll handle him. I'm sure you have better things to do." Kat touched the lieutenant's arm in the same way she sometimes touched *his* arm, and Alex's chest exploded.

"Thank you for taking me today. Is it okay if I come find you if I have more questions?" Luke was staring at her like she was a decadent chocolate cake and Alex made his hands into fists to keep from striking the man. *Breathe, Alex.* His reaction was totally overblown; the soldier had done nothing wrong. Knowing that intellectually didn't stop the surge of anger in his chest.

"I do hope we get to see each other again,"

he said unabashedly. Alex took a step closer, but Luke walked away.

Alex turned to Kat, ready to give her the lecture he'd been practicing all afternoon. Before he could get a word out, she stepped forward and threw her arms around him. He was so stunned that she was pulling back by the time he managed to snake an arm around her waist.

"Do you know how worried I was with you out there?" he whispered into her hair. She felt warm and soft in his arms, and he wanted to feel every inch of her.

"Without you?"

"Yes, without me. I'm here to protect you."

"You can do better than a whole unit of army men?"

"They don't…"

"What?"

"They don't work for your father—they're not as well motivated as I am." He released her and she stared at him. He reached back and gently dislodged her arms from his neck.

"Don't do it again, Kat."

He turned away, but she grabbed his hand. "Doesn't it all seem petty to you, Alex?"

He stopped and swiveled back to her. "Doesn't what?"

"People die here, they lose their limbs, loved

ones leave them one way or another, and we go about our lives eating fine foods, thinking about how the universe has done us wrong. We're both attracted to each other. Why aren't we together? Why are we standing around fighting when any second, our lives could be obliterated? So what if I can never be your first lady? Is it really that important?"

No, it's really not. He gazed into her eyes, which were as inviting as the warm Caribbean Sea. Every cell in his body screamed *kiss her* but he recognized the fire raging inside him. He was too close to the precipice, and once he fell off, he'd never recover.

ALEX TURNED AND stepped away from her, and Kat's heart sank to her toes. She'd never done anything like this in her life; never stood in front of a man and offered up her heart on a plate, never begged for affection. Perhaps she shouldn't have now. She dropped her gaze to fight the tears welling in her eyes. Alex was not worth crying over. Reza's pain was worth crying over. Watching starving children devour MREs like they were the best food they'd ever tasted was worth crying over. A stubborn man was not worth her tears. And yet, to her horror, a whimper escaped her lips. She put a hand to her mouth.

Alex let out a guttural moan and suddenly he closed the distance between them. He embraced her and she looked up in surprise to see his mouth come crashing down on hers. Lifting herself onto her tiptoes, she circled her arms around his neck, wanting to hold him close, to feel his strength. His lips were hot on hers and she met his hunger with her own. Moving her hand to his heart, she felt its beat and connected it with her own. He moaned again, and she knew in that instant that he felt it, too, the magnetic force that pulled them together no matter how hard they tried to tear away. For the first time in her life, she felt a man's love inside her soul. She wanted Alex more than she'd needed anything in her life. It felt good to finally let go of the shackles she'd placed around herself, to open her heart to someone. He plundered her mouth and she pressed against him, eager to savor every moment. She whimpered when he broke the kiss. He let go and stepped back. "Kat, I can't." His eyes fell to her lips and she touched them instinctively, knowing they were swollen and raw.

"Alex, let yourself be with me," she said softly.

He shook his head. "I can't control myself around you, and it scares the hell out of me."

"Alex, it's okay. I'm not scared of you."

He shook his head. "That's not the man I want to be. I'm sorry." He walked away and she was left standing there wondering what had just happened.

CHAPTER ELEVEN

THERE WAS NO room in his head to think about Kat. The general had arrived and Alex needed to bring his A game to their meeting. He'd talked to the senator earlier in the morning and learned that the EAGLE managers had set up a meeting with him while Alex was in Iraq. If he didn't get the general's endorsement, Senator Roberts would not continue the fight; he was starting to grow weary of the number of favors they'd promised for the bill. Roberts might not see it, but Alex knew the law would be the senator's legacy—and his own. It would change the face of the war.

General Bouchard was a surprisingly small man, several inches shy of six feet. Yet his presence was no less commanding than the title implied. He greeted them efficiently and got right to the point.

"I'm not supporting the bill."

"Can you share your concerns?" Alex kept his voice calm; he expected this to be a long, drawn-out conversation.

The general laid out his concerns, which were arguments Alex had anticipated. Bouchard had a long list of items he needed for the troops in addition to the new IED technology. Alex was prepared for them and dealt with each one in turn.

"Dr. Driscoll, why don't you tell me why you lectured against this bill?"

Kat sat up straight and Alex met her gaze for the first time since yesterday. He silently pleaded with her.

"General, my concerns regarding the bill are largely academic. This is my first trip to Iraq, and I think my inexperience in the field should be taken into account when considering those lectures."

Alex stared at her. Was this the fake Kat he'd seen back at headquarters after the dinner with her father? Or was she just being gracious? He hadn't talked to her since the kiss. That soul-shattering kiss that had nearly made him lose his mind. In that moment with Kat, all he could think about was how much he wanted to make her his. Nothing else had mattered. He'd felt like a man who'd been roaming the desert for days and had been presented with a lake full of fresh water.

Things he'd never considered before had flown through his mind. *Will Mom like her?*

He'd never introduced a woman to his mother. *What if I took one of those jobs the lobbying firms are always offering me?* For an insane second, he had entertained the thought of having a different life. All because of her. It had taken every ounce of self-control he had to break the kiss and walk away; even more not to turn back when he heard her whimper. He couldn't be with a woman who affected him like that. If that kiss was any indication of the kind of passion Kat held inside her, he knew without a doubt that he'd never be able to control himself with her. There was only one true nonnegotiable for him, and that was how he would treat a woman.

The general cleared his throat, forcing Alex to refocus his thoughts. "Son, I need some time to think about this. Let's meet again tomorrow morning. I'll even let you keep the clothes as a souvenir."

Alex smiled politely at the attempted humor. As they left, he felt Kat beside him. Their arms touched as they exited the general's office and wordlessly made their way to the mess hall. They each poured themselves a cup of coffee and sat down.

"Thank you," he began.

"What for?"

"Supporting me in there."

"I was toeing the party line." Her lips twitched, and he smiled.

"Good job."

"Thanks, boss." This time there was no mistaking the sarcasm.

"About yesterday…"

She raised a single eyebrow, and for the first time in his life, he squirmed in his seat. The words of a former governor came to him. *Sit still, boy. Someone who can't sit still is either about to lie or screw you. Glue yourself to your seat.* Somehow, he couldn't tamp down the restlessness. This was what Kat did to him; he'd been right to walk away.

"I'm sorry I let things get too far. We work together. You're the senator's daughter. I shouldn't have…"

"Excuse me, Alex."

He realized he'd been staring over her shoulder to avoid looking straight into her electric-blue eyes. Now she pinned him with her gaze and he was unable to turn away.

"I know exactly why you stopped."

He waited.

"I'm not the trophy you want on your arm, so you're afraid of getting involved with me. If it ends badly and I go crazy on you, it could really jeopardize your relationship with the senator."

When she put it that way, he sounded like a jerk. He opened his mouth to correct her, but he couldn't find the words. What was he supposed to say to her? *I'm afraid of losing control around you and I want a woman who doesn't drive me crazy?* Her assessment, as harsh as it sounded, wasn't incorrect. He did want a woman who could support him; a future first lady who understood the need to sacrifice and compromise. Most important, someone with whom he could keep complete control over himself.

Apparently, Kat had no shortage of words. "You need to get your head out of your you-know-what. Look at where we are." She waved around her. "These soldiers might not come back from patrol alive this evening. You said yourself we could've been in danger yesterday. What if we get killed on the way back to the airport? What if I had gotten hurt in the village?"

He regulated his breathing. He'd already lived through that nightmare yesterday as he'd paced the control room for hours like a caged animal. He never wanted to feel that desperation again.

"Life's unpredictable," she continued. "Can't we try to enjoy what we have?"

He shook his head. "I can't be irresponsible like that."

She laughed mirthlessly. "I don't think you have an *irresponsible* bone in your body. I bet when you were growing up, you were in charge of the cash at the lemonade stand."

"When I was a child, I stole food from those boxes people put out to collect donations so my mother and I could have dinner." He never discussed his childhood, but he needed Kat to know that he wasn't a good guy. His DNA was flawed; she deserved someone better.

She reached out and touched his arm. "I get it, Alex. I've been taking care of my mother since I was six years old. When she couldn't hold down a job, I filled out the WIC application to get food stamps. It was never enough, though, so I lied about how old I was so I could get a job. We all do things to survive—it doesn't define us."

Her hand felt comforting and he wanted nothing more than to pull her in his arms and take care of her like she'd never been taken care of before. He wanted to give her everything she'd never gotten in her life. But he couldn't, and it would serve him well to remember that. He withdrew his hand.

"That's our problem. We're too alike, too independent, too headstrong."

She shook her head. "Fine, be this way. I'm not going to argue with you. I see Lieutenant Luke—I'm going to ask if I can go on another patrol." She stood and he was up in a flash, grabbing her arm.

"Alex!"

He released her and swore under his breath. There was a clear pink mark where he'd gripped her way too hard. This was exactly why he couldn't be with her.

"You don't get to tell me what I can or cannot do."

She was right. He watched her walk over to Sergeant Hotshot and his blood boiled as he said something that made her laugh. She followed Luke out, shooting Alex a withering look as she passed him.

It was just as well. He needed to get the general more data and make some calls to the Pentagon. There was no time to babysit Kat.

He clenched his fists. "Lieutenant." Luke turned to him, a clear challenge in his eyes. "I'll join you in whatever patrol you're doing." What was he saying? He couldn't whittle away the day following her around like a puppy dog.

"I'm sorry, but I can't take another person. There's no room in the Jeep." Luke gave him a disarming smile, but Alex could plainly see the smugness in his eyes. He looked at Kat, whose face tilt told him his protests were just firming her resolve to torture him further.

"You two have fun, then," he said easily. He would not go to the command room today. Kat was on her own.

CHAPTER TWELVE

KAT COULDN'T BELIEVE how brazen she'd been with Alex. The trip home from Iraq had been uneventful aside from the fact that she never did get her luggage. The security company sent some clothes to wear on the flight. Alex needed to stay an extra day but insisted on sending her back early due to "security concerns." She had no doubt he was avoiding her because he'd felt the nuclear connection when they kissed. Things had changed between them. A new charge electrified every encounter, and he couldn't take the heat.

She wasn't going to worry about it. For her, the trip had awakened a desire to do more with her life, to get out of the rut she'd let herself get used to. Being in Iraq, seeing the devastation, feeling the pain and suffering of everyday people ignited her. That kiss, the one that lit her very soul on fire, had blasted the cobwebs off her heart.

The taxi had just dropped her off at home, and a breeze was cooling the hot evening air.

It was still light out even though it was almost dinnertime. She stared at her house, purse in hand.

How could she be content lecturing on things she'd read about in books, being the good daughter and going to bed wondering if there was more to life? There was. There were people who lived their lives even in the most austere environments, fighting against the odds. She'd always seen her glass half empty instead of considering it half full. The very fact that she was healthy and had food and shelter left her better than many people in the world for whom each of those things was a daily struggle. She wasn't going to let the excuse of her mother's illness dictate her life.

"Hi, Rex," she yelled to the neighbor's yippy dog who'd started barking as soon as she crossed the street and stepped onto her driveway.

She frowned, noting the blue car parked there. It didn't belong to her aunt, and it wasn't time for the nurses, either.

Her pulse kicked. Did her mother have a visitor? And where was her aunt? The door opened just as she stepped onto the porch.

"Crista!"

"Welcome home." She gave Kat a hug.

"What're you doing here?"

"A pipe burst in your aunt's house and she had to go, so I came to check on your mom."

"Is she—"

"She's okay. She's taking a nap in the bedroom."

Kat went to her mother's room and gingerly opened the door. Her mother was sleeping, the rise and fall of her chest steady. She looked good; her cheeks actually had some color to them.

Closing the door softly, she returned to the living room, where Crista was closing her laptop. "When did Aunt Luce leave?"

"Day before yesterday."

Kat took a sharp breath. "Why didn't you call me?"

"Because there was no point in worrying you. Nathan and I have been taking turns visiting your mom when the nurses aren't here. She's been great. We didn't want to worry you."

And there it was, reality crashing down on her. She couldn't rely on others to take care of her mom.

"Thank you, Crista. I appreciate you and Nathan doing this, but…"

Crista crossed the room and placed her hands on Kat's shoulders. "You're not used to someone else helping you, I get that, but stop with just the thank-you. We do this for each other, all of us. You had enough going on in Iraq, and you didn't need to spend twenty-four hours in transit worrying about your mom. She's okay. She really is."

Kat nodded. She made a mental note to pick up a gift for both of them but knew it wouldn't be enough. She'd been through this before. It started in college when well-meaning friends would offer their help so she could go out on a date. But then came the inevitable request for something in return that she couldn't give. Not that she could blame them. Friendships were not about always taking and never giving. It had felt good, for a little while, to feel as though there was a chance she could have a normal life, that all she had to do was seize the day.

"How did it go with Alex?" Crista gave her a meaningful look.

Kat began to form her lie, got ready to tell Crista that she was reading too much into things between her and Alex.

"He doesn't want to get romantically involved," she said simply. It was easier to tell the truth.

"I don't think it's a matter of want, more a deep-seated fear of dating a woman who holds him accountable for how he behaves."

"That's the nice way of putting it."

Crista linked arms with Kat. "If you ask me, you've dodged a bullet. As mean as he sounds in the office, he's an incredibly gentle and thoughtful boyfriend. If you think you've got it bad now, it would be a whole lot worse for you later."

Kat wondered whether Crista knew about Alex's history with the girl he claimed to have hurt. She'd seen the gentle Alex that Crista was talking about. She couldn't imagine him ever hurting a girl. There had to be more to the story.

"How about we go out for a girls' dinner one night and do an Alex detox?"

Kat smiled. "Why don't you stay? I can order pizza or Chinese."

Crista looked at her watch then bit her lip. "Ugh, I wish I could but I have to get back to the office."

"This late?"

"Nathan has been rewriting the donor briefs with the general's endorsement. I've got to approve them tonight."

And yet she'd driven all this way to check on her mother. Crista put the laptop in her bag and hoisted it on her shoulder. "So Nathan and I are going hiking tomorrow morning."

"You're taking a day off?" Kat feigned shock.

Crista laughed. "I know, but it's Saturday and I've realized that all I do is go to work. I can't remember the last time I had a home-cooked meal, got more than five hours of sleep or had a real friend."

Kat tilted her head. What could she say? It wasn't as if she could give Crista any advice. "Listen, nothing changes until you do something differently. Taking the day off and going out with Nathan is a start. Who knows where it'll lead. Stay here a second."

She went to her freezer and pulled out a Tupperware container. She handed it to Crista. "I freeze meals for nights when I don't feel like cooking. It's not the same as a fresh-cooked dinner but it is homemade."

Crista smiled widely, put down her bag and gave Kat a hug. "Oh, my God, that's the most thoughtful thing anybody has ever done for me."

"It's nothing, really, especially considering what you've done for me."

Crista stepped back, surprised. "Friendships aren't quid pro quo, Kat."

Kat had never seen it that way, but the words were nice to hear. Maybe things would be different with Crista.

She had just closed the door after wishing Crista goodbye when there was a knock.

She smiled when she saw Crista. "Did you change your mind about ordering in?"

Crista bit her lip. "There's something you should know."

Kat motioned for her to come inside but Crista shook her head. "I was specifically asked not to tell you, but..."

Kat's stomach flipped. It had to be something related to her mother.

Crista shifted on her feet and Kat placed a hand on her shoulder. "Crista, please. I've been taking care of my mom since I was six. I've been worried about her, so if you know something..."

"She's been talking to the senator."

Kat had been expecting any number of things; that her mother had been hiding her medications, watching horror movies, which gave her nightmares, online shopping for things they didn't need again. But this was a shock.

"What? How?"

"I'm not sure when it started, but she's been talking to him on the phone at night. He stopped by to see her when you were gone."

"About what?"

Crista shrugged. "I wasn't here when he came. I only heard her side of the phone conversation, and it seemed like they were making plans but I didn't get any details." She looked around as if she was waiting for someone to come arrest her. "I shouldn't have said anything." She turned and left.

Kat stared at Crista's retreating figure. Why was her mother talking to her father after all these years?

The sound of the bedroom door opening grabbed her attention. Kat gave her mom a hug and was surprised to see clear eyes and pink cheeks. If she wasn't mistaken, her face even seemed a little fuller.

"Mom, you look great."

Her mother smiled. "I thought you might be hungry. I made dinner—your favorite macaroni and cheese. It's in the refrigerator."

Kat's eyes widened. She couldn't remember the last time her mother had cooked. Macaroni and cheese was the only meal that ever tasted good when she was a child. It was the only dish Kat could make without burning. Emilia took it out of the fridge and put it in the microwave. After it was done, Kat forked a bite into her mouth, not knowing what to expect. It was delicious, made from scratch.

She took the container to the living room, where her mother had turned on the TV. "Mom, this hits the spot. Thank you so much." Kat gave her a kiss on the cheek.

Her mother beamed. She'd obviously been

taking her medications while Kat was gone. The nurse knocked on the door and Kat let her in. It was her mother's usual nurse, Carol, and Kat greeted her warmly.

The nurse checked her mother's vital signs. "She's doing really well. I was concerned when she went off the lithium, but after the first night…"

"Wait—what? She hasn't taken her lithium?"

The nurse shook her head. "She wouldn't take it the first night you were away. Your aunt was here and said she'd handle it. When I came back the second night, the day nurse had left a note that she'd talked to the doctor and he okayed her going off it because she was on such a low dose to begin with."

Kat took a deep breath. It had taken her months to get her mother to agree to go on lithium to help control her moods. She had strict instructions for the nurses to make sure she took it. Aunt Luce had no right to undo all the work she'd done to help her mother stabilize. It had taken weeks to get her mother's levels right, and now Kat would have to call the doctor to start all over.

Anger bubbled inside her, but she resisted the urge to yell at the nurse. It wasn't her fault; it was Kat's fault for leaving her mom. For thinking she had a chance at normalcy. Then a thought hit her: Did all this have something to do with the visit from her father? Now the other shoe had really dropped. No matter how genuine a friendship Crista might offer her, no one could protect her mother. It was Kat's responsibility; one that she could never take a break from, even to seize the day.

"For what it's worth, your mom actually seems to be doing better."

Kat looked at Emilia, sitting on the couch with a smile on her face. She did seem to be doing well. The last time she'd gone off the lithium, Kat had come home to find she had dumped two ten-pound bags of potting soil on the kitchen floor, convinced they'd be better off creating a garden in the kitchen so they could have fruits and vegetables in the winter. Her mother had tracked dirt all over the house, and Kat had spent over a week cleaning it all up.

This time, her mom had made dinner. Something was going on between her and the senator, and Kat needed to find out what it was before her mother went into another downward spiral. It was only a matter of time before she'd go from the happy side of normal to full-on mania. Kat knew the crash back to a depressive state would be bad. The trip to Iraq had been a departure from her routine, but it was time to get back to reality, and she couldn't change the life she had. It had just taken her longer than Alex to figure this out.

CHAPTER THIRTEEN

Are you coming into the office today?

KAT GLARED AT the text. It was Saturday; were they really expecting her to work? What was Crista doing at the office? Why wasn't she out hiking with Nathan?

You need to come in. ASAP.

Had something happened? She drove as fast as she dared and arrived at campaign headquarters to see the entire place hopping. Not only were the usual staffers there, but they seemed to have multiplied. She caught Nathan on his way to the coffeepot. "Who are all these people?"

"Volunteers, to deal with the situation and press coverage."

"What situation?"

"Heard what?"

Nathan stopped. "You haven't heard?"

"Heard what?"

"I'm going to go get Crista. Don't move."

Kat stood there feeling stupid. All around her, the cubicles were abuzz, people moving with a sense of purpose. They were obviously in crisis mode, and Kat felt wholly inadequate. She clicked on her BlackBerry, belatedly realizing she should have checked her emails. There were several from Crista marked urgent.

"Hey!"

She looked up to see that the person who had snatched the phone from her was none other than Crista.

"You haven't seen your emails."

Kat shook her head. Crista grabbed her hand and pulled her into Alex's office, closing the door behind her. A cold dread spread through her.

"Just tell me, Crista."

"Alex's transport to the airport encountered some IEDs. He and the two security personnel that were escorting him are missing."

Her heart stopped. She grabbed the desk and sank into a chair. Somehow she found her voice. "What does that mean? Missing?"

"We don't know. They could've been kidnapped, or they could've died and the car could have been stolen." Crista was talking so fast, Kat could barely keep up. "There's no specific information, but the senator has talked to the general directly and asked him for his help. The army has sent out patrols to see what they can find."

Kat's knees were shaking so badly she was afraid to stand up. "When will we know?"

She placed a hand on Kat's shoulder, but the slight shake in her voice made Crista's words less reassuring. "It could be any moment, or we might not hear for days. These situations are highly volatile, but we're doing everything we can."

"What can I do?"

"There's a lot, and nothing to do. We're getting a lot of press calls about the IED bill. Alex's transport wasn't the only thing ambushed— there were twenty simultaneous IED attacks. We've lost a number of soldiers."

"What can I do?" She knew she sounded like a broken record but she had to do something.

"The senator's appearing on the Sunday morning shows tomorrow. Can you write some counterpoints for him on the IED bill so he's prepared to answer questions?"

Kat nodded even though that was the last thing she wanted to do. Couldn't the campaign stop for just a minute?

"I have to go, but stay here, take your time." Crista closed the door behind her.

Kat didn't know how long she sat in the office. Her entire body felt numb. She looked at Alex's chair, picturing his smiling, smirking, smug face. The warmth of his dark eyes pierced her soul. He was alive. Maybe it was just wishful thinking or faith, but if he had died, she was sure she would've felt it in her heart.

She went to her desk and booted her computer. The chocolates he had sent almost a week ago on the senator's behalf sat there taunting her. Hours passed before she completed the talking points. She'd been arguing these points relentlessly, but instead of focusing on writing them out, she kept refreshing her email to see if there was any news.

Each minute seemed maddeningly slow, yet the day went by quickly. Kat called her aunt, but she couldn't leave her house. Closing her eyes, Kat tried to think through all her options. She didn't want to leave headquarters in case something happened. But could she leave her mother alone? The nursing agency was already scheduled to do the nightly check. Her mother seemed to be doing well, didn't she? She hadn't had a chance to talk to the doctor, but if her mother had been off lithium for days now it didn't matter if she was off for a few more since she seemed stable. As it was, they had to wait for an appointment before the doctor would put her back on the meds.

Kat decided to stay at headquarters. It was more important for Kat to be here for Alex.

"Kat, there's news."

She stood so fast, her head spun. She raced into the conference room, where Crista had the phone on speaker. Nathan was there, too, along with several other campaign staffers. The senator was still on the campaign trail but had called in.

"They found the car Alex was traveling in. We're on the phone with the senator and First Lieutenant Luke Williams."

Hope bloomed in her chest. She'd seen Luke in action. He was a man who genuinely cared. "Go ahead, Lieutenant."

"We tracked the GPS locator in the car. They disabled the navigation feature, but this is one of the newer models that has redundancy built in. The car was in a chop shop in Baghdad. We were able to recover it and there was some blood in the vehicle, but not a lot. Our best guess is someone was injured, but not seriously."

"What about the occupants?"

"We don't have a lead on them. They were most likely kidnapped."

"Alex always has his BlackBerry on him.

Can you track him with that?" Kat didn't know where she found the presence of mind to make the suggestion.

"Kat, is that you?"

"Yes." Kat was impressed he recognized her voice, given the circumstances.

"We've tried tracking his BlackBerry and the cell phones for the two security firm personnel, but they're completely dark. My guess is whoever grabbed the men took the batteries out of the phones."

There was a collective sigh of frustration in the room.

"For what it's worth, we're preparing for a ransom demand. If they were dead, we would've found their bodies by now."

The senator thanked Luke. Crista stabbed the end button on the phone. Kat caught her eye and could see the other woman's frustration mirror her own. She remembered Alex's laser-sharp focus when they'd traveled together to the base. Had he been distracted when this incident happened? Could it have something to do with the kiss they'd shared? She'd been so focused on her own needs, so overcome with the devastation in Iraq that she needed to make sure her heart was capable of feeling something positive. She'd gone to Alex because she knew he'd ignite her soul; she wanted to know that she wasn't dead inside, that she was capable of loving again. If the kiss hadn't made him so uncomfortable, they'd have come home together, with extra security.

"You're blaming yourself, aren't you?" Crista was gathering her papers. Kat realized with a start that everyone else had already left.

"If I hadn't come back early, if I'd insisted on returning with him, we would have had extra security…"

"He was going to go to Iraq with or without you. And I'm the one who arranged the security detail. Alex always wants to go with the cheapest option and you were the high-value target. We'll go crazy with the what-ifs."

Kat shook her head. "I pushed it with him. That's why he sent me home earlier."

"He wouldn't have been desperate to get the general's endorsement if it weren't for me."

The catch in Crista's voice made Kat look up. She went to her side and placed an arm around her.

"The senator asked me to keep an eye on Alex. I've been monitoring the campaign emails and looking through his files."

Ice chilled her veins. She dropped her arm from Crista's shoulders.

"I told the senator that Alex was using too much political capital on the IED bill, that we were losing donors and spending too many favors."

So the senator's waning enthusiasm for the bill had nothing to do with Kat's conversation with him. Crista had been sabotaging Alex's efforts.

"How could you? I thought you cared for him, Crista," Kat said quietly.

Crista lowered her head, obviously fighting tears. "I feel horrible about it. If he comes out of this alive, I'll tell him everything."

Kat left the conference room feeling numb. She wanted to blame Crista, but she knew it wasn't her. If there was one thing she'd learned, it was that they were all playing a game, one where each person hated the rules, but no one had the courage to change those rules by breaking them.

Around one in the morning, someone handed out space blankets, the thin aluminum sheets used by runners to keep warm after a marathon. Staff found places to nap: in their seats, heads on tables, even the floor. Kat didn't know of any other workplace where people put their lives on hold to stand in support of their boss, especially not a man who drove them harder than anyone she'd ever encountered. It wasn't about Alex, though; it was about the camaraderie of the campaign. They were friends who were bonded closer than family, even if some members were backstabbing each other.

Around four in the morning, the senator quietly arrived. Kat was the only one who noticed because she couldn't sleep. He went to his office and she followed.

"You can't sleep, either?"

He nodded. His tie was loose, his usually pressed suit crumpled. "This is on me. I told Alex I was wavering on the bill. If I hadn't, he wouldn't have stayed to convince the general."

"You had Crista spying on him."

His brows furrowed as he studied her with dull blue eyes. "That's a little harsh—I told her to watch out for him. He's too emotionally involved in this bill, and I'm rapidly losing friends and supporters."

Kat thought about Alex's reasons for fighting for the bill. He truly believed in it, and the senator was going to undo all of his work, all of his sacrifices. Her hand flew to the pendant at her neck, and she let the silver cool her fingers. "Senator, this bill means everything to Alex. When he was in Iraq…"

"I know all about his personal experience with IEDs. He's the one who convinced me to pursue this in the first place."

"So you don't believe in it."

"I believe in supporting our troops and

doing everything we can for them. Alex persuaded me that this bill was the way to do that. But the bill is not worth all the other things I'm trying to do."

Her stomach hardened. She was a grown woman, and yet she'd created a fantasy about the type of man her father was. About the woman she'd become because of the genes she'd inherited. Alex revered this man.

"And it's not worth the election," she said stonily.

He rubbed the back of his neck. "Katerina, I want to clear something up. If I lose my supporters and therefore the election, my opponent becomes the junior senator. He's a first-timer—he'll take the first six years just to make space for himself in the Senate. He won't do anything for the people of Virginia or for the troops because he'll have no clout. I'll remind you—I am a ranking member on the Appropriations Committee."

Kat knew the point he was trying to make. Each state got two senators and the one with a longer tenure in Congress was known as the senior senator. That was currently her father. The longer a senator remained in power, the more plum the committee assignments they received. The Appropriations Committee was arguably one of the most powerful since they determined how much money each agency and program received. Someone elected for the first time would get put on the least popular committees.

"And that's exactly why you can afford to do things no one else can. You control the purse strings of the biggest bank in the world. If you're so easily bullied, what chance does anyone else have to—"

The senator stood. "Katerina, I'm going to chalk up your comments to stress and naïveté. Things in DC work differently than in college, where you analyze people's moves as if they are pieces on a chessboard. That's not real life."

"I may be naive, but I'm also a voter, and an average woman who believes that if you make a promise, you keep it. You've made a promise to the troops by making this your signature legislation. The soldiers in Iraq—they're already waiting for this technology. They're risking their lives every day. Their lives! Nothing here, not even the loss of an election, measures up to that."

The senator sank back in his chair. Kat stood and left. There was no point in continuing the conversation. Men like her father, and Colin, didn't believe in the greater good if it meant personal sacrifice.

The next several hours were the longest of her life. Despite it being daytime in Iraq, there was no news. No ransom demand and no sign of Alex or the other two men. The security company was also doing its own investigation, and no one had found a single piece of information to tell them where the men might be. Kat distracted herself by writing. As the words of her book flew out of her, she realized she was being a hypocrite with her father. She still believed that the IED bill was wrong, but she was tempering her words, letting her time in Iraq, her feelings for Alex and how important the bill was to him cloud her analysis. She stopped writing.

By nine in the morning, the entire staff was exhausted.

"I'm sending everyone home!" Crista announced. "The phone tree is active. As soon as I have news, I'll call. Get some rest. Alex needs you at your best."

Almost everyone cleared out. Kat, Nathan and the senator stayed. Someone put out cots that were only slightly more comfortable than their chairs. Mellie entered through the front doors wearing jeans and one of the blue-and-red Roberts for Senate T-shirts that had been distributed earlier. Mellie's hair was in a ponytail and her face devoid of makeup. Kat barely recognized her.

She greeted Kat coldly. "Why did you come back early?"

Kat knew Mellie was only asking the question, not presenting an accusation, but she couldn't help feeling defensive. "Alex insisted. He and I weren't getting along." It was the line she'd given everyone else.

"Did he push you away?"

"Excuse me?"

"That day you were in DC, Alex was buzzing with electricity. We had dinner together before he left for Iraq. Do you know how long I've been asking him out? He finally accepts and all he could talk about is how frustrating you are."

Kat stared at Mellie. Alex had dinner with her?

"Alex doesn't let a woman turn his head. Believe me, I've tried."

Kat resisted the urge to roll her eyes. Was there any woman who didn't have a thing for Alex? Except, as she looked around, she realized she had something in common with the other women in the room. They didn't just have a crush on Alex. They loved him.

"There's nothing between us," Kat said quietly, more to herself than Mellie.

"If you want my advice…" Kat bit her lip to stop herself from telling Mellie to keep her opinions to herself. "Don't let him push you away."

"Excuse me?"

Mellie put a hand on Kat's shoulder. "He doesn't let a woman get too close, but don't give up. A guy like him is worth fighting for."

The day ticked by slowly. Exhaustion finally won and Kat managed to sleep for a few hours in the evening, which left her refreshed to continue working on her book late into the night. But her thoughts kept wandering back to Alex. Kat wondered whether his not letting women close to his life had anything to do with his father. *Oh, my God!*

"Crista!" Kat screamed, aware of the hysteria in her voice. Crista stood, hearing her call, and Kat made a beeline for Nathan's cubicle. "Has someone contacted Alex's mother to let her know what's going on?"

Crista slapped a hand over her mouth. "I totally forgot. I'll call her now." She reached for her BlackBerry, but Kat placed a hand over hers.

"You can't tell her over the phone."

Crista swore under her breath. "She lives four hours away. I'm too tired to drive this late at night."

"I'll go."

Kat grabbed her purse and stopped at the twenty-four-hour café next door and bought two cups of espresso to combat her fatigue. But she needn't have bothered. During the long drive, she went over what she'd say to Alex's mother, the only woman who mattered in his life. Her apprehension kept her wide awake.

The GPS led her to a small town house in an area that looked much like her neighborhood, with neat yards overflowing with summer flowers. Kat had no idea if Mrs. Santiago would be home. She'd debated calling but then realized that even setting up a meeting would have the woman stressing for the four hours it would take her to get there. So she'd brought her computer and was prepared to wait if she needed to.

She parked the car on the street and took a deep breath. It was a dewy morning, and the air smelled fresh and bright, as if the day promised to bring good news. Kat's hands were clammy as she rang the bell, and she wiped them on her jeans, wondering whether she should have changed her clothes.

When there was no answer, she rang the bell again. It was early morning; maybe she was still asleep? Kat turned then heard the door open. The woman looked exactly like the picture she'd seen on Alex's desk. Mrs. Santiago was dressed in a gray uniform with a name tag pinned to her chest. She had black hair peppered with gray and dark eyes that beamed with kindness.

"Can I help you?"

"Mrs. Santiago, I'm Kat Driscoll. I work with Alex."

The woman smiled widely. "Kat! I know all about you—come in." She was a soft-spoken woman with a Central American accent. Kat followed her into a cozy kitchen that had a table with two chairs. "I had the night shift, so I just got home. I'm making breakfast—would you like something?"

Kat shook her head. The two cups of espresso were churning in her stomach like a stormy, frothy ocean.

"Where do you work?" Kat knew she was stalling, but she couldn't just blurt out information she knew would destroy this woman's world.

"At the Hilton hotel in town. I'm the head of housekeeping. I usually don't work nights—one of the advantages of being a manager—but one of my girls had a sick baby last night. I figured it was easier to do it myself than ruin someone else's plans."

She put two plates of scrambled eggs on the

table. "You look like you haven't had breakfast. Eat—that's an order."

Kat looked up in surprise, suddenly and irrationally angry that her mother had never made her sit down and eat breakfast.

"So you're the girl Alex is in love with."

Kat dropped her fork. "I think you have the wrong..."

Mrs. Santiago reached over and patted her hand. "Alex hasn't stopped talking about you. All he's said is how difficult you've made his life. I know my son. Only people he cares about get under his skin."

Kat opened her mouth then shut it. "I have something to tell you."

She nodded. "He hasn't called me in two days and his phone goes straight to voice mail. You're here to give me really bad news, else Crista would've called."

Kat swallowed. There was no easy way to do this. She told her the whole story. To Mrs. Santiago's credit, she remained calm. Dabbing at the tears in her eyes, she asked the same questions the campaign staff had been asking for the past several hours. It somehow felt even worse relaying the unsatisfactory nonanswers than hearing them.

"I'm so sorry—it's my fault. If I hadn't come

back early, maybe the extra security could have prevented this."

"Katerina, how do you feel about my son?"

Mrs. Santiago sat silently, content to wait for whatever answer Kat was willing to give. What was she supposed to tell Alex's mother? She couldn't even describe their complicated relationship to herself.

"I like Alex. I'd like to see what there could be between us, but he's pushing me away. I don't understand his excuses."

Mrs. Santiago finished her eggs then wiped her mouth and peered at Kat.

"Alex doesn't believe in love. His father was not a good man, and life wasn't easy for us when he was growing up. He's always been very driven and he doesn't want to do anything that will jeopardize his career."

Kat nodded. That much she'd figured out for herself.

"You will have to show him."

Kat looked at her quizzically. "Excuse me?"

"When he returns, you will show him what love is."

Kat put a hand on her stomach. Alex would return. He had to. But she'd already told him how she felt and he'd rejected her. She couldn't keep throwing herself at him. Besides, what did she know about showing someone how to love?

She stood. "Mrs. Santiago, I promise to call you as soon as we have news, but let me give you my cell-phone number. Call me anytime, day or night—"

"I wish to show you something, Katerina."

Kat nodded but had to suppress a sigh. She didn't want more questions she didn't have the answers to. They walked up the narrow staircase to what was obviously Alex's child-hood bedroom. Kat walked in, studying everything with interest. There was a twin bed that seemed impossibly small, even for a child-size Alex, a set of dresser drawers and a little desk. The walls were lined with formal pictures of presidents. There were no toys, no teddy bears, no posters of rock stars or turtles dressed like ninjas.

"Does this look like the room of a child to you?"

Kat shook her head.

"I tried to protect Alex, but he saw more than he let on. I was a young woman when I came to America. I didn't speak English properly. I trusted Domingo, Alex's father, but he was a very violent man. It took me too long to find the courage to leave him. The women's shelter got me a job at the governor's mansion."

Kat put her arm around the tiny woman as she stared off into the distance. Her own throat closed, her breaths coming in short bursts.

"The governor expected certain favors from me, and I gave them. Domingo couldn't get to us in the governor's mansion. We had a place to live, food every day. Alex was a growing boy…" She clasped her hands and looked down.

Kat tightened her embrace. "You did what you had to do to protect your son. It's more than most mothers could stomach."

"We've never talked about it, but I know Alex knows." She lifted her sleeves and Kat's stomach roiled as she saw the scars on the woman's wrists and upper arms. "Alex would insist on changing my bandages. I told him these were just accidents, but it's a little hard to keep burning yourself with cigarettes, especially when you don't smoke."

Bile rose in her throat. She could picture Alex changing his mother's dressings with warm, gentle care.

"Alex was an angry young man growing up. He never threw temper tantrums, but there was always a darkness around him. When he was a teenager, he was sweet on this girl—she was the head cheerleader in his high school.

He was in love, but she was playing some kind of joke on him. Her boyfriend and some of the other kids ganged up on Alex and he got into a fight. In the tussle, the girl was hit. I know in my heart it was an accident—Alex would never hurt a girl—but she made a big deal saying he did it on purpose. Convinced him of it, too, even though Alex's friend later told me it was definitely an accident."

She shook her head. "The governor called the principal personally and we kept it quiet. In an odd way, the incident seemed to change his life. He took it hard. I think he saw too much of his father in himself, and he's worked hard to find inner peace. He's become a man I'm proud of, but he's still afraid he'll turn out like his father."

And suddenly it clicked into place for her. Why he wasn't willing to be with her. "He's afraid of hurting me."

His mother nodded then shook her head. "That's what he thinks, but I know that the truth of the matter is that he doesn't know how to love. He needs someone to teach him." She looked meaningfully at Kat.

What do I know about love? She'd spent her entire life trying to make friends and unable to keep any of them. How was she supposed to show a tough-as-nails man how gentle he really was?

Thankfully, Alex's mother didn't expect an answer and began telling her about Alex's school days.

They chatted for another hour, neither one saying out loud what was on both of their minds. *Is Alex even alive?*

CHAPTER FOURTEEN

ALEX LOOKED AT his watch, the only electronic device he had access to, wishing he had bought one of the new ones that was also a phone. When their car was ambushed, he'd been on his BlackBerry and dropped it to grab the gun in the seat pocket so he could shoot back. By sheer bad luck, the two other security guys had damaged their phones in the scramble to escape.

So they were all stuck in a mud pit, now exhausted from debating whether the man who'd given them shelter would turn them in before a friendly force found them. They were resigned to waiting for their fate, something none of the men were programmed to do.

He found a corner that was relatively dry and sat down, his pants still damp from sleeping on the cold, wet earth. He closed his eyes and let his head rest on the stone-and-mud wall behind him. His skin crawled, itchy from the bites of various desert creatures. He knew scratching would just expose his skin to more bacteria and invite insects to come for a bite, so he sat still, gritting his teeth.

He closed his eyes and the image that had comforted him for the past week blissfully filled his mind. Taking a contented breath, he watched Kat's blue eyes smolder in anger, ice with determination and sparkle with anticipation. Her lips brushed against his cheek; the scent of her hair tickled his nose.

Alex felt the fire she ignited inside him. Here in this muddy hole, staring down at the very real possibility that he'd never get out alive, he needed to feel the flames he'd been running from all his life. It was the only thing that would keep him alive as night descended on them and the cold wind set in. All they had were threadbare blankets, and one of the guys was already shivering.

They'd promised to pay the informant an exorbitant sum of money to hide them. That was on top of the cash they had already given him, a substantial sum the security guys had been carrying to bribe their way through insurgent checkpoints. Alex didn't trust the man who was hiding them. The mudhole was a basement of sorts beneath his house. The only access point was a trapdoor above their heads. There was no other exit. If he sold them out, they'd be like sitting ducks. The first few nights, the men had taken turns keeping watch until they realized they were all sleeping with one eye open.

Alex studied the two other men in their corners. They'd all talked about their families. Roger, who was currently praying, was an ex-Delta guy who had a wife and two teenage kids at home. He'd taken the security job for a two-year stint to earn his kids' college tuition. He was a month away from finishing his contract. Larry, the guy with his eyes closed, was a divorced recovering alcoholic whose grown kids wanted nothing to do with him. He had taken the job to find something that made his life feel like it was worth living. Roger and Larry had significant life-insurance policies, so their families would be financially set if they died. Alex's mother would be okay on that front, too; he had saved money for her and bought the house she lived in. But would she ever recover from his death? Kat would go to his funeral, and she'd meet his mother there. Somehow he knew the two of them would bond. That was the kind of woman Kat was.

He closed his eyes again, reliving the kiss at the base, when she'd come to him with abandon. When she'd freed herself from whatever hold she'd put on her heart. Here in a literal hellhole, he wanted to feel what it was like to lose control with a woman he loved, to imagine what a mundane nine-to-five life would be like with her.

A loud noise above them had all three men on their feet in an instant. Alex's pulse kicked into high gear and he knew without a doubt that the time had come. The make-or-break moment when they'd know their fate for sure.

A gunshot rang out, shattering the door in the ceiling.

CHAPTER FIFTEEN

KAT DIDN'T KNOW how she'd gotten through the week. She walked through campaign headquarters and sat at her desk numbly. Staffers were buzzing with their usual energy, but the air felt different. The senator had resumed his campaign schedule, and the media had moved on from both Kat and Alex. The story of his disappearance had lasted only one news cycle. Kat was writing policy memos and talking points on the IED bill to lend a hand. She seemed to be the only one who didn't care about the campaign anymore. Everyone else was going about their business, marching forward with life; she was the only one standing still.

They had a daily briefing with the base in Iraq, but the calls had gotten shorter and shorter, with yesterday's not even lasting five minutes. There were only so many ways to say "There's no news. He's likely dead and there's not much more we can do."

It seemed the only two people who were holding on to hope were Kat and Mrs. Santiago.

"Kat."

The tone in Crista's voice made Kat pause before she turned in her chair. Her hand flew to her face, tears welling in her eyes. *It can't be!*

Crista lowered her gaze. "I'm moving into Alex's office."

Kat's head snapped up. "How could…?" She barely got the words out.

"Someone has to sign checks and make decisions. If he comes back…"

"If?" Kat put a hand to her stomach, trying to calm the storm raging in her body. There was no point in taking it out on Crista; she hadn't created the circumstance they were in. They had no idea how long it might take for him to be found, and it wasn't Crista's fault they had no leads. "I guess I work for you now," she said testily and turned to face her computer. She heard Crista leave and blinked against the sting of tears in her eyes.

Kat stabbed at the keyboard, trying to focus on the inane document she was working on. Crista put a hand on her shoulder and Kat turned to see her green eyes shining.

"I haven't given up on him, Kat—I'm just trying to make sure he doesn't come back to a big mess."

Kat blinked. "He'll be back," she said, unsure whether she was trying to convince Crista or herself.

"Are you looking forward to dinner at the senator's?"

Kat closed her eyes. She'd almost forgotten about it. Senator Roberts had invited her and Emilia to dinner at his house to meet his other children. She'd been so focused on Alex that she hadn't figured out what was going on with her mother and father. Whenever the senator stopped by campaign headquarters, their conversations were perfunctory, and talks with her mother were no better. Even yesterday, when her mom informed her that the date for dinner at the senator's had been set for tomorrow, Kat hadn't had the energy to get into it. Of course Crista knew about the dinner.

Kat shrugged. "I just hope my mother doesn't get hurt in all this."

"She still loves him, doesn't she?"

Kat nodded. It was a fact made painfully obvious by the glow in her mother's face every time she talked about him.

"For what it's worth, I think he cares about her. I haven't seen him this happy, ever. And he's down in the polls—usually that makes him unbearable."

She knew Crista was trying to make her feel

better, but somehow the knot in Kat's stomach just grew bigger.

She finished her work with record speed and tore out of headquarters. When she saw the senator tomorrow, she would tell him she was quitting. She didn't care if she didn't have enough to write her book. The book, her faculty job, nothing meant anything anymore. Academic discourse wouldn't change the lives of people like Reza or save those babies on Guam.

She'd parked on the street, and as she reached her car she stopped, her hand frozen on the handle. The back of her neck prickled. Her heart exploded in her chest, the release so intense she wasn't sure her legs would carry her any more. Then his arms were around her, supporting her, just like she knew they would be.

"I knew you were alive," she whispered as he held her, her back to his chest. He pulled her closer, propping her up as every muscle in her body released the tension of the past ten days.

"I came back for you, Kat."

Something pulsed inside her and she spun, lifting her face to meet his waiting lips. He moved his hands to her face and kissed her with a sweetness that melted her core. She let his lips warm hers, savored the feel of his scratchy face as he kissed the salty tears from her cheeks. She leaned against him, needing to feel the beat of his heart, the strength of his touch. In that moment she understood that she'd never loved anyone this way, had never seen into another soul or been connected with a force so strong that breaking it would shatter her very being.

When she finally pulled back to look at him, she felt a stabbing pain in her chest. It wasn't the stubble that had scratched her skin or the wild hair that caught her eye. It was the bandage on his forehead and the scabbed cut above his cheekbone.

She ran her fingers over it. "Alex…"

"Shh, it's okay. I'm fine. I'm alive."

He bent and picked up her keys; she hadn't even realized she'd dropped them. He opened the car door and helped her get in.

"Will you wait while I go tell everyone I'm all right? Then I want to take you out to dinner." He grinned, and a fresh volume of tears filled her eyes. She must have nodded because the next thing she knew, he was kissing her on the forehead and then walking into headquarters.

She rested her head against the seat and took

some deep breaths before calling her mother to tell her she wasn't going to be home until very late tonight. There wasn't a late-night nurse scheduled, but she didn't care. Alex was safe and they were having dinner together. Her mother had been doing well and perhaps it wouldn't be the end of the world if Kat took a night off.

It seemed like forever before Alex returned and climbed into her passenger seat. Her phone buzzed and she turned it off.

Alex grinned at her. "It could be important."

She shook her head. "For one night, the world can take care of itself. I need you."

He DIRECTED KAT to a 24/7 diner where he knew the owner wouldn't mind them sitting in a booth all night talking. Kat ordered them both burgers and fries even though he wasn't hungry.

"You look like you've lost weight," she commented, touching the heart-shaped pendant on her neck. She wore it all the time even though it was often tucked underneath her shirt. He'd found himself wondering what she cared about enough to keep so close to her heart.

"Who gave you that necklace?"

She looked up, obviously surprised he'd

asked. He pinned her with his eyes, letting her know he wanted the full story, not whatever standard answer she had on her lips.

"I went through a rough patch in high school. Mom was off her meds and really difficult, and, well, you know... I had the usual teenager problems. I came to the point where I couldn't handle it anymore. I took a bottle of my mom's sleeping pills."

His heart lit up, filled with the need to go back in time and comfort that struggling girl. He moved from his seat in the booth and slid in next to her, pulling her close, savoring the rise and fall of her breathing body next to him. She buried her head in the dip between his shoulder and arm.

"Lucky for me, I immediately puked them all out," she continued. "My mom had the presence of mind to call 911. They kept me at the hospital for a few days and there was this nurse who took care of me. She had moved to our city from California after her twelve-year-old daughter and her husband were killed in a car crash. The only reason she wasn't driving with them was because she'd been visiting her injured sister. She gave me this necklace. It had belonged to her daughter, and she said it gave her the strength to survive after seeing the dead bodies of the two people she loved most."

She lifted her head and touched the necklace. "She saved my life, in more ways than one."

"I'm glad she found you."

"She said it was time for her to give up this necklace, her safety blanket. She had recently found love and didn't need its comfort anymore."

His heart contracted at her words. "Why do you still need it, Kat?"

"Because I don't know how to love."

He kissed the top of her head. "Yes, you do. You've opened my heart."

She looked at him with shining eyes. "What happened to you in Iraq, Alex?"

"Don't worry—it was nothing bad. At least, nothing worse than I've already seen. We got another flat tire on the way back and our cars got ambushed. This flat was deliberate. We fought our way out and escaped."

She gasped and he could feel her tense. He rubbed her arm.

"One of the guys knew an informant and we hid at his house. We didn't have our phones and couldn't risk coming into the open to find communications. We were literally holed up in a dug-out basement."

He felt a heavy breath leave her body, and she collapsed against him. "It wasn't too bad, aside from getting up close and personal with two very smelly dudes. First thing I did when we got to the base was take a shower."

"How were you found? Why didn't anyone call us?"

"Turns out your hotshot lieutenant also knew the informant, and during one of the routine patrols, he slipped word to him. They pulled us out and shipped us home. They didn't want to tell anyone stateside until we were wheels down. Apparently the ambush was payback against the security company for killing one of the local warlords. There was a lot of heat on one of the guys I was with. The army didn't want a leak."

"You could have called when you were in the air."

"And miss seeing your face when I returned?"

"You had me worried sick." She punched him playfully in the arm.

He caught her hand and held it, letting himself drown in the ocean blue of her eyes. Without the distraction of the BlackBerry buzzing in his hand, voices demanding results in his ear and the chaos of the campaign and senate staff, he'd had a lot of time to do something he'd avoided for years. Let his guard down. Trust. The informant who he'd been sure would sell them out hadn't. Not to say he hadn't taken advantage of the situation; he'd managed to squeeze money out of the army in addition to the money the security company had already promised. But he'd sold them to the good guys. Something Alex hadn't believed would ever happen.

"I didn't think love was in the cards for me," he whispered, barely hearing the words that were coming from someplace deep inside him. A part he hadn't known existed. He'd started out as an angry young man and developed into a cold, calculating one. Aside from his mother, he didn't love anyone. He'd tried hard to get close to Crista, to find a place in his heart for her, but he'd failed. For a minute he'd thought it would be easier with a practical woman like Mellie who was okay with the fact that he didn't believe in love. And maybe, if he hadn't met Kat, it would've been.

She nestled deeper into the crook of his arm. "Neither did I."

"So how do we do this?" He hadn't thought about what they'd do after he got home. Through the rescue and the long flight back, all he'd thought about was seeing her again.

She lifted her head and gave him a slow

smile. "I already made the first move." She rested her forehead against his. And there it was, the fire in his belly that coursed through him like molten-hot lava. He put his hand on the back of her head.

"I don't know whether I'm capable of this, Kat," he murmured. "That's why I've kept away from you. I don't want to hurt you."

"I can take care of myself, Alex."

But he didn't want her to take care of herself anymore. He wanted to be the man to protect her, to make sure no one hurt her. He hoped to God he was capable of being that kind of man.

They talked well into the night, about nothing and everything. "Did you keep in touch with the nurse who gave you the necklace?"

She shook her head. "We were close initially. About a year after the incident, Jill invited me to be a junior bridesmaid at her wedding. If I took the bus, it was going to be three hours from where we lived. The morning I was scheduled to leave, Mom had a bad night and I didn't want to leave her. Jill said she understood, but our emails and phone calls became fewer and further apart and we just lost touch. It's how it always is."

He wanted to take her in his arms and promise her that was not what it would be like with him, but an unseen force held him back, pushed him away from the shining blue eyes that still held the pain of the memory. The diner owner saved him from making promises he couldn't keep by slapping down two plates of complimentary breakfast on the table. They looked at each other and laughed.

Kat checked her watch and groaned. "I need to get home." Her eyes were wide and full of the kind of sparkle he'd dreamed about in that hole in Iraq. "We're going to the senator's house for dinner tonight. I want you to come."

He tensed. He hadn't figured out what he would say to the senator. He wasn't prepared to deal with the consequences of being with Kat.

"I want to tell him," Kat said softly, as if she'd read his mind. "I want to go all the way in. The campaign staff already know how I feel about you—I'd be shocked if the senator hasn't heard."

He took a breath. It was a big risk. The senator was very protective of his family; what if he saw this as a betrayal? *You don't mess with the candidate's family.*

"What're you afraid of?"

That I'm not good enough for you.

"I need you to do this with me, Alex. Go all in."

"Okay."

Her smile made it all worthwhile. It was time to face the music.

CHAPTER SIXTEEN

KAT REGRETTED AGREEING to meet Alex at the senator's house. She'd spent the two-hour drive telling her mother about her new relationship; something that she could hardly define, let alone describe. Her mother had been surprisingly accepting, more focused on the upcoming dinner at the senator's house than on what Kat was saying. Emilia continued to be cagey about her own relationship with the senator, insisting there was nothing to say. But it was hard to ignore how much her mother seemed to have changed.

Kat had picked out a dress for Emilia at the mall, but her mother had pulled out a gown from her old wardrobe. Every time they had moved from one house to another, Kat wondered what was in the brown-and-black suitcase her mother never opened. Today, she'd come home from her dinner-slash-breakfast with Alex to find her mother trying on various dresses. She'd picked a royal blue one, made of elegant silk with silver beading on the waist. It had been meticulously kept in a plastic bag in the suitcase.

Her mother had even gotten ready herself, adding silver ball earrings and makeup. She looked beautiful, like the woman Kat had seen only in pictures.

Reluctantly, Kat had put on one of the outfits the campaign had bought, a shimmery deep maroon dress that she'd fought with Elle not to buy. But having come home so tired that she'd fallen right on her bed to catch a nap, she hadn't had time to figure out what else she could make work from her meager closet.

As they rolled up to the massive, wrought-iron gates, Kat's mouth dropped open. The senator's *house* was in McLean, Virginia, in the older part of town on Chain Bridge Road. This was his Washington, DC, home, just a few miles outside the city. Most long-term congressional representatives kept a residence close to the capital, where they spent most of the year, and a family home near their constituent base. The senator had a second house near the state capital of Richmond, close to headquarters, but given the amount of time he'd been in DC, this was where he spent most of his time. It could conservatively be called a mansion. *I am way out of my league.*

She turned to look at her mother and saw her eyes misting over. "Mom, did you ever live here?"

Her mother shook her head. "We had a smaller house a mile down the road, but we were here so much, it might as well have been home. This was his father's place. His mother hosted a lot of campaign fund-raisers here."

Kat swallowed. She never would have pictured the woman who bought their clothes at Goodwill to live in this type of house. She drove through the gates to the circular driveway. She half expected a valet to come out and take her keys, but not seeing any, she parked in a small lot adjacent to the six-car garage. Her economy-sized, budget car looked like an ugly coffee stain on the front of a beautiful white wedding dress.

Alex's car wasn't there, and Kat fought the panic rising in her chest. She couldn't do this without him. It took her a few moments to realize neither she nor her mother had made a move to exit the car. "We don't have to do this, Mom. We don't owe him anything."

Emilia sat frozen and Kat felt her pulse quicken. She'd thought her mother had been doing well. What if it had all been a mild manic episode? Kat was used to full-blown events where it was obvious her mother was off the rails, but there had been times when she was a child that her mother had been functional. Times when she'd gotten herself dressed and shown up to parent-teacher conferences and actually signed report cards so Kat didn't have to fake her signature.

Kat clicked her seat belt back in place and turned the key in the ignition. She needed to get her mother out of here. It was one thing for her to deal with her mother coming off a manic episode, but she didn't want Senator Roberts and his perfect family to witness it.

She put her hand on the clutch to move the car into Reverse, but her mother touched her shoulder to stop her. "I'm ready. I want to do this."

Kat searched her mother's eyes but saw none of the wildness, none of the deep despair.

They walked up to the stone-front house and stepped up to the covered portico. Kat looked for an additional bell on the double door. She'd already rung one bell when she pulled up to the gate. There was a giant knocker on the door that seemed heavier than what Kat could possibly lift. The door opened.

It was the senator himself, polished and stately in a light blue shirt worn open-collar, without a tie. "Emilia, Kat, it's so good to see you." He widened his arms to welcome them. Kat stepped through the door first to give her mother a moment to get used to the sight of him. He was an imposing man and stood in a marble foyer in front of a grand double staircase. He kissed Kat on the cheek. "I'm so pleased you accepted my invitation."

She nodded. "I hope you got my message about Alex… I…"

"Ah, yes, sorry—I didn't get a chance to call you back, but I spoke to Alex and told him he was more than welcome. He's running a little late."

She turned to see her mother still lingering at the threshold. The senator held out his hand and she took it, stepping into the house. "Emilia, you look lovely as ever. Is that the blue dress you wore—"

Her mother nodded at the senator, finishing his sentence. "At our engagement party."

"I love that dress on you."

Her mother smiled and Kat had to stop her own mouth from falling open. It was the most brilliant smile she'd ever seen.

All those dresses her mother had kept locked away in the suitcase. They were all from when she'd been with her father. Kat's throat tightened as she watched the senator take her mother's elbow and usher her gently down the hallway. They looked like the perfect couple. She clasped her hands together, hoping she hadn't set her mother up for the second heartbreak of her life.

As they walked through the house, Kat tried to keep her eyes focused on the senator and her mother ahead of her and not let her jaw hit the floor. The entire town house they were renting could have fit into the living room they entered.

Her half brother and sister were already there. Vickie greeted her first. She was a tall, elegant woman with bright green eyes and strawberry blond hair that was wrapped in a chignon at the nape of her neck. She was wearing casual linen slacks and a green blouse that made Kat feel like she was trying too hard in her ridiculously expensive designer dress.

She turned to meet Walter, who was dressed in a polo shirt and slacks, his light brown hair and blue eyes mirroring the look of a younger Senator Roberts. He went to the bar in the corner of the room and brought them glasses of white wine.

Kat fought the urge to check her watch. *Where is Alex? Why didn't he call* me *to say he would be late?* she thought irritably.

They sat on an ivory-and-pale-gray tufted sofa with high arms. Kat perched on the edge, unable to get comfortable and careful not to tip the crystal glass that held her wine. Somehow, the senator and Vickie filled the room with conversation. Emilia, seated beside Kat, appeared perfectly comfortable. Silence was never good, but her mother seemed to be enjoying the banter, nodding and smiling at the appropriate times.

Kat nearly jumped for joy when the doorbell rang. The senator returned a couple of minutes later with Alex. Kat was on her feet, but not before Vickie and Walt, who rushed to hug him. It was the first time they'd seen him since his disappearance. Kat stood back and watched the ease with which Alex interacted with the senator's family. He accepted Vickie's hug and peck on the cheek with familiarity and bumped fists with Walt, accepting the good-natured ribbing that came his way. He walked over and gave Kat a kiss on the cheek and did the same to her mother. The senator excused himself to go check on dinner. Alex easily filled the role of host, refreshing everyone's drinks from the bar and chatting lightly with Vickie as if he'd been doing it for ages. Her stomach churned. *He wants a first lady.*

When the senator announced dinner and invited everyone to the kitchen, Alex placed his arm around Kat's waist as they filed out of the living room. "How are you doing?" he whispered.

The warmth of his breath in her ear sent her nerves tingling all the way to her toes. She could do this. With Alex at her side, she could face the life she would have had.

"Kat, I hope you like pot roast." Senator Roberts was wearing a cheesy Kiss the Cook apron. They were in an enormous room that served as a kitchen and family room. The new term was *great room*. A giant granite countertop island had been set with plates.

It was all too much. The sight of domestic normalcy in a house that looked like Buckingham Palace.

"It's your famous pot roast, isn't it?" Emilia exclaimed. She was grinning from ear to ear. *Where has this woman been all my life?* Kat thought.

The senator nodded and everyone turned to stare at him and her mother. Their eyes were locked on each other as they obviously shared a moment.

"Right after we were married, I hosted our first dinner party," Emilia began.

"She forgot to tell me that she didn't know how to cook," the senator continued.

"I thought it would be simple enough to follow a recipe for coq au vin." Was her mother giggling?

"An hour before dinner, I come home to see if Emilia needs a hand and all I see is smoke billowing out of the oven. Emilia is nowhere in sight."

"I was upstairs getting dressed." Her mother was definitely giggling.

"She was so distraught when she found out."

"His mother and father were among the guests, and I so wanted to show them I could host a party. So Bill gets right to work and whips up this delicious pot roast. It was a total hit and it became one of my favorite dishes." Kat watched her mother's face transform as she relived the memory. The twinkle in her eyes told the story far better than words.

The senator set a serving tray on the kitchen island and Vickie pulled out a bowl of spinach salad from the fridge. Everyone took a seat at one of the bar stools.

"The pot roast is one of our favorites, too." Vickie's lighthearted comment deflated Emilia. Kat's heart clenched painfully as her mother averted her eyes, focusing on getting onto the bar stool.

Conversation at dinner centered around Alex's disappearance and the senator's IED bill. The senator, Vickie and Alex carried the conversation. Walt chimed in from time to time, but he seemed to be the silent observer. Kat wanted to find fault with her father's family, to see them as taciturn children whose daddy had been too focused on his career to pay attention to their well-being, or else spoiled brats who'd been handed everything on a silver platter, but they seemed to be genuinely kindhearted, well-adjusted and accomplished people. Their love for each other and the senator was obvious. Kat couldn't get rid of the lump in her throat.

Alex squeezed her hand every few minutes, even if he was in the middle of a sentence or in the throes of an animated story, but Kat felt cold. Alex was a part of this family; these were his people, not hers. She hadn't had much to eat, yet dinner churned in her stomach.

They'd scheduled an early evening since Kat and Emilia had to drive home. She hadn't accepted the senator's invitation to stay overnight—baby steps—and she was happy to use the excuse of the long drive to say goodbye. Vickie and the senator hugged her, and Walt gave her an awkward kiss on the cheek.

When they were at the door, the senator turned to her. "Why don't you bring the car around, Kat. I want to chat with your mother a few minutes."

Kat glanced at Emilia, who nodded. Alex walked her to the car.

"You okay?"

It seemed that was all he'd asked her all night. This time, she shook her head. "What am I supposed to do with that?" She gestured to the front porch, where her mother was laughing at something the senator had said. "What's the point of all this? To show me what a happy little family he created once he left my mother? And why is she—"

"Taking it so well?" he finished for her.

She nodded. "I sound like a horrible person, don't I? I should be happy it went so well, that she seems happy, but…"

"You're waiting for the other shoe to drop."

She nodded, and he pulled her into his arms. She focused on the comfort of his hard muscles beneath her fingertips, the steady beat of his heart. The world seemed to melt away when he held her like this, and she wanted to stay here for the rest of her life. In this moment, he felt like her Alex, not the man her father was grooming.

"It's okay to be angry," he told her. "To feel a sense of loss. Don't be mad at the senator—he would've given you this life if he knew. He wants you to be a part of all this now. That's why he wanted you here tonight."

She pushed against him, breaking their embrace. "Is that what you think this is about? That I'm jealous of the wealth those kids enjoyed?"

Unlocking the car, she slid into the driver's seat and slammed the door behind her.

ALEX WATCHED KAT collect her mother and drive away, debating his next move. What exactly had he said that set her off, and how was he supposed to fix it? He returned to the house. Senator Roberts had asked him to stay so they could have a chat. It wasn't an unusual request; Alex often spent time with the senator, and he even had an assigned guest room in the twelve-bedroom house. But he knew this time was different. The senator had been short with him on the phone when he'd told Alex that he was welcome to come to dinner as Kat's guest. Then he had tasked Alex with an assignment that he knew would make him late.

After that awkward conversation, Alex's next phone call had been to Crista, who had tearfully admitted that she'd been spying on him at the senator's request. Alex shouldn't have been surprised. How many times had he spied on his staff? It was the way the game was played in campaigns; loyalties were constantly shifting. It was the nature of all temporary work. Any staffers who weren't already looking for other positions would be soon. Regardless of what happened in November, most of them would be out of a job.

He met the senator on the deck off the great room. The senator offered him a brandy, which he declined in favor of coffee. Depending on how the conversation went, he might have to drive a couple of hours tonight and he was already exhausted.

"When I was a kid, there was nothing but woods and the Potomac River back here. Now all that's left is a few trees. They pack houses onto every square inch of available land."

The senator started every difficult conversation with meaningless small talk. He knew from experience the lead-up could go on for the better part of an hour. It wasn't as if Alex was expecting the senator's blessing to date his newfound daughter. He cleared his throat.

"Sir, I didn't mean to spring my relationship with Kat on you. The truth is, it sneaked up on both of us."

The senator turned and sat in a rocking chair. Alex followed suit.

"I was surprised. Heard you went on a date with Mellie."

"I've been trying to avoid getting involved with Kat, sir, for the obvious reasons. But after my time in Iraq, I figured life's too short not to explore our feelings for each other."

"And what would those obvious reasons be?"

"Excuse me?"

"You said you didn't want to get involved with Kat for the obvious reasons. What are those?"

"Well, for one, she's your daughter, sir, and you may not approve of her dating someone who works for you." Alex knew his place; it had been ingrained in him since childhood. *You're the son of the cleaning lady.*

The senator laughed. "To be honest with you, Alex, I was rather hoping you and Vickie would get together."

Alex sat up straighter. *What?* He'd always assumed the senator wouldn't want him getting involved with his family. He'd never considered Vickie. "Sir, Vickie is much younger than me."

"Hardly—only seven years. A decade ago, when you were in your twenties and she was a teenager, I'd have taken issue, but you're both adults now."

"Sir, I've always seen Vickie as a kid, a sister of sorts. I've never felt for her romantically." *Why am I discussing the merits of dating a daughter I'm not interested in?*

"I think Kat's a fine young woman." The senator picked up his snifter and swirled it around. Alex knew what he was going to say and prepared his response.

"…but she's not the type of woman who can support your plans."

"I think we've underestimated her. She's bright and articulate. She did well with ad-libbing the troop speech in Iraq. We can work with her on media presence and tempering her statements…"

Even as he said the words, he realized he was talking about changing Kat fundamentally. What drew him to her was her fire, her insistence on sticking to her guns.

"She's a lot like her mother, and Emilia was—still is—the greatest love of my life." Alex stared at the senator. It was obvious he cared about Kat's mother; he could see it in the way he'd looked at her tonight, but he'd had no idea that the senator's feelings ran that deep. "Learn from my experience, son—I tried really hard with Emilia, and I was ready to give up my dreams for her. But it never would've worked."

Alex leaned forward. "Why not? Surely there was a way to compromise?"

Senator Roberts shook his head. "This is who I am. I could've done other things, but I wouldn't have been happy. Emilia tried, she really did, but she couldn't change who she was, either. And I probably wouldn't have loved her if she became a different woman." He looked at Alex with shining blue eyes. The same intense blue eyes that Kat had. "I was foolish and in love when I married, convinced that we'd find a way to make it work. But reality, it has a way of coming crashing down on you, to remind you that nothing ever works out that perfectly. You have to decide what you want to give up."

And you weren't willing to give up your political aspirations for love. The words were on his lips, but he didn't dare say them out loud. Who was he to judge the senator? He hadn't had that conversation with himself. But he also didn't believe there wasn't a way. He spent his life negotiating compromises; there was always a middle ground, a way to give from each side.

"She looked beautiful tonight. All the stuff in the reports about her bipolar disorder, I didn't see any of it. She seemed like the woman I married, the one who broke my heart."

The senator was a million miles away. Alex had shared the reports on Kat and Emilia with the senator when the story first broke. They hadn't discussed it except for the senator's insistence on getting to know Kat. He'd told Alex he had already set up a trust fund for her, similar to what he had for his other children.

"If you could go back in time, would you do things differently, sir?" Alex couldn't help asking the question he was sure the senator didn't have an answer for.

Bill Roberts shook his head and took a sip of the dark amber liquid in his glass, scrunching his nose as he swallowed. "I thought she'd come back. I figured if I kept her at arm's length, she'd realize she couldn't live without me and come back, ready to compromise, to do things my way. I was an arrogant young man. By the time I realized she was gone for good, I was so angry, all I wanted to do was show her I could move on."

"So you married Carol."

He nodded. "I'd known her all my life. We were family friends and she stepped right in when Emilia left. It was the easy thing to do. Don't get me wrong—I loved Carol. I took care of her..."

"I don't doubt that, sir," Alex said quickly. The senator's marriage with Carol was legendary, and for once in political history, it wasn't spin. He'd never cheated; he genuinely spent time with his family and actively parented his children. In fact, he'd been asked to be on the vice presidential ticket when Vickie and Walt were in high school, and he declined. He'd wanted to be present to mentor his kids through college.

Alex hadn't believed it when he'd first read the articles; that was how all politicians' biographies read. "Family reasons" were always a subterfuge to avoid scandal and hide betrayal. But once he met Vickie and Walt, he saw that the senator was the real deal. It was a big part of what Alex loved about the man. His question about whether the senator regretted giving up on his marriage to Emilia had been genuine; he'd seen the senator pass up opportunities for his family's sake. He declined meetings with heavyweight donors because he had dinner plans with his children. He never missed graduations and college events no matter how difficult they were to fit into his schedule. And he regularly put on an apron and cooked for his family. How had he given up on love?

"Love is not enough, son. Don't get me wrong—you need to respect and care for your partner, but a life in politics is stressful. You need to have support from your better half. Emilia was so volatile—I didn't think back then that it was more than just a fiery personality. I didn't want to spend my life arguing about policies, controlling chaos and strife in the house. People often called me and Carol an old, boring married couple. I preferred to think of us as stable."

Alex's chest burned, and he wanted nothing more than to tell the senator he was wrong, that he'd miscalculated what life with Emilia would've been like, but he couldn't. Aside from dinner and breakfast this morning, he'd never had a conversation with Kat that didn't result in an argument. What would he do when she riled him up? When her strong temper lit up his explosive side?

"You're going to be president one day, you know." The senator's voice was soft, mellowed by the cool night air and the brandy he'd been sipping.

Alex laughed. "How about we focus on getting *you* elected first."

But the senator wasn't listening. "I hear there might be some openings soon. One more high-profile position, then you run for governor of Virginia in four years—you'll need it to win the presidential. It's going to be a purple state for years to come."

In any election, the states were identified as red or blue depending on whether they tended to vote Republican or Democratic. Purple states were battleground or swing states. Virginia had been firmly red, but in recent years, with the increasingly liberal influence of Northern Virginia, which bordered Washington, DC, and Maryland, the state was beginning to polarize. The last few elections had all been within five polling points.

Alex and the senator had the conversation about his career once a year, usually with Alex drinking coffee and the senator sipping brandy, but the tone was different this time. The senator wasn't just sounding off. He was laying out timelines and details with a level of specificity they hadn't discussed before. All of a sudden, the hypothetical was becoming real.

But the more the senator talked, the more the knot in Alex's stomach twisted, sending a burning sensation up through his belly and into his chest. *This is what I want, isn't it?* He should be grateful, and he was. Every man he'd ever worked for had tried to hold him back, keep him in a position where Alex wouldn't overshadow him. They were never going to let Alex become one of the elite. The senator had treated him like a son, taken him under his wing and shaped his success. He was the only person who accepted what Alex aspired to be. *Why can't I just be happy? Because he doesn't fully trust me. If he did, he wouldn't have had Crista keep an eye on me for him.*

The senator's next words pulled him out of his internal musings like the ringing of a fire alarm.

"Vickie's career can be fast-tracked if she's the governor's wife first."

Suddenly, things clicked into place for him. "You've been grooming me to set the path for Vickie."

The senator winced at Alex's tone. "I've invested in your future."

"Is that what you were doing when you asked Crista to spy on me?"

"I asked her to watch out for you, make sure you didn't make foolish moves. You had too much of an emotional stake in the IED bill," he replied with the smoothness of a practiced politician.

Alex took a breath to calm himself. There was no point in arguing with the senator. He was playing the game.

"How long have you had this plan?"

"Don't get testy with me, Alex. I hired you because you were qualified. I promoted you because you were good. Vickie's always liked you—don't tell me you haven't noticed her being sweet on you. You two would be very good for each other."

"You'd want me to marry your daughter, knowing I don't love her."

The senator stood, swirling the dredges of amber liquid in his snifter. "Until you told me about Kat, I thought you got along well with Vickie. She has feelings for you."

And until he'd met Kat, he would've welcomed this conversation with the senator. "Sir, I love Kat. Like the love you had for Emilia."

"But if you married Vickie, it would be like my marriage to Carol. It's your decision, son. Know this, though—if you want to be with

Kat, you have to be willing to give up on becoming president. I'll give you my blessing either way. Love only comes once in a lifetime, but a presidency sets you up for generations."

An uneasy feeling settled into his stomach. He wanted to take the senator at his word, but years of experience had taught him to read between the lines.

He'd never considered Vickie for a life partner, in large part because he assumed she was off-limits, but she was exactly the type of woman he had always wanted. *This is the kind of deal I've been waiting for my whole life. He's giving me an inside ticket.*

CHAPTER SEVENTEEN

SOMETHING WAS GOING on with Alex. He'd been avoiding her for a week. His claim that he had a lot of work to do in DC seemed legitimate, but Kat couldn't shake the feeling that he was pulling away from her. He'd made a surprise announcement the morning after the dinner with her father that he was delegating his campaign responsibilities to Crista so he could focus on the IED bill, which was coming up for vote soon. The vote was scheduled for tomorrow. Something was up, and it bothered Kat that she didn't know what.

Her mother was being similarly aloof. Emilia had been positively giddy after the dinner with the senator, but she still refused to open up about what they were privately discussing, first at the house and then on their nightly phone calls.

"What are you working on?"

Kat jumped at Crista's voice behind her. "Just an analysis of what the passage of the IED bill might mean for future spending."

Crista rolled her eyes. "Is this for your book?"

Kat nodded. She'd written two versions of a critical chapter on the IED legislation. One continuing to argue how wasteful the spending would be, and the other analyzing it from Alex's perspective. Reading each chapter multiple times, she'd finally gone with what felt right to her.

She was grateful that it had been slow at the campaign office the past few days. Congress was almost ready to go to recess, so all the action was in Washington, DC, where they were trying to get a budget passed in addition to the IED bill vote. The senator was down ten points in the polls, a significant hit. Crista was hoping that the passage of the IED bill would get them back on track. Until then, there was nothing to do.

"So, are you and Nathan ever going to take that hike?" Crista and Kat had gotten closer since Alex's return. They'd even gone out to lunch this week.

Crista sighed dramatically. "He hasn't brought it up, and the one time I did, he changed the subject. I think he's intimidated by my new role."

"But not much has changed—you were running the place before, too."

Crista stared at Kat. "Do you not get how big a deal it was for Alex to delegate primary responsibility to me?"

Guess not.

"I was his right-hand woman before, but he was the boss, making the strategic decisions, having the difficult conversations. Now I do that, and it's not an easy role. It often creates tension with the staff. Like yesterday, when I asked Nathan to redo his research on the policy statement the opponent put out on military spending because I didn't think he did a good job."

Kat swallowed. She hadn't really absorbed the news that Crista was now her boss. But more important, was it a demotion for Alex? Had the senator punished him for being with her?

"And in four months, the campaign will be over and we're all going back to our previously scheduled lives," Crista continued.

Kat sat up. She knew her time here was limited, but she hadn't thought about what it meant for everyone else. "So where are you two going?"

"I have a couple of offers in DC, but I haven't decided what I'll take. Nathan is going to get his PhD. He's already been accepted to Berkeley. In fact, he'll be leaving the campaign in a few weeks."

"But…"

Crista stood. "He has different goals than I do. He wants to work for a think tank or possibly even do TV reporting." She widened her arms and gestured to everyone around her. "I love this, the energy, the life-changing work. Our paths are diverging, that's all."

Something twisted inside Kat's chest and she sat up straighter. "Listen, that's not true. There are a ton of schools and think tanks around DC. With his background, he could become a political correspondent."

"Campaign romances are always temporary," Crista said dismissively, walking away. Kat wondered whether she was looking for an excuse not to get involved with Nathan...and whether it was one of the reasons Alex had pushed away from her.

The day went by quickly. Though she had been with the campaign for only a little over a month, her book was due to the publishers in under four weeks. The dean had called to say they needed it as soon as possible to get it into circulation before the election. She still hadn't dropped that bomb on Alex, but knew she had to say something the next time she saw him. More important, she needed to tell him what she was writing so he wouldn't feel blindsided. Her BlackBerry buzzed and a shiver of excitement went through her as a text from Alex popped up.

Go to primail.com and set up a free email account. Send me the address.

She frowned. What was this about? Somehow she'd been expecting something a little more romantic from him. And why couldn't he just call or email her campaign account? Then she remembered the campaign emails were monitored. Probably by Crista. She sighed. Alex would probably say this was just how the game was played, but she didn't believe it. Surely there was another way to run a campaign, one where friends didn't feel the need to spy on each other.

Still, she wanted to hear from him, so she followed his directions and texted him the address she'd set up. The website said it was private, encrypted email. She went to the account and a message popped up from Alex. She looked over her shoulder then opened it.

From: Alex.Santiago@primail.com
To: Kat.Driscoll@primail.com
Subject: We need to talk

I'm in back-to-back meetings and can't call. Just found out the senator is going to your house tonight. You need to talk to your mother.

It's not my place to tell you what I know, but she's been keeping a secret from you.
—Alex

A bitter taste filled her mouth. She had bitten the inside of her cheek. Something was going on with her mother and Alex was keeping it from her? How could he? Knowing how much she worried about her mother, why would he torture her like this?

From: Kat.Driscoll@primail.com
To: Alex.Santiago@primail.com
Subject: This is not funny.

Do you really think it's okay to send me an email like that? Call me or do some fast typing. Tell me what's going on.
—Kat

She refreshed her screen several times, but it took a full ten minutes to get a short email that simply said I can't. I'm sorry. Go home and talk to your mother.

And just like that, she knew what was going on with her and Alex. He'd picked sides, and it wasn't hers. She grabbed her bag and let Crista know she was heading out. While driving, she tried Alex on his BlackBerry, his office phone, even the private phone she knew he kept in the car in case his cell ran out of battery. She gave up when she passed by a police cruiser. The last thing her dwindling savings account needed was a texting-and-driving ticket.

Parking in the driveway, she took a breath and went to her front door, ignoring Rex's barking. Did it smell like…*apple pie*? She walked into the kitchen to find her mother wearing one of her pretty dresses under an apron. Her hair was done; she even had lipstick on. She looked like she could be on the cover of *Good Housekeeping*.

"Kat, you're home early."

"Mom, what're you doing?"

"Your father is coming over for dinner. I made his favorite apple pie. I was thinking we could go have dinner at that nice Italian place then come back here for dessert."

Kat stepped into the kitchen. "Mother, why is he coming here?"

She shrugged, washing out a mixing bowl in the sink. "Oh, who knows. Probably just to say hello."

Kat took a breath to keep herself calm. "Mom, I've had enough. You need to tell me what you've been discussing with my father."

Emilia turned off the water and stood with

her arms on the kitchen sink. "Put on a pot of coffee."

They sat in the living room. Kat warmed her hands on her mug. Despite the warm day, she felt a chill in her bones.

"I've been keeping something from you, Katerina." Her mother's hands shook as she picked up her own mug and took a sip. "Remember three years ago when you took me to see the doctor?"

It could've been any number of trips. Kat didn't specifically remember, but she nodded. She had yet to drink any of her coffee; she was so nauseous, she was sure anything she sent to her stomach would come right back up.

"I asked to speak to the doctor privately."

Kat narrowed her eyes. She vaguely remembered that visit… It might have been the first time her mother had requested privacy, but Kat hadn't thought much about it since the doctors always talked to her about treatment plans anyway.

"I'd been having some symptoms, and I didn't want to worry you, so I talked to the doctor and she ran some tests."

Kat set the mug down. She didn't have the strength in her hands to hold it. "What kind of symptoms?"

"There's no easy way to say this, so I just have to tell you. I have Parkinson's."

This can't be true. Her mother must be mistaken. How could she have hidden this from Kat for three years?

"Mom, I'm sure that's not right. I would've seen the signs. Not once have I seen your hands tremble."

"I've been having trouble sleeping and writing."

Kat knew her mother had insomnia; she had assumed it was a side effect of the psychiatric medications. She'd even mentioned it to the doctor, who had subsequently changed her mother's dosages.

"Does Dr. Leventhal know about this?"

Emilia nodded. "I asked him not to tell you. She's bound by doctor-patient confidentiality."

Doctor-patient confidentiality? Since when was her mother in charge of her own health care? How could the doctors keep something like this from Kat? While she didn't have power of attorney over her mother, Kat had always been her primary caregiver and the doctors consulted her on everything.

Kat had a million questions. She grilled her mother about the details, of which there were few. She was in the early stages but would get worse as the years went on. That was why the doctor had authorized taking Emilia off the lithium and refused to put her back on even after Kat insisted. The doctor had recently put her on new medication. Medication that her mother took without Kat's knowledge, sometimes with the help of the nursing company. Nurses that Kat sacrificed her own needs to pay for, but who were asked to keep Kat in the dark.

"Why didn't you tell me?"

Her mother sighed. "You've spent your whole life taking care of me. I found out right when Colin left. You were already hurting—it was time for me to start being your mother."

Kat put a hand to her mouth to stifle a hysterical laugh that threatened to escape. What world was her mother living in? Hiding critical medical information from Kat so she couldn't properly manage her bipolar disorder was parenting?

"I know you're upset. I wasn't going to tell you, but I didn't want you to hear it from your father."

"*He* knows?" Now the tremble in Kat's hands was from the rage burning inside her.

"Kat, I need to make sure someone will take care of you if I die, and who better than your father?"

Kat couldn't take it anymore. "My father?" she sputtered. "When did you tell him?"

"About a year ago. We were trying to figure out a way to talk to you when the story broke."

"Is that why he's coming to dinner? So you can tell me about your illness before it's broadcast on the news? I'm a grown woman, Mom. I don't need a father—or a mother, for that matter. The time for needing a parent is long gone."

She picked up her purse and walked out. She didn't want to see the senator. Did Alex know about this? Was that why he sent her home to talk to her mother? So he'd hidden it from her, too. She got into her car and slammed the door shut. She wasn't going to cry. She'd used up all her tears the last time she was betrayed. The one constant in her life, the one person she knew would never betray her, was her mother.

A knock on the window made her head jerk. She hit the button to roll it down. "What're you doing here?"

"I came to make sure you're okay."

She opened the door and got out.

"Did you know, Alex?"

"Kat."

Of course he knew. That was what the email had been about. She wasn't going to cry. She knew how to deal with a man betraying her.

"Alex, I need an honest answer. How long have you known?"

"I just found out this morning, I swear. If I'd known earlier, I would've told you. The senator said he was coming over for dinner and that he and your mom planned to tell you. I sent you the email because I wanted you to be prepared."

"So why are you here? Why didn't you just call and tell me?"

"Crista said you tore out of headquarters. I got worried."

Kat pointed to the house behind her. "She lied to me, Alex. You lied to me."

He placed his hands on her shoulders. "Kat, I didn't know before today, I promise."

She placed a hand on his chest and her heart leaped into her throat as she felt the rise and fall of his breaths. Was he telling her the truth? Her mother had revealed that she'd called her father nearly a year ago. They had been talking since well before the news story broke.

"The senator told me this morning after he had me shuffle around some very important meetings so he could come down here. He's set up a trust fund for you—your mother asked him to make sure that you were taken care of, like the rest of his children."

She turned away from him. "Tell him I don't need his money."

"Believe it or not, I tried. He said you can access it, but only if you want to. If you don't, it'll become part of your estate when you die."

"I'm not some little girl. I can take care of myself."

"I think this has less to do with you and more to do with the senator needing to absolve himself of guilt for not being a part of your life. And I think he really loves your mother."

She buried her face in his chest. What was she supposed to do? Could she really trust Alex?

"Kat, talk to me." He rubbed her arm.

"Why have you been avoiding me?"

"Kat." His hand was still on her arm. She didn't need to see his eyes to feel the tension in his body.

"You haven't found a way to tell me this isn't going to work out."

"Kat, I love you."

"But…"

"It's not a simple answer."

She locked her gaze with his. She was tired of not having answers. "It's not that complicated. Be a man and tell me to my face."

He clenched his jaw. "Fine. I'm going to run for office one day, Kat. That's my life.

It'll mean having the media in your face all the time. It'll mean charity dinners where you can't talk about how you really feel. How could you be a political-science professor and not talk about your husband or say negative things about the Republican Party? Can you really give up everything for me? Give up your beliefs?"

She stared at him. He couldn't be serious.

"Why do you assume I'm the one who has to give something up?"

The look on his face told her he hadn't even thought about it. Her chest hurt. Why was she the one who was expected to go with the flow? To accept the decisions others made that affected her life. "I am a good professor, on my way to becoming an excellent one. I can influence the hearts and minds of the next generation. After my book comes out, I may even have opportunities at some big universities. Can you give up your dreams and support *mine*?"

She didn't know how long they stared at each other. "This is not the time to have this conversation," he finally said. He turned but she sidestepped and got in front of him. She placed a hand on his chest, this time with firmness.

"No, Alex, I want to have this conversation. Now."

"Kat, now is not the time," he said through gritted teeth.

SHE WASN'T GOING to let it go. He could see the cold stubbornness in her eyes. He took a breath to calm the inferno that was flowing through him. The senator was on his way here and had specifically asked Alex not to say anything to Kat. He had already jeopardized everything for Kat; the last thing he needed right now was an open confrontation with the senator.

"Tell me, what are you willing to give up for me? You're asking me to give up my life. What will you do for me?"

Deep breaths, Alex. You're in control of your anger. There was another reason they couldn't be together, one he had allowed himself to forget in the adrenaline rush of acknowledging his feelings for Kat. Without calculating the risk, considering the costs and benefits, and thinking of the long-term strategy, he had acted impulsively.

She stepped away from him, her eyes blazing. "Tell me, Alex, what is it that you even like about me? Or have you just been using me? Manipulating me to get ahead in your career. What is it that you're going to take away from me?"

How dare she? Was she equating him to the likes of her former scumbag fiancé? Something erupted inside him. He grabbed her arm. "Is that the kind of man you think I am?"

He didn't know how long it took him. Far too long to see that the ice in her eyes had melted. Replaced by something he never wanted to see. Fear. He let go of her arm and looked down to see her fair skin had reddened from his touch.

"I'm sorry, Kat." His voice cracked.

"Alex!" She reached out to touch him but his feet were moving faster than hers.

He was already in his car turning on the engine when she caught up to him. He put it in Reverse and screeched out of her street. He couldn't let his emotions rule him anymore.

CHAPTER EIGHTEEN

I GUESS THIS day can get worse. Kat stared at the senator and her mother. As if fate were conspiring against her, just as Alex left, the senator had arrived to find her standing frozen on the edge of the driveway. At a loss for what to do, she accepted his invitation to come to dinner. Now she sat across from her parents in a romantically lit Italian restaurant where a musician keyed a love song on the piano. Her brain was still processing the words her father had said.

"I'm sorry—I must have misheard. Can you repeat that?" she asked just to make sure her brain wasn't playing tricks on her.

"Kat, I know this must seem sudden to you, but I think your mother and I should marry again."

"*Sudden* is not the word I was thinking," she muttered as she took a sip of her wine. She looked at her mother, who must've known this was coming because she seemed remarkably composed, even excited. The senator had led

up to his explosive statement with a long preamble that Kat had largely missed as she went
over her conversation with Alex. What had she
done? She had been spoiling for a fight with
him, taking out the anger she couldn't unleash
on her mother. Not that he didn't deserve it,
the way he assumed *she* would have to make
sacrifices for them to be together.

The senator was looking right at her. "I
know this must seem…"

"Crazy? Impulsive? Nonsensical?"

"Kat!" The admonishment came from her
mother. Kat gave her an icy glare.

"Please, Mother, tell me what else you've
kept from me. I'm obviously missing some
pieces of the puzzle here."

"Kat, let me explain." The senator's sooth-
ing voice broke the staring contest between
her and her mother. He took a breath and put
his hand on Emilia's. She rewarded him with
an adoring look that made Kat's stomach bot-
tom out. "Your mother called me almost a year
ago. She was worried that if her Parkinson's
got worse, you'd work yourself to the bone to
take care of her. She wanted to make sure I
knew about you and that I'd be there to take
care of you."

Kat took another sip of her wine to keep
from making a biting comment. She needed

to hear the full sordid story, understand the full depth of her mother's betrayal.

"I was angry at first, but then I realized that I wanted to know you, to be a part of your life. We were talking about the best way to tell you all of this."

"And you figured CNN could do your dirty work?" The words were out of her mouth before she could bite her tongue. Her mother flinched and the senator pursed his lips but continued on.

"I had pictures of you, and a letter from Emilia when she first contacted me. I must've been careless with it. I didn't think about the documents until the story leaked."

She narrowed her eyes. It seemed too convenient.

"So why not come clean when the story broke? Why not tell me everything?" She directed the question at her mother, who had been lying to her for three years about the Parkinson's and for months about everything else. She shouldn't be surprised. This was the woman who'd managed to keep the identity of her father secret for thirty-five years.

Emilia dropped her gaze. "I didn't know how to tell you. It seemed easier to go along, to encourage you to get to know your father."

"So what's the grand plan here?"

She looked at both of them. A man she hardly knew and the woman she thought she knew.

"Kat, your mother and I share the kind of love most people never get in their lives. Reconnecting with her has brought me more joy than I've had in years. I don't want to waste another minute. I want to be with her."

"How does she fit into your election plans? And your run for president?" She gave her mother a look. "All of a sudden you're okay with dealing with the media? Hosting fundraisers? Being Martha Stewart?"

The senator leaned forward. "Things are different than they used to be. A candidate's wife doesn't have to do as much as she used to, not if she doesn't want to. Emilia can stay in the background."

Kat shook her head. Her mother couldn't possibly be falling for all this. *Nope, she is*. The adoring puppy-dog eyes her mother was giving him said it all.

"What's the rush?" she asked, changing tack.

"There's none. We're not talking about getting married tomorrow. But we wanted to tell you what we're planning. I asked your mother to move into the house with me."

Kat focused on the chicken marsala she'd ordered. None of them had touched their entrées.

She speared a piece and put it in her mouth, chewing slowly, trying to find the words that would magically make her mother understand reality. They ate in silence.

"So let's play this out here. You're going to move into the big McLean mansion. Who will take care of you? Make sure you take your pills?"

Her mother's eyes flashed to her, a clear warning.

"I'm capable of taking care of myself. I've been honest with Bill about my conditions."

"Really? You've told him all about how I have to cancel plans or put my life on hold to make sure you take your meds? Or how you pretend to take the pills and I come home to find ketchup all over my bed?"

Her mother set down her fork and knife with a clank. The senator set down his own utensils and reached over and squeezed her mother's hand. Emilia gave him a grateful smile and Kat's heart contracted painfully.

"All these years, Kat, I've been enabling you to use my illness to avoid getting close to anyone. I want you to live your life."

Kat shrank back, tears welling in her eyes. *I'm the one in the wrong here?*

"Mom, that's not fair. All I've ever done is protect you."

"Is that what you think you're doing now?" Her mother's eyes shone and the senator put an arm around her.

He looked at Kat. "Your mom has been honest with me about everything. There's nothing you can say that'll scare me away."

What did she need to say to get through to them? She turned to her father. "How will you continue to campaign? Will she sit at home while you traverse the state leading up to the election? If she's not going on the campaign trail with you, she'll be at home, all alone."

Her mother shifted in her chair. "How's that different from what I do now? You go to work all day and I sit alone in that house with nothing to do. These last few months, I've had purpose, a reason to live."

She couldn't deny that, against all odds, her mother was doing far better than she had in years.

"And I don't plan to leave your mother all alone in that big house. She doesn't have to get in front of the cameras, but she can travel with me when I'm gone for long periods."

Kat shook her head. They made it sound so easy. Her mother had kept secrets from her for years. Kat's entire life had been planned and organized around her mother. The career in academics where time away from home was minimal, superficial friendships, the constant worry. She'd done it all for her mom.

She lined up her fork and knife neatly on the plate, wiped her mouth with her napkin then set it on the plate and stood. "I wish you both the best of luck. Let me know when you're moving out."

CHAPTER NINETEEN

"ALEX, M'BOY, I NEED to talk to you." Alex looked up in surprise at the senator's jovial, booming voice.

He had barely spoken to Alex in the past few weeks. Alex had heard about the senator's plans to marry Emilia during a senior staff meeting. For two years, he'd been the senator's confidant and adviser. Senator Roberts didn't make a move without running it past him. Now Alex was nothing more than the hired help. He'd made a mistake in being honest with him. He had been firm in saying that he could never consider a future with Vickie, especially knowing how he felt about Kat. As a result, he was no longer the senator's inside man.

He stood as the senator walked up to his desk. He waved to the couch and the senator sat, unbuttoning his jacket as he did so. "Six points down in the polls and only three months to go," he said without preamble.

Alex nodded. They'd expected a bigger bump after the IED bill passed, but the bill had actually backfired; with the country's tolerance for troop deployment at an all-time low, voters were seeing Senator Roberts as way too war friendly. Yet another reason why the senator had cooled toward Alex. Crista had the senator making nonstop stump speeches; his kids were campaigning; there was a full schedule of media interviews.

"I wouldn't be doing anything differently," Alex said quietly.

"Oh, I know Crista's doing a bang-up job, but I was thinking, it might help if we had some other folks campaigning for me."

"We've already done appearances with the governor, major city and town mayors, and the congressional representatives."

The senator nodded. "What if we brought old Lacey out of retirement?"

Alex's stomach clenched, sending a fire into his chest. He dug his fingernails into his hand.

"Sir, Lacey hasn't been governor in twenty years."

"Yes, but he has been the most popular governor Virginia has ever had. He's the only modern governor to have successfully won two terms."

Virginia gubernatorial terms were limited to four years with no succession. A governor could run again after a four-year hiatus, but

Lacey was the only governor to have done so successfully in recent years. The man was so popular that he'd been encouraged to run for a third term, but had instead gone for a presidential nomination, which he lost.

"So have Crista schedule it with him."

"She's tried, but he won't do it."

And that was why the senator had come to Alex's office rather than summoning him to his own.

"You've got history with the governor. I understand your mom worked for him. Could you call him?"

Alex shook his head, using every last ounce of self-control to keep his voice even. "Sir, we didn't exactly part on good terms. I don't think it would help to get me involved."

The senator furrowed his brows. "Is this about me taking you off campaign duty?"

Alex sat up straighter. "No, sir. I..."

"Because I called the governor when I hired you. It was in your background report that you lived in his house as a child, and I wanted his impression of you. He had only good things to say about you and your mother."

His mouth soured. Of course the man had only good things to say about them. Alex was a well-behaved boy. He'd sat silently while his mother was taken advantage of and hadn't acted out of turn by pounding his fist into the man, no matter how many times he'd wanted to.

"Alex, I'm going to trust you to convince the governor to join me at the big speech I'm giving in Richmond next week."

He didn't need the senator to say the next part of the sentence. The *or else* was understood. The senator stood to leave. "Oh, and another thing—I asked Crista to plan a wedding for me and Emilia. I'm thinking mid-October. It'll be good press coverage."

Something squeezed deep inside his chest. He knew he should keep his mouth shut, but he couldn't help it. "Sir, are you sure this is a good idea? Would a public wedding help Emilia's mental state?"

The senator waved his hand dismissively. "She'll handle it."

Alex closed his eyes and took a deep breath. He'd given up too much to throw it all away now.

CHAPTER TWENTY

ALEX PULLED INTO the driveway and pinched the bridge of his nose. This would not be easy.

He had managed to avoid Kat for three weeks. Not that it was hard; there wasn't much for him to do at campaign headquarters these days. His stomach roiled as waves of acid ate him alive from the inside out. It had nothing to do with Kat. Or with not seeing Kat. The door opened as he stepped onto the porch, as prepared as he could be to face his mother.

"Mama, *cómo estás?*" He gave her a hug and a kiss on the cheek, and she ushered him in. The house smelled like it always did, of fresh baked pupusas. The entire house could fit into his one-bedroom condo in Arlington. He'd tried several times to convince his mother to move into a bigger place that he'd pay for, but she insisted on staying in the small house he had grown up in.

"I made your favorite—tres leches cake."

He sat down at the small Formica table in the chair that had been too small for him for many years, but he knew better than to complain.

"Tres leches? Must've finally done something right."

She handed him a plate and fork. "I thought Kat might be coming with you."

His antennae went up. "Why would you think that?"

"She hasn't called me in a week and last time she promised to come see me soon."

He knew his mother and Kat had met while he was holed up in Iraq. "You two talk regularly now?"

She sat down with a cup of coffee and cut herself and Alex a piece of cake, sloshing it onto the plate with an extra scoop of the milk sauce. "We talk once or twice a week, but she hasn't called for several days now. When are you going to show me the ring you bought her?"

"*¡Dios mío*, Mama! When did I say I bought her a ring? In fact, when did I ever even say we were serious?"

"Do you think I don't see how much she loves you, or how much you love her? *Mi hijo*, why are you running away?"

"Because you have to make sacrifices in life, Mama. You know that better than anyone. I stay with Kat and I lose everything I've worked for."

She gave him a stern look. The one he got when he did something she didn't like. "And what is that, exactly, Alejandro? What is it that you're working for?"

"How can you ask me that? You've seen how I've struggled." He pushed his plate of tres leches away. "I want to create a family legacy, so my children—your grandchildren—and all the people who come after us aren't treated like the hired help."

Turning away, she opened a drawer and threw a newspaper at him. He flinched. It was the local Richmond paper. The front page was a picture of the senator with former governor Lacey and Alex. The three of them were smiling into the camera. Alex didn't even remember the picture being taken. That whole day had been surreal. He'd gotten through it by taking a lot of deep breaths and keeping his eyes on the prize. On top of playing nice with a man he reviled, he'd gotten a phone call from the chief of staff for the vice presidential nominee, who'd just found out he had terminal cancer. He'd called Alex to say the job was his. If the senator gave him a good recommendation.

"How could you?"

He looked down. "I had no choice, not unless you wanted me to tell the senator our sordid history with this man."

"Alejandro, you were a sixteen-year-old boy when you told me that I had a choice. You made me see how my decisions affected you, how they shaped you. You made me see that in order to raise the boy I wanted to be proud of, I had to do things differently."

She jabbed at the paper. "This is not the boy you promised me you'd be."

He crumpled it in his hand. "What do you expect from me? You think politics is easy? You think at my level I can afford to say no? After everything I've done, I should throw it all away?"

"*Querido!* That is a mistake I have made all my life, believing there is no other way."

She took his face in her hands, the way she used to when he was a little boy. "You are a good man, one I am proud to call my son. Do what you feel in your heart, not what you fear in your brain."

He spent the night on the tiny twin bed in his old room. They'd moved here after leaving the governor's house. It was part of the reason his mother refused to let him upgrade her house. This was the first place she'd felt safe, the first place he'd been able to sleep well at night.

He woke early the next morning, left a note for his mother and drove on autopilot. Despite the fact that he'd been to her house only a couple of times, he knew the way; it was burned in his memory.

Her car was in the driveway. The neighbor's dog barked when he got out. By the time he got to the front door, it was already opening.

"Ms. Driscoll, hello."

Kat's mother looked well, dressed in jeans and a plaid shirt, her hair neatly combed into a bun. Her face showed none of the gauntness he'd seen when they'd first met. "It's nice to see you, Alex. Is everything all right?"

He hesitated. What if he was wrong? The senator's attentions seemed to agree with Ms. Driscoll.

"Alex."

There she was, the woman who had permeated every cell in his body. He stepped closer, wanting to be within touching distance of her, but Emilia stood in between. "Well, I'd better finish packing—today is the big moving day." The excitement in Emilia's voice was palpable.

"Can we go get a cup of coffee?"

Kat nodded. "Can you meet me at the coffee shop on Market and Crescent? I have something to give you. I need a few minutes to gather my stuff."

He was on his second cup of coffee by the time Kat burst through the door. She was wearing jeans and a sleeveless blouse, her hair loose around her shoulders. She carried a backpack and looked more like a college student than a professor. Her face, freshly scrubbed and free of makeup, was one of the most beautiful sights he'd ever seen.

She stopped a foot short of his table.

It took everything he had to keep himself firmly in his seat. He wouldn't touch her; he'd promised himself he wouldn't get close. So focused was he on staying seated that he didn't see her take the last step toward him. She flung her arms around his neck and he froze. The scent of her shampoo teased his nose; the softness of her cheek caressed him. He closed his eyes. "Kat!"

"Don't push me away, Alex."

He gently pried her arms off him, unable to look at her. She set down her backpack and sat across from him. They gazed at each other for what seemed like an eternity. She finally spoke. "If you asked me to, Alex, I'd do it for you."

He frowned. "What do you mean?"

"I'll dress the way Elle taught me, paint my face, host dinner parties. I'll do the media interviews."

"I can't ask you to do that. I don't want you to change who you are."

A tear escaped her eye and he longed to kiss it away. "I lashed out at you, Alex. I'm not even sure I want to keep on teaching. This whole summer has changed my perspective. I want to do something meaningful with my life."

It was tempting, so tempting. He leaned forward. "Kat, I can't."

She blinked several times, wiped her cheek then reached into her bag. "I came here to talk to you about something else." She pulled out a thick sheaf of papers. "This is my manuscript, the book I'm writing on the senator."

"You're finished with it already?"

"What can I say—I'm not getting a lot of sleep."

He picked it up and thumbed through the pages, used to speed-reading a few lines per page to get the gist of a document. Most bills and briefs that came across his desk were large and unwieldy. It was an early survival skill he'd learned. But the words swam before his eyes. He patted the manuscript and nodded. "I'll try to read it in the next few days and get back to you."

"You're not going to like it, and it'll be published before the election."

He leaned forward.

"The dean of my school has a connection at Harvard University Press. They're fast-tracking it."

He waited for the familiar thunder in his ears, for his muscles to tense up, but nothing came. All he felt was a deep ache in his chest, his body leaden with an overpowering desire to take her in his arms and tell her he didn't care about any of it; that all he wanted was to have her in his life and in his home. Had he lost his fight?

"Why didn't you tell me before?"

"I...I don't have an excuse. I..."

"You wanted to make sure I wouldn't stop you."

Shifting in her chair, she gave him a pleading expression and a weight settled on his heart. What did it matter? So what if the senator lost the election? Was it worth seeing this look in her eyes?

"All that talk about how you hate manipulations—how is this any different?"

She swallowed. What was wrong with him? This wasn't even his problem now that the senator had taken him off campaign duty. He could let Crista handle it. "Did you come out against the bill?"

She nodded. "I tried to see things your way, Alex. I really did." Motioning toward the manuscript, she flipped it open. "I wrote this chapter two ways, one in support and one against. I included both chapters to show there is no right answer and my analysis is just one opinion."

In an odd way, he was proud of her. She didn't

compromise her ideals, didn't sell out or take the easy route. He cringed. It was more courage than he had shown.

"Have you considered what this will do to your father?"

Another tear fell as she nodded. He gripped his coffee cup, glad he'd asked for the ceramic and not the paper one.

"I'm going to give him a copy of this so he knows what's coming. I can only hope he respects the fact that I'm standing up for my ideals."

"Even if it means losing your relationship with him."

She straightened. "There are a lot of things in life I can't control. My integrity isn't one of them."

His stomach bottomed out, leaving him hollow.

He didn't know how long the silence stretched between them, but she broke it. "What did you want to talk to me about?"

Right. The reason he was here. "Your mom and the senator."

She pressed her lips together, an expression he'd come to recognize as barely contained anger. He'd thought about a way to tell her without sounding like a complete jerk, even practiced the words, but they escaped him now as he gazed into her clear blue eyes. Worry lines were etched in her forehead. "I'm concerned that the senator might not have thought this marriage through."

"You think?" she scoffed. Leaning forward, she tapped the table. "It's a campaign stunt, isn't it? He's using my mother. She'll get hurt and I'll have to pick up the pieces."

He didn't disagree with her, but he also didn't know how to make it better. "I think he genuinely cares about her, but…"

She waved him off. "You're not telling me anything I don't already suspect, although I do appreciate the effort. I've tried, but I can't talk her out of it."

Walk away, Alex. He'd done more than he ever would have before. If the senator found out, Alex could not only kiss his next job goodbye, he'd also be blacklisted. He was putting a lot on the line for Kat, and she'd just admitted she hadn't been completely honest with him.

"Well, I'd best be going, then."

"Alex, you drove all this way just to tell me my mother marrying the senator is a bad idea? Come on."

She was right. Why hadn't he simply called, emailed, even texted her? His revelation was hardly earth-shattering. He had come for something else. To see the bruises on her arm and know that he was the wrong man for her. With a heavy heart, he brought himself to do the one thing he'd been avoiding. He looked at her arms.

CHAPTER TWENTY-ONE

"HAVE YOU READ this manuscript?" Crista screamed in his ear as he shut down his computer for the night. Alex checked his watch. It was past midnight and the caller ID on his phone told him Crista was at the campaign offices.

"It's late, Crista. Can we discuss this tomorrow? It's not like it's hitting the bookshelves right this minute."

"If this comes out before the election..."

"I know. He'll never win."

She sighed. "I can't believe she did this. And when I asked her not to publish it before November, she flat-out refused. Refused!"

He didn't expect anything less from Kat. To describe the book as a scathing review of the senator's policies was an understatement. Kat had shredded him. But she'd done so in a fair manner, legitimately analyzing the weak spots in all of his policies and pointing out the strengths brilliantly against the backdrop of the human cost of the war. It was an unusual political analysis, one written with heart. She even had statistics, no doubt from Captain Atao, on the number of babies that could be saved in Guam and around the world if they left Iraq.

"Did you see the last page?"

Frowning, he unlocked the desk drawer where he'd put the copy Kat had given him. Crista had the scanned version he'd emailed her. He had stopped reading when he got to the references. He flipped to the last page now, which had a handwritten note from Kat.

I'm not afraid of you, Alex.

"Is she taunting us? I just can't believe it. Here I thought we were friends. She knows how important it is for me to prove myself in this new role."

"She's not taunting us, Crista. The note was personal, meant just for me."

"Are you two still dating?"

He didn't know how to answer that question. *I'm not afraid of you.* How could she say that? She'd tried to hide it from him. The hint of a healing bruise on her arm. She'd rubbed makeup on it, but he had seen it with the practiced eye of someone who knew what to look for.

"No, we're not really on speaking terms."

"So how do we handle this?"

He took a breath. There was only one way

to handle this if he wanted his life back. The life he had before he met Kat, back when he was sane and knew where he was headed professionally.

"We have two options. Option A, we wait until it publishes and then do damage control. Option B is leak it and spin the analysis." Bitterness filled his mouth.

"Okay, let's leak it to the media. She won't give an interview, so the only narrative they'll hear is from our side. And we can use the fact that she's against the wedding to create some buzz. It'll be a lot of press coverage for the senator."

"Be careful, Crista."

"At this point, it's about name recognition. You know that, Alex." It was common knowledge within campaigns that those who followed an election closely made up their minds months before voting day, after reviewing policy issues and a candidate's qualifications. The casual voters, those who mainly came out for presidential elections and almost never showed up for local ones, tended to vote along party lines...or for the names they recognized.

Name recognition was now make-or-break for the senator. He was polling within the margin of error with his opponent. The photo op with the former governor, the one that Alex had sold a piece of his soul for, had the intended result of boosting the senator's numbers. Senator Roberts had kept his promise of getting Alex the job as the vice presidential nominee's chief of staff. But how far was Alex willing to go? How badly did he want this?

"Discuss it with the senator. The last thing you want is for the strategy to backfire on you." It was a lame attempt at absolving his guilt, putting it on the senator to protect his daughter. He hung up the phone feeling like he needed a shower. He should warn Kat; he'd made her a promise not to expose her to the media. Stabbing the power button, he tapped his foot as the computer booted up.

From: Alex.Santiago@primail.com
To: Kat.Driscoll@primail.com
Subject: Watch your back

Your manuscript is making waves. I suggest you work something out with Crista or else you'll be facing the media.
—Alex

His finger hovered over the send button. He closed his eyes and took a breath. The bruise on her arm filled his vision. There was no way for him to keep away from Kat. He knew without a doubt that she would pull him back. The only way to make sure he never hurt her again was to drive her away from him. Shifting over to the delete button, he sent the email to the trash.

CHAPTER TWENTY-TWO

"THIS IS ONE of the best manuscripts we've received in recent history."

Kat nodded at the jolly old man who was the senior editor at Harvard University Press. True to his promise, Dean Gladstone had gotten her a publishing contract in record time. They were discussing the final details now.

"Normally, I have pages of edits that need to be made, but aside from some proofing, I think this is ready to go. Now, getting it out before the election is a bit challenging..."

Kat leaned forward. "Sir, if Senator Roberts loses the election, this book will be worthless."

"Yes, but if he wins..."

"It's rare to produce a piece of writing that'll affect a voter's decision. I wrote this book so that the people of Virginia, those who care to, can make an educated decision. I was critical of the senator's war policies until I visited Iraq to see the on-the-ground impact of our work there. I truly believe there is no right or wrong side, just an informed one."

"Dr. Driscoll, have you considered running for Congress?"

She laughed, but stopped when she saw the earnest look in his eyes. "You're serious?"

"This manuscript—" he stabbed at the thick sheaf of papers in front of him "—it moved a surly old man like me to tears. You have empathy and a strong sense of right and wrong, something I wish more of our leaders had." He pointed to the newspaper lying on his desk. "Surely you know that the incumbent from your very own district had to resign because of allegations he laundered money. The Democratic Party is in a bit of a scramble trying to find a suitable replacement this close to the election. You already have name recognition. And once this book comes out, you'll win."

She stared at the editor. *He's serious!* "I'm sure they have a plan, and it does not include the media-shy daughter of a Republican senator."

He raised his bushy brows then took a card from his desk drawer and slid it toward her. "The DNC chair is a friend of mine. He'll happily take your call if you want to consider it. Think of it this way—you won't have to go back to working for Gladstone the bear."

She stifled a laugh; the nickname fit. *It's a*

crazy idea. I'd be in the spotlight constantly.
She pocketed the card.

"Okay, so if we want this published before the election, our work is cut out for us," the editor said, moving on to the task at hand.

When the meeting was finished several hours later, Kat touched the card in her pocket. Writing the book had reminded her of the speech she'd given to the troops in Iraq. She had notes, tons of them, but the reason she'd written it so quickly was because she hadn't needed them. The words flew out with brutal honesty, from her heart. When she'd pictured her father as an unknown politician, she envisioned a man who spoke the truth, someone who declined campaign contributions and didn't promise chits he couldn't morally justify. A man who would save those babies in Guam. She'd come to learn that such politicians were only figments of her imagination. They didn't exist in real life. But *what if...*

She shook her head. It was a crazy thought. She remembered how she'd felt seeing all those ugly pictures of herself when the CNN story broke. She could never go through that again.

Her flight from Boston to Richmond was late. Normally she'd be worried sick about her mother, but she was free from that now. Her mother was safely at the senator's mansion in

McLean planning a "small but tasteful" wedding. The last guest list Crista had shared with Kat, back when they were on speaking terms, had well over five hundred names. Kat was not going to interfere. Her mother was flourishing, and that was all she cared about. Emilia seemed happy without the manic euphoria that usually followed a good mood. Emilia was taking her medications and the senator seemed genuinely happy to have her with him. Though Vickie and Walt didn't live in the house, they'd called Kat to assure her that they, too, would check on her mother every chance they got.

It seemed her mother didn't need Kat anymore. Emilia's words came back to her. *"You're using me as an excuse not to get close to anyone."* Was that what she was doing?

She made her way to the airport gate, found a seat in the crowded departure area and opened her laptop. She could use the time to finalize the syllabus for her fall classes at the college, a task she'd put off as long as she could. Going back to a lecture hall and talking about laws and policies seemed hypocritical. What was the point in philosophizing about how the world could be a better place if politicians did things differently? She felt for the card in her pocket again. *What if?*

She opened her laptop and saw an email

marked urgent from Crista on her college email account. *Delete!* After Crista asked, then insisted and finally threatened her not to publish the manuscript, Kat had quit the campaign. Just like that, their friendship was over. The request Kat had been waiting for, the one she knew she wouldn't be able to fulfill, had come.

"Are you Kat Driscoll?"

A flash blinded her as she looked up. She blinked several times to see a large, redheaded woman holding out a cell phone.

"I knew it was you. Oh, my God, can we take a selfie?" Before Kat could protest, the woman wrapped an arm around Kat and positioned the phone in front of their faces. Kat forced herself to smile when she saw the picture on screen, grateful that she'd dressed up and put on some makeup for the meeting with the editor.

"I just can't believe it's you."

There hadn't been any stories about her in almost two months. She was surprised someone had recognized her.

"I mean, what are the chances. I'm sitting here watching TV and suddenly I see the person they're talking about."

Kat went cold. Several people were starting to stare at her now. "What do you mean?"

"Oh, honey, you're all over Fox News. They're talking about how you're getting revenge on your daddy for breaking your mama's heart."

"Excuse me, Kat Driscoll?" This time it was a young woman with a baby balanced on one hip and a phone out in the other hand. Kat shook her head, stood and grabbed her stuff. She finally found an empty gate and did a Google search for her name. There were several news items about her from the past hour or so. Different headlines, but the gist was always the same: pieces of her manuscript had been leaked. News outlets were openly debating whether she had written the book because she was opposed to the senator's marriage to her mother.

Retrieving her phone, she realized she'd put it in flight mode when she entered the airport. When she set it back to cellular, it lit up with dozens of missed calls, including several from her mother, the senator, Crista, Vickie and quite a few unknown numbers.

Alex had betrayed her. She had purposely given him a paper copy of the manuscript and he hadn't wasted any time in sharing it with Crista. The two of them had leaked it. He'd chosen the senator and his career over her. He'd broken his promise to protect her from the media. Yet another betrayal.

The TV screen caught her eye and she

stared at her picture. At least this time it was one of the shots the campaign had taken, far more flattering than her college mug shot. She waited for the familiar tightening in her chest, but it didn't come.

She slammed the lid of her laptop and silenced her phone. It was time to stop being the victim. Retrieving the card from her pocket, she dialed the number.

CHAPTER TWENTY-THREE

"You have got to be kidding me."

Alex didn't know whether to console Crista or laugh. They were in the campaign-headquarters conference room. Crista had rallied the troops to capitalize on the leaked manuscript story. Except, it hadn't turned out as Crista planned.

The senator stormed into the room. He had heard the press conference on the radio on his way over.

"How did this happen?"

He was greeted with silence. Crista finally broke it. "The DNC orchestrated it. This is to slam you in the polls."

"Is this real? Can she do this?"

Crista nodded unhappily. "The DNC got a ruling from the Virginia Board of Elections to get her added to the ballot even though it's after the filing deadline. The RNC didn't know."

The senator turned to Alex. "Did she tell you she was going to do this?"

He shook his head and stared at the TV.

Kat didn't look glamorous; she didn't sound adequately rehearsed. But just like the speech she'd given the troops, her sincerity carried her through. And he knew without a doubt that she'd make the best congresswoman the United States had ever seen.

All eyes turned to him. "Alex, you have to fix this."

He faced the room. His eyes locked on the senator's. The first boss he'd ever respected, and still did. Except somewhere along the way, Alex had sold out and really become one of them. With a clarity he hadn't had since he met Kat, he knew what he had to do.

"KATERINA, WHAT HAVE you done!"

What is she doing here?

Kat stared into her mother's wild eyes, then pushed past her into the house. She set down her purse and went into her bedroom. She'd known it was only a matter of time.

Her mother followed her. "And what have you done with my furniture? Where is the couch?"

"In storage," Kat said calmly. She had gotten a nice advance from the publisher for her book, so she'd redecorated, buying new furniture and hanging pictures on the walls, making the place hers. "You moved out, remember."

"I have a dinner party tomorrow and nothing to wear!" her mother screamed. She lifted Kat's bedspread, throwing it onto the floor. "Have you seen my suitcase? I can't find it anywhere."

Kat stepped on a stool to retrieve the box she kept on the top shelf of the closet.

"I don't want that." Her mother grabbed her hand but Kat was quicker. She deftly clasped the prefilled syringe from the box and stepped down. Her mother screamed and ran into her former bedroom. Kat had removed the lock from that room when they first moved in. Her mother was in the bed hiding underneath the covers. Kat double-checked the dosage in the syringe and primed it. She'd been expecting this. The big wedding the senator was planning had been taxing her mother. How many times had she asked her mother to come visit, hoping to give her a break from the wedding preparations? But Emilia always made an excuse. This episode was weeks—even months—in the making.

"Mom," she pleaded softly. "We've been through this before. You know the medicine makes you feel better." Most of the time she could talk her mother into it. If not, she'd have to call the nursing company to watch her mother until she was reasonable enough to take the medicine.

Emilia emerged from underneath the covers and held out a phone. "You can't do this to me."

Kat frowned at the phone as she heard the muffled sound of her name being called. She put the phone to her ear. It was the senator. Kat stiffened. She hadn't talked to him since he'd called to congratulate her on running for Congress, even joking about being the first Republican and Democrat to break bread together. Despite his cheery facade, she could tell the senator was upset. Crista had stopped talking to her altogether, and all she'd gotten from Alex was a text that said "nicely done" and a box of dark nut chocolates.

"Kat, I understand there's a problem with your mother."

Kat took a breath. "My mother is having a manic episode and I need to give her a shot of Haldol to stabilize her before she hurts herself or someone else."

"Your mother doesn't wish to have the treatment, Kat."

Of course she didn't. "Fine, then. You come here and deal with it." She ended the call without waiting for an answer.

She closed the door behind her and put the

syringe on top of the refrigerator. She retrieved her new tablet computer from her purse and took a seat on her new couch. There were a ton of emails and text messages to respond to along with a number of media requests. She took care of those first. The DNC had advised her to get a campaign manager soon. Running for Congress was a big risk, but for once in her life, it felt good to be the one calling the shots. The one dictating what happened in her life.

Her mother's condition would normally have her in a frenzy, calling doctors, prefilling syringes, preparing to call in sick for work. No more. Kat didn't need to be her round-the-clock nurse. She had chosen that role because it was easier to be needed by her mother than rejected by her friends.

The senator must have been at campaign headquarters because the doorbell rang an hour later. Kat shouldered her purse.

"She's in the bedroom. Her doctor's information is on the refrigerator and the syringe of Haldol is on top. Good luck."

"Kat, I need you here."

"No, you don't. You want to marry my mother—learn to take care of her."

She walked out, leaving the senator standing in her living room.

It was a good opportunity to drive to her

faculty office to pack up. Much to the chagrin of Dean Gladstone, she'd officially resigned from her position. The manuscript leak had backfired on the senator's campaign. They had counted on Kat's silence to direct the narrative, but when she made her announcement to run for Congress on the Democratic ticket, the conversation changed. Her publication date had been pushed up to capitalize on the press, and though she'd made her announcement only a week ago, the publisher was already reporting record-breaking preorders.

Dean Gladstone had called to offer her a promotion, which she politely declined. With the senator taking care of her mother's medical bills, Kat could comfortably support herself with the projected royalties from her book. If she didn't win the congressional seat, there were several universities that would hire her.

While she was packing up, various faculty members stopped by to wish her well. The DNC thought she had a fair chance at winning the congressional seat. Without even starting her campaign, she was already ahead in the polls, thanks to the leaked manuscript. Donors were mailing checks to the DNC in her name, and she didn't even have a bank account to deposit them in yet. Before shutting down her computer, she searched her name. There were multiple articles on her. Even more pictures.

It hadn't been easy, standing in front of the cameras, blinking against the constant flash of lights. Her mouth had been so dry that for several seconds she couldn't even choke out the words she'd practiced. Then she'd remembered the last time she'd given a speech she didn't want to give. It had been at the base in Iraq. At the time, she had looked at Alex and found the strength to continue.

But Alex hadn't been with her during the first press conference of her life. And yet it had been the thought of him watching her, the way he'd looked at her in Iraq, that got her through it.

She closed the computer without reading the articles. It didn't matter what they said; she was going to do things the way she wanted to, live her life according to her own rules. But could she do it without Alex? More important, did she want to?

It was bittersweet to pick up the cardboard box that contained her meager office knick-knacks and walk out. Somehow she knew she'd never return to teaching.

She pulled up to her house, and the neighbor's dog barked as she stepped onto the driveway. She had been gone only an hour, but it was the first time her father had come face-to-face with what it really meant to take care of her mother. Kat was prepared to find him running far, far away. No one ever stayed to pick up the pieces.

She marched over to the fence and stood on her tiptoes to peer over it. Rex was a small rottweiler. She realized she'd never actually seen the dog, just heard him barking every time she came home. The dog had brown eyes, and he moaned as he looked at her, tilting his head. He gave a small yelp and pawed at the fence. She reached over, getting her hand as close to him as she could. Rex stood on his hind legs and put his nose in the air, sniffing.

She shook her head, smiling. "You just want me to come say hello, don't you?" The dog yelped. "You bark because you're scared and alone."

Rex gave a short bark and licked her hand.

She found her mother and the senator sitting on the couch. He had his arm wrapped around her.

"So you got her to take the Haldol."

The senator shook his head and Kat went to the refrigerator to see the syringe still full.

"I was waiting for you before I take her to the doctor."

Kat considered the two of them. She'd never

brought her mother down from an episode without drugs. Her parents exchanged glances, then stood.

"Kat, I know you love your mother very much, and you're trying to protect her. I really do love her, and when I said I wanted to take care of her, I meant it. No matter what it takes. I hope I've shown you that today."

This was what she wanted more than anything, to have the freedom to live her own life. To see her mother happy. And yet she felt gutted.

"Katerina, it's time, baby. It's time to let go of me."

But if I let go of you, Mom, I have no excuse.

She stepped up to the senator. "I didn't mean to hurt you with that manuscript. I wrote it honestly, from my heart. And I didn't plan to run for Congress—it fell in my lap." The senator's polls were bad. Since her announcement to run and the interviews she'd done, he was so far behind, losing the election was a foregone conclusion.

He nodded. "I know. Truth be told, you might have done me a favor. I've been too scared to consider what it might be like not to be a senator. Being in office has been my entire life."

"I'm sure you can recover in the polls. You

said so yourself—a newcomer wouldn't be good for the state."

He shook his head. "You reminded me, Kat, of how little power I really have. I've been at this game so long, I've forgotten why I got into politics in the first place. Losing the seat is not as scary as I thought it would be." He took her mother's hand. "Maybe it's a blessing in disguise. All my life, I've been so focused on following and then exceeding my father's footsteps, I didn't stop to consider what was truly important to me." He looked pointedly at Emilia.

"You're willing to give up your career for my mother."

"She was the love of my life first, before she was your mother." Kat searched his eyes but all she saw was the clear truth. He wasn't going to betray her mother.

He leaned over and kissed her forehead. "You'll make a great congresswoman, Kat. You remind me of myself when I first ran. I'm proud of you."

She watched them leave then threw out the syringe and emptied the rest of the emergency medications she kept in the box. She'd given her mother away, and with her, every excuse she had.

CHAPTER TWENTY-FOUR

ALEX RAN HIS hand over the picture of him and the senator. "Do you need help with the packing?"

He turned to see Crista and smiled. She came and gave him a quick hug. "I can't believe you did that," she said.

"You deserve it. Just do me a favor and stay with the senator through the election. I already took responsibility for him losing."

She nodded. "So, don't keep me in suspense. You wouldn't have given up the chance to be the next VP's chief of staff unless you had something bigger. So what is it?"

He shook his head. "First off, there's no guarantee the Republicans will win. But I have nothing. I don't want this anymore."

The look on her face mirrored his own. He'd been equally surprised when he'd impulsively told the senator he was quitting. He had been sitting in on a constituent meeting and watched the senator make non-promises to "look into" an issue. All Alex could think about was how

Kat hated the way politicians handled such meetings and realized he didn't want to do the job anymore.

Shortly after, the vice presidential nominee had called and officially asked if Alex would be willing to become his chief of staff. The words to accept had been on his lips, but he'd recommended Crista instead. In that moment, all he remembered was his phone call to the governor, shaking the hand of a man he loathed, watching his mother's face as she threw the newspaper at him. It was not the person he wanted to be.

He needed to be a man worthy of a woman like Kat, someone she'd be proud of. A man who didn't compromise his ideals. A man who could protect the ones he loved.

"What are you going to do?"

He dropped the picture into one of several cardboard boxes. "I'm not sure. I'm going to take some time to figure it out."

"Does this have anything to do with a certain media-shy secret daughter?"

He laughed. "I haven't spoken to her."

"Why not?"

"Because…"

She raised her eyebrow and he shook his head. How could he describe all the reasons he and Kat couldn't be together?

"You know there's always a middle ground, a compromise." He looked at her quizzically, and Crista smiled shyly. "Nathan and I are going to do the long-distance thing. He'll get his PhD and I'll hopefully end up in the White House. We want to see what we have."

Alex reached out and squeezed her hand. "I'm happy for you."

"She forgave me, you know. For being a crappy friend. Relationships are not just about give-and-take, Alex. Sometimes they're about admitting you're wrong and asking forgiveness."

She stood to leave.

"Close the door behind you. I need to get packed up."

She'd been gone only a second when there was a knock on the door. He crossed the room to open it. "What did you forget—" He stopped.

How did she do it? Take his breath away. He stepped aside as she entered the room, not waiting for his permission. She was dressed in a pale peach dress, her skin glowing with the hint of a summer sun.

"Kat, you look beautiful." His voice was whisper-soft as she breezed past him.

"I figured since you're so insanely stubborn, it was up to me to make the first move. Again."

He wanted nothing more than to take her in his arms and tell her he wanted nothing more than to be at her side for the rest of his life.

"I don't ever want to hurt you." His voice caught, but he didn't care. She needed to see the raw pain in his heart.

"What're you talking about?"

"I saw the bruise on your arm."

She frowned. "What bruise?"

He pointed to the spot on her arm where he'd grabbed her.

"There's nothing here, Alex."

"It's healed by now."

"Look at me."

He looked up to see her eyes big and wet.

"There was never a bruise. I swear to you! Do you know why I haven't let a man get close to me since Colin?"

He lowered his eyes, but she reached out and stroked his cheek. He leaned into her caress, desperate for her touch.

"It's because all I felt with them was fear and a sickening repulsion. I'm not afraid of you, Alex. You don't hurt me—you can't hurt me. Because all I feel when I'm with you is love."

She wrapped her arms around him and her goodness filled his heart. He needed her to make him the man he wanted to be. Pulling her close, he bent his head, just enough. She stood on her tiptoes and kissed him with abandon, her fierceness matching his own. The familiar fire she ignited burned through him, shattering every bit of his control. But this time, he let her soul embrace his; let himself feel her love, let it bloom inside him.

"I did say I like dark and nutty," she said breathlessly, when they came up for air.

He laughed, and as he looked into her eyes, he knew that he could never be whole without her. "What am I going to do with you?"

"Be my campaign manager."

"Excuse me?"

She stepped back and he immediately missed the feel of her pressed against him. She linked her fingers with his. "Do you know why I decided to run?"

He pulled her close. "Because you want to be a different kind of politician. One who only takes the morning meetings and runs her campaign with honest contributions. You want to save the babies in Guam and show the rest of Washington, DC, that it's not about the game, but about serving people."

She smiled. "That's why I need a campaign manager. To make sure I get elected so I can actually have a chance to do those things. I need someone who believes in me, who'll understand where I'm coming from."

He shook his head. "This is a step down for me, managing an unknown candidate's congressional run."

She let go of his hands. "My father said you quit his campaign."

"He's your father now? Not the senator?"

She smiled, her eyes full of sparkle, like the shining blue surface of the Caribbean Sea.

"I'm warming up to him. Believe me, he won't be getting the Senator of the Year award from me, but I think he's trying hard to be my father. He moved the wedding, saw how hard it was on my mother, so he did the right thing."

"He asked me to marry Vickie." Alex didn't want there to be any more secrets between them.

"I know—he told me. He also said that he handed you the path to the presidency on a silver platter and you turned it down. Because of me. He doesn't have any hard feelings—he made a plan and struggled to regroup when things shifted around him. I think he's still getting used to the fact that I'm a Democrat." She said the last part with a smile so mischievous that he couldn't help bending his head and giving her a kiss on the top of hers.

"That's another reason not to be your campaign manager. We'll always be arguing."

"At least dinner won't be boring." She grinned, but then her tone grew serious. "Alex... I want you in my life. Tell me what you want and we'll work it out. If you want to run, I'll stand beside you. The media doesn't scare me anymore."

He didn't know why he'd done it, but the day he returned from Iraq, he'd passed by a store at the airport and made an impulsive purchase. It had been burning a hole in his breast pocket ever since. He knelt on the floor.

"Katerina Driscoll, you are the only woman who has ever made me lose my mind. You threaten every fiber of my self-control, and I want nothing more than to have you keep doing it. I won't be your campaign manager because I want to be your husband. Will you marry me?" He opened the box, which held a deep blue sapphire ring. Somehow, she didn't seem like the type of girl to want diamonds.

She stared at him, her eyes big and filled with tears.

"Kat, don't keep me waiting."

She dropped to her knees and cupped his face. "Oh, my God, you stubborn man. Yes.

Yes, I will marry you. I thought you'd never ask."

He kissed her, letting go of every bit of self-control he had.

EPILOGUE

"IN A SURPRISING VICTORY, Katerina Driscoll will be the new congresswoman from Virginia. Ms. Driscoll—excuse me, Dr. Driscoll—left shortly after her victory speech to be the maid of honor at the wedding of her father, former senator Roberts, who lost his senate seat by a narrow margin to a newcomer. The former senator is remarrying his first wife and Congresswoman Driscoll's mother in a private ceremony. The details are sketchy, but we know that only immediate family members and close friends have been invited."

Kat ignored the TV blaring in the background as she helped her mother with her makeup. The lessons she'd received on her makeover day were proving useful after all.

"Okay, I have something blue," Crista said. She had come early to help get her mother ready. She held out her hand and Kat laughed. It was a Kat for Congress button with the blue colors of the Democratic Party.

Her mother snatched it out of Crista's hand. "I think it's perfect."

"Okay, so we have you in your old wedding dress, a new pair of shoes and the something blue. What about borrowed?" Crista asked.

Kat touched the pendant on her neck then reached back and unclasped it. "Here's her something borrowed."

"Your necklace," her mother whispered reverently.

Kat smiled. "I don't need it anymore. I want you to wear it." She clasped it around her mother's neck, hoping it would help her find strength and happiness.

Kat's phone rang, and she looked at the number before excusing herself.

"Captain Atao."

"Congratulations on your win, Congresswoman." Her voice sounded muffled, and Kat knew her connection from Brazil might be unstable. They had been playing phone tag for weeks. "I hear you've been trying to get hold of me. Is this about the literature I sent?"

"Your information was very useful. I'd like to go to Guam in the next few months and bring some media attention to the issues we've been discussing," Kat told her. "I'd like you to come with me."

All she heard was faint crackling.

"Captain Atao, did I lose you?"

"I'm here. I…I can't go to Guam."

Kat frowned at the phone. Anna Atao had been so helpful in sending her documents and spending countless hours talking to her about the situation in Guam. She was obviously passionate about the place and the people there.

"I'm sorry, but I can't go back there, Congresswoman. No matter what." The panic in her voice was palpable.

"What happened there, Captain?" she asked in a soft voice.

"I can't talk about it. Please. I'll send you anything else you need. This is an important issue, but I can't…" Her voice cracked.

Kat's mother motioned to her. "Captain, I have to go now, but please just think about it." It was one of the first issues Kat hoped to fight for. She knew no one else would take it up. The few members of Congress she met were focusing on "high priority" issues, which was a nice way of saying those things that would get them more power. No one cared about babies in a US territory that had no delegates to the electoral college or congressional voting rights. That was why it was her top issue.

"Please, make a visit there…" Anna implored her. "Don't give up on the issue because of me." They disconnected, but Anna's broken voice stayed with Kat. She wondered what had happened to Captain Atao that she couldn't go back to Guam.

"Look, Kat!"

She turned to see Crista had put the veil on her mother's head. Emilia was a stunning sight of beauty and elegance in a vintage-inspired dress with long lace sleeves and a lace top that cinched at the waist with a silver brooch. The cream silk skirt fell to the floor.

Kat escorted her mother to the garden, where the senator stood with the priest. As Kat handed over her mom, her father smiled at her gratefully then turned his attention to the woman he loved. Vickie and Walt were by his side. She smiled at her half brother and sister, looking forward to the upcoming holidays, which they'd all agreed to spend together, as a family.

She took her place next to her mother. Alex was standing on the senator's side of the garden. Her eyes found his and he mouthed, "I love you." He had taken a position as the CEO of a nonprofit organization that defended abused women. Vickie had become Kat's chief of staff after managing her campaign so beautifully.

As the small wedding party danced underneath the stars, Alex pulled her close and pressed his mouth to her ear. She let the warmth of his breath tingle all the way down to her toes. "A week is too long to wait to make you my wife."

She smiled. She had everything in the world she ever wanted.

* * * * *

LARGER-PRINT BOOKS!

GET 2 FREE LARGER-PRINT NOVELS PLUS 2 FREE MYSTERY GIFTS

Love Inspired®

Larger-print novels are now available...

LARGER-PRINT BOOKS!

GET 2 FREE LARGER-PRINT NOVELS PLUS 2 FREE MYSTERY GIFTS

Love Inspired®
SUSPENSE
RIVETING INSPIRATIONAL ROMANCE

Larger-print novels are now available...

LISLP15

WESTERN (WP) PROMISES

YES! Please send me **The Western Promises Collection** in Larger Print. This collection begins with 3 FREE books and 2 FREE gifts (gifts valued at approx. $14.00 retail) in the first shipment, along with the other first 4 books from the collection! If I do not cancel, I will receive 8 monthly shipments until I have the entire 51-book Western Promises collection. I will receive 2 or 3 FREE books in each shipment and I will pay just $4.99 US/ $5.89 CDN for each of the other four books in each shipment, plus $2.99 for shipping and handling per shipment. *If I decide to keep the entire collection, I'll have paid for only 32 books, because 19 books are FREE! I understand that accepting the 3 free books and gifts places me under no obligation to buy anything. I can always return a shipment and cancel at any time. My free books and gifts are mine to keep no matter what I decide.

272 HCN 3070 472 HCN 3070

Name	(PLEASE PRINT)	
Address		Apt. #
City	State/Prov.	Zip/Postal Code

Signature (if under 18, a parent or guardian must sign)

Mail to the **Reader Service**:
IN U.S.A.: P.O. Box 1867, Buffalo, NY 14240-1867
IN CANADA: P.O. Box 609, Fort Erie, Ontario L2A 5X3

* Terms and prices subject to change without notice. Prices do not include applicable taxes. Sales tax applicable in N.Y. Canadian residents will be charged applicable taxes. This offer is limited to one order per household. All orders subject to approval. Credit or debit balances in a customer's account(s) may be offset by any other outstanding balance owed by or to the customer. Please allow 4 to 6 weeks for delivery. Offer available while quantities last. Offer not available to Quebec residents.

Your Privacy—The Reader Service is committed to protecting your privacy. Our Privacy Policy is available online at www.ReaderService.com or upon request from the Reader Service.

We make a portion of our mailing list available to reputable third parties that offer products we believe may interest you. If you prefer that we not exchange your name with third parties, or if you wish to clarify or modify your communication preferences, please visit us at www.ReaderService.com/consumerschoice or write to us at Reader Service Preference Service, P.O. Box 9062, Buffalo, NY 14240-9062. Include your complete name and address.

WPBPA16R

LARGER-PRINT BOOKS!
GET 2 FREE LARGER-PRINT NOVELS PLUS
2 FREE GIFTS!

HARLEQUIN

super romance

More Story...More Romance

HSRLP15